HAUNTED: PURGATORY

LEE MOUNTFORD

FREE BOOK

Sign up to my mailing list for free horror books...

Want more scary stories? Sign up to my mailing list and receive your free copy of *The Nightmare Collection - Vol 1* as well as *Inside: Perron Manor* (a prequel novella to *Haunted: Perron Manor*) directly to your email address.

The novel-length short story collection and prequel novella are sure to have you sleeping with the lights on.

Sign up now.

www.leemountford.com

1

THE HAZELNUT COFFEE Sarah sipped was piping hot and full of flavour.

Her sister would have hated it.

The last time Sarah had been in the *Hill of Beans* was with Chloe. And back then, the man she was now due to meet had received a tongue lashing. All because he had delivered a warning Sarah and Chloe should both have heeded.

David Ritter entered the coffee shop and quickly spotted her. He was dressed in a dark t-shirt with the logo of a classic rock band blazed across the front, black jacket, blue jeans and scruffy trainers. He was of below average height, slightly overweight, with greying, brushed-back hair. However, he had a kind face and was as unthreatening as a person could be.

He spotted Sarah and gave her a sad, sympathetic smile —followed by a wave—and walked over.

'I'm sorry to hear about what happened to your sister,' he offered.

Sarah just gave a tight-lipped smile and small nod in

return, then gestured to the empty chair opposite her. He took it.

'It was an accident,' Sarah lied. She didn't want him to know the full details of the story, nor the true danger Perron Manor actually posed. Not when she needed something from him.

It wasn't an accident. She had been killed. By something not of this world.

'So it *was* the fall that killed her?' David asked, seeming a little surprised. 'I'd heard that was the case, but thought maybe...'

'No, that much was true,' Sarah lied again. 'But before the fall, things happened we didn't tell the police about.'

David gave a solemn nod.

'So,' he started, 'you said in your message you wanted to talk to me about something?'

'Yes.' Sarah took another sip of her drink. 'Chloe and I got into a fight that day... before everything happened. She believed what you told her about Perron Manor, and I... well, I had a hard time with it. But Chloe did let something interesting slip. She said that, according to you, the only way to free the souls trapped at Perron Manor was... with an exorcism?'

'Possibly,' David said. 'But it was more an educated guess, to be honest. Why do you ask?'

Sarah took a breath. 'After Chloe died, I saw her again in the house. Upstairs. She seemed like she was in pain.'

David's eyes widened, but he then just nodded again. 'The house has her,' he stated.

That threw Sarah. She'd expected the revelation to be more of a surprise to him. *Does he know more about that place than he's letting on?*

'I believe it does, yes,' Sarah continued. 'But I can't let it keep her. I won't allow it.'

David paused for a moment. 'So... you want the place exorcised?'

'That's right,' she said, then added, 'and I need you to help me do it. Will you?'

David didn't consider the question for very long. 'Yes,' he said enthusiastically. 'I'll help you.'

Sarah felt a wave of relief, then smiled. 'Good.'

There was a momentary break in the conversation, and David used it as an opportunity to get himself a drink. When he walked back over, his face was a picture of seriousness.

'Do you think an exorcism is the best way to help Chloe?' Sarah asked.

He considered that for a moment, then nodded. 'I think so. As I said to her when I last saw her, there are no guarantees, and I want you to know that up front. However, I would say that is the best way to free her. Theoretically, it should release *all* the souls trapped inside.'

Sarah took another drink and considered his words. It all sounded so crazy. Ghosts, spirits, and demons? Those things shouldn't be real. However, Sarah's reality had changed now. She knew the truth. Things she had previously dismissed as make-believe were something much more real.

In fact, Chloe had been killed by a demon, and now her soul was trapped in the house she and Sarah had recently inherited.

Perron Manor.

'Can you help with the exorcism?' Sarah asked. 'I mean, is it something you can carry out?'

David's eyes went wide. 'Me? God, no. We'd need a priest, as well as the permission of the Church.'

'Okay. So how do we get permission and a priest?'

'We ask,' was David's response. 'I know of a priest local to the area, Father Janosch. He has experience in the supernatural and the occult. First, we need to convince him that you are telling the truth. He then convinces the Church. Hopefully, we can then get the exorcism officially sanctioned.'

'And what do we need to do to convince them? Provide proof?'

David nodded. 'Exactly. But it isn't always an easy thing to accomplish. However, I think I can help.'

'How so?'

'With my team. This is the kind of thing we do: investigate paranormal phenomenon and catalogue evidence of it.'

Sarah was vaguely aware of the team. After all, she'd read the book he'd written about Perron Manor, and in it there were details of a previous investigation in 2014 they had carried out there.

'Then,' David went on, 'I go to Father Janosch with what we have gathered. I know him pretty well, so I'm sure he'd help us. Plus, he's already aware of Perron Manor.'

'Has he had any experiences there?'

David shook his head. 'Not that I know of, but most people around here know of the house.'

Sarah drained the last of her coffee. 'Okay,' she said. 'That all sounds good to me. So... when do we start?'

'Well,' David began, 'I'll need to run it past the team to make sure they are all on board, though I can't see that being an issue. Considering the things we saw during our last investigation, I'd imagine they'll be chomping at the bit to get back inside. Then we need to arrange dates—'

'As soon as possible,' Sarah stated. 'We can get in there today if need be.'

Perron Manor was Sarah's now, and hers alone. However, she hadn't set foot back inside since the night her sister had died—three weeks ago. In truth, going back there scared the hell out of her. But she didn't have a choice.

David held up his hands and gave a friendly smile. 'Woah,' he said, 'that is a little too fast. It could be a few days at least, to be honest. Like I said, I need to get everyone on board; some of them have day jobs and they would need to request time off. How about we aim to start this coming weekend?'

'Fine,' Sarah replied, a little disappointed it wasn't all happening sooner. The fear of going back was overshadowed by the need to help her sister. 'How long will all of this take?'

David shrugged. 'That's the rub. There's no telling, really. As long as it takes to get what we need.'

'Then how long does it *usually* take?' she asked. A growing level of frustration started to rise up within her.

David gave her another sad smile. 'Hard to say. It depends on what we get from the house. Could be one night, or it could be much, much longer.'

'You'll appreciate the situation my sister is in, David. She's suffering, so time is of the essence.'

Sarah tried to keep a lid on her bubbling anger. However, it was difficult to do so given Chloe's death was so raw. Sarah was still in the early stages of grief, but that was only exacerbated by knowing Chloe's soul somehow lived on in torment. Sarah pictured in her mind what she'd seen that night at Perron Manor: Chloe, twisted and rotted, staring out from a window and mouthing the words *help me*.

'I get that,' David gently said. 'Believe me, I do. And I'm

sorry I can't make things go any quicker. But we will work as fast as we can, I promise you that.'

Sarah could only nod in response. He was being perfectly reasonable, yet it was hard to be patient.

'Okay,' she said, repressing the urge to sigh.

'We'd need full access to the building. I assume that won't be a problem?'

'No, not at all,' Sarah replied. Then she asked, 'Would you all be living there while you investigate?'

David nodded. 'To an extent. My team are all volunteers, so they'd give as much time as they could. But some would need to take time out of the investigation to deal with their work and personal lives. Same with me. But we'd spend as much time as we could there, which would involve sleeping at the house for the foreseeable future.'

To Sarah, their personal distractions sounded like it would just slow things down. 'I could pay you all for your time,' she offered. The inheritance money she'd received along with the house was still sitting in her bank account, mostly unused.

David raised his eyebrows in surprise. 'That's... very generous of you. But you don't need to do that—'

'I insist,' Sarah cut in. 'Seriously, if it helps speed things up, it'll be worth it. I'll also pay for everyone's food the entire time, if that works?'

David took a moment. 'That's very kind,' he said. 'But... are you sure?'

Sarah gave an assertive nod. 'I am.'

'Okay,' he said, unable to hide his smile. 'I've never been paid for this service before. It's always been voluntary.'

'Well, help me save my sister, and I'll even throw in a bonus. When can you get everyone on board?'

'I'll call them straight away,' he said. 'Hell, even if it's just me and no one else, I'll still start this weekend. Will you be staying at the house with us?'

Sarah nodded. 'Is that okay?'

'Of course,' he replied. 'But... you aren't going to be living there in the meantime, are you? I wouldn't advise it. I think the house could be dangerous.'

'I'm at a hotel at the moment,' Sarah told him. There was zero chance of her staying in that house alone.

'That's good. So, I'll pull the team together and speak to Father Janosch as well, just to forewarn him.'

'And I'll see you at the house on Saturday. Does midday work?' Sarah asked.

'It does,' David confirmed. He then held out his hand to shake. 'I promise I will do everything I can to help you and your sister,' he told her. 'I mean that.'

'I know you do,' Sarah told him and shook his hand. She was appreciative of the sentiment, but she needed him to do more than just try. She needed him to succeed.

And she would do everything in her power to make sure that happened.

I'm coming for you, Chloe.

2

THE DAY WAS FINALLY upon them and David was shaking with a nervous excitement. The team were all packed into David's transit van on their way to Perron Manor.

'I can't believe how anxious I am,' Ralph Cobin said from his position behind David. Ralph was a big guy, too, so for him to be feeling that way spoke volumes of what lay ahead. Though considering what had happened during their investigation back in 2014, David could hardly blame him.

The transit van was a six-seater. It was just big enough for all of the team and their equipment, but it was extremely cramped inside.

Jenn Hogan was seated up front in the passenger seat, which was apt considering David always looked upon her as his right-hand woman. Not that he ever admitted it to the rest of the group.

Ann Tate sat next to Ralph, and in the very back seats were Jamie Curtis and George Dalton.

David's vehicle had certainly seen better days. It was

close to ten years old and there was an audible squeak down by the passenger-side wheel as they drove. However, the van had served David well, and he didn't have the money to upgrade yet. Though, perhaps the money he and Sarah had agreed upon would go some way towards changing that.

David was splitting the fee equally with everyone, of course, minus a little bit he insisted go towards upgrading their equipment. Their operation had thus far been completely self-funded—by *him*—and was a true labour of love. If things went well at Perron Manor, and they were successful in helping Sarah, then maybe, just *maybe*, he could turn the venture into something more.

Of course, that wasn't David's main reason for being here. Or why Perron Manor was such an obsession. He had personal business to settle with that house.

In addition, there was the incident from their last investigation in 2014, where a ghostly voice had sent him a message: '*Return here. Help another in need.*'

Another in need.

He'd had years to think on that, and to David it could only mean one thing.

'I think we're all feeling that way,' Jenn Hogan said, replying to Ralph's comment. 'But this time at least we know a little of what to expect.'

Jenn had been with David the longest out of everyone and was every bit as passionate about the subject of the paranormal as he was. She had a strong build to her—no doubt a product of her day job in a warehouse, humping around boxes for hours on end—wavy red hair, light freckles on her face, and brown eyes. She wore a thick blue jumper with the sleeves rolled up to the elbows.

'And how is the client holding up?' George Dalton asked

from the back. He was the baby of the group at only twenty-three years of age. 'I mean, is it right to be doing this so soon after her sister died?'

'It's what she wanted,' David answered. 'You all know the reason we are here.'

'Yeah, but I mean... doesn't it seem a little farfetched?'

David frowned at him through the rearview mirror, but it was Ann who responded.

'How can you say that after what we saw in there?' she asked, bewildered. 'We *know* the house is haunted. We saw it with our own eyes.'

'I get that,' George said defensively. 'And I'm not denying it. But for her to see her sister so soon after death... I dunno, does that seem right to everyone?'

'There's no reason to disbelieve the client,' David stated. 'If we didn't have our own experiences with Perron Manor, then I get why we might be sceptical. But, come on... you remember what happened.'

George shook his head and shrugged before rubbing a thin hand over his patchy goatee. He had angular cheekbones, a long and sharp nose, pronounced upper front teeth, and was dressed in a smart, grey suit jacket with a black t-shirt beneath. While he shared the same love of the paranormal they all did, his other passion was the tech they used during their investigations. He was also a freelance IT consultant and worked a lot of jobs with David.

That was how they'd first met.

The weekend they spent at Perron Manor in 2014 had certainly left its mark on the group, and was the cause of the anxiety that now rippled through them.

Getting access back then hadn't been easy.

David had tried for years to arrange an investigation at

that house, with no success, but had eventually managed to get the former owner—Sarah's uncle, Vincent Bell—to agree to let them stay for a few days. And while they had originally gotten some impressive results, it was the last night that would live in their collective minds forever.

They had used a demon board down in the basement in an attempt to communicate with the dead. And it had worked... a little too well, in fact, as it wasn't just the dead that had come through. There was something else.

A demon.

David believed it was the demon that was behind everything at Perron Manor, and the reason all the other souls were trapped there and unable to move on. By exorcising the demonic entity completely, David hoped the damned at Perron Manor would finally be able to move on.

However, trying to do that could be incredibly dangerous.

Sarah had told David that her sister had died when fleeing the house. A genuine accident, where she'd tripped and fallen down a flight of stairs.

But David had to wonder about that.

Still, it didn't change anything for him. The others might think differently if he shared his doubts, so he'd decided against that. It would have undoubtedly led to some of the team dropping out, which was not ideal. A place like Perron Manor demanded a full contingent.

Besides, they were experts in their field, and if proper caution and restraint were exercised, they were perfectly capable of handling whatever the house might throw at them.

'We're nearly there,' David said. He turned the vehicle off the winding country road they were on and down a narrower track. The house came into view up ahead.

'Starting to feel a little more on-edge now,' Ralph admitted.

'We'll be fine,' David assured him. 'This could be the start of big things for us.'

3

SARAH STOOD with her back to the house, looking down the long driveway as the sound of a vehicle drew closer. She saw a blue transit van turn in through the open security gates.

The team had arrived.

She was relieved. Waiting out front on her own at the bottom of the entrance steps had been unnerving. Sarah had only been there for a little over ten minutes, but that was ten minutes too long to be standing alone at a place like Perron Manor.

Get a grip. You're going to be living back here, for a little while at least.

The cloudy sky was grey and accompanied by a drizzle of rain so light it was more like a blowing mist of precipitation. A musky, earthly smell from the muddy grounds around her permeated the air.

While standing and listening to the light wind, it had been hard for Sarah to resist the temptation to turn around and look upon the house again.

She knew what the building looked like well enough: stone construction and tall, narrow windows, with the most striking feature being the three peaks high up above that sat central along the length of the building and cut into the roofline. The building had an elegant if simplistic design, one Sarah had always liked.

However, the reason for not wanting to gaze upon the impressive architecture once more was a simple one—she was scared of what she might see looking back.

The last time Sarah had been at the house, her sister had been killed by the things inside. Sarah had held Chloe's lifeless body for a long time before finally dragging herself away, feeling utterly crushed and alone in the world. And, when outside, she'd had an overwhelming urge to turn and look back. It was there, in an upstairs window, she'd once again seen her sister.

Chloe had looked like a corpse that had been dead for years. And she'd mouthed a desperate plea for help.

That sight had plagued Sarah's nightmares ever since. It was the reason she was here again now, and the reason she'd enlisted the help of David and his team.

But she didn't think she was quite ready to see anything like it again, so she refused to turn her head and look back, despite a strong feeling of being watched.

The royal-blue vehicle drew closer, kicking up spray from the wet gravel it rolled over. Sarah noticed patches of orange rust around the wheel arches and edges of the doors, and there was a dent to the side near one of the front wheels.

The group didn't exactly travel in style. However, Sarah liked that. It seemed to suit David's personality somehow, judging by the brief interactions she'd had with him.

The van pulled to a stop in a covered car port which sat beside the house. Sarah's own car—a small, sleek, and sporty model—was parked there as well. She held her breath as the doors opened and the team emerged. She was surprised at the rag-tag appearance of them all.

For whatever reason, Sarah had expected them to be much like David: middle-aged white men, all with a nerdish quality to them.

But that was not quite the contingent standing before her. For one, there was one guy among them who was huge. He was tall, stocky, and relatively young—she guessed in his early thirties—with a thick but stylish black beard. His bulk was just about contained within a light-grey sports jumper with a logo she did not recognise stencilled in blue on the front.

A rather stern-faced lady with red hair jumped out of the front passenger seat, and David emerged from the driver's side.

There was also another woman, this one tall and thin with jet-black hair, matching black lipstick, and nose and lip rings. She wore dark eye shadow and her skin was as pale as moonlight. In addition, she was dressed in black trousers and a long purple coat with black patterns to it.

A pair of men completed the group. One of them had long blond hair pulled into a ponytail, an angular face with a serious expression, and brooding eyes. He also wore predominantly black, like the dark-haired girl.

The final man looked rather bookish, sporting a goatee and glasses, and he wore a grey suit-jacket over jeans in a smart-casual look.

David strode over to her first while the others spread out behind him. While their leader wore his usual friendly smile, none of the others really made eye contact with Sarah, instead either looking to the ground, to each other, or to the building behind her. All of them appeared awkward and uncomfortable.

Sarah knew why. It was a reaction she'd seen far too often in the three short weeks since her sister's death. People just didn't know how to act around someone who was grieving.

But Sarah didn't have time for that. She stepped forward and shook David's hand.

'Thanks for coming,' she said with as big a smile as she could muster, before lifting her head and standing tall to address the rest of them. 'Thank you *all* for coming. It really is appreciated. I take it you know why you are here?'

David paused, looked back to his team, then turned again to Sarah. 'They all know why they're here,' he confirmed. 'I briefed everyone.'

The woman with the black hair and purple coat stepped forward. 'And can I just say,' she began, her voice soft but even, 'I think you are extremely brave for doing this.'

Sarah quickly pulled her lips into a tight smile, more so to stop herself gritting her teeth in anger. The comment, while intended as kind and understanding, came across as patronising, like someone giving fake praise to a child for the most mundane of accomplishments. On top of that, there was an insincerity, almost a performance to the words.

'Thank you,' Sarah eventually said. The dark-haired woman gave a large smile in response.

Idiot.

'Well, let's get you introduced to everyone,' David said. 'That was Ann Tate. This,' he pointed to the big guy, 'is Ralph Cobin.' Ralph gave a polite smile and wave. After him was the redhead, Jenn Hogan, the guy with the goatee, George Dalton, and lastly, the tall man with the long blonde hair, Jamie Curtis.

Sarah did a double-take at that name but tried not to let her surprise show. Evidently, she failed.

'Don't worry,' Ralph cut in. 'His middle name isn't Lee.'

Jamie just shook his head and rolled his eyes. 'That got old the first seventy times you used it, Ralph,' he chided. 'I have a similar name to the girl from *Halloween*. Big deal.'

'Okay, I think we have more pressing matters,' David said in an admonishing tone. He then turned to Sarah. 'How about we go inside and start getting set up? Then I can go over what we have in mind.'

'Sounds good,' Sarah said.

But that was a lie. It didn't sound good at all, because it meant once again entering Perron Manor. Just the thought of that was enough to cause a stabbing pain in her chest. She took a breath and turned around, allowing herself to take in the details of the great house once again. She dug her hands in her pockets and pulled out the keys, waited a moment to try and compose herself, then started up the steps to the front porch.

She heard the footsteps of the others follow behind, drawing to a stop when she stood before the front door. The brass door knocker with the snarling lion's face looked back at her.

Ugly thing.

She slid the key into the lock and took a breath. *Here we go.* The door unlocked with a small squeak of sliding metal and she pushed it open, revealing the entrance lobby inside.

The very spot Chloe had died.

Sarah's gaze was immediately drawn to the floor at the foot of the stairs, and she remembered holding Chloe there as her sister grew colder in her arms. It had been all Sarah could think about for the last three weeks—being here now still felt like being punched in the gut. She had an urge to cry, one that was growing stronger by the second. However, she hated the thought of the others seeing her that way.

Keep it together.

Though a little more dust had gathered since her last visit, nothing else had changed: there was still grey marble-tiled floor with subtle whites and yellows, dark oak panelling to the walls, and a grand staircase that ran up to a half-landing, where it split off both left and right to walkways above. The air inside smelled stuffy, and the space had an oppressive feel.

'Just as you remember it?' David asked. Sarah turned around to answer but saw that he was instead talking to the rest of his team. They all looked anxious to varying degrees.

'Pretty much,' George said, his voice soft and almost feminine.

Sarah was aware they'd all had their own experience in the house. Not to the extent Sarah had, but she knew theirs was traumatic nonetheless. David had written a book about Perron Manor, one that detailed its storied history but also recounted his team's investigation in 2014. Sarah had read that book, so she knew most of what had happened to the group.

It was fantastical stuff, but now she believed it wholeheartedly.

The team fanned out, all taking in their surroundings. The entrance lobby was a grand space, but now felt small with seven of them inside.

'Where do we set up our headquarters?' Jenn asked. 'Same place as last time?'

'Makes sense,' David said. 'That seemed to work okay.'

'Headquarters?' Sarah asked.

David nodded. 'We'll have cameras mounted around the house, so will need a room where we can set up the monitors and computers, as well as store our equipment. A kind of base of operations.'

'I see,' Sarah said. 'So then, what... you capture something on video, send it to your priest friend, then they call in the exorcist?'

'Well, that's a very basic way of putting it, but not completely inaccurate. One video probably won't do it. We need to compile as much as we can and make our case watertight. Video is the best evidence we can hope for, but to be honest, everyone knows footage can still be doctored or faked. So, our best bet is to compile as much evidence as possible: video, audio, personal experiences, temperature fluctuations—we'll try and log everything. And, if we are lucky, it would be even better if Father Janosch witnessed something himself. That would carry a lot of weight.'

'Understood,' Sarah said. 'Do you know this Father Janosch well?'

'I guess.'

'So if he believes what you're saying, what are the chances he'd tell a little fib on our behalf? It would save us the trouble of gathering evidence.'

David paused, studying her face, probably trying to work out if she was joking or not. Sarah wasn't even sure about that herself.

'Lie?' David eventually asked. 'You *know* he's a priest. That... isn't exactly something he would be comfortable with.'

Sarah forced a smile. 'I'm just pulling your leg.'

David's eyes slowly widened in realisation. He let out a chuckle. 'I see. Very funny. Well, I suppose you could ask him that question yourself. I've arranged to meet him here in a little while, just to get things moving as quickly as possible. He knows roughly what we're doing, and has agreed to give the house a blessing. That's an important step. In truth, that alone *could* put an end to the haunting here. At least, in theory.'

'Really?' Sarah asked, surprised. 'Seems a little... easy.'

'I didn't say it would definitively work,' he replied. 'In fact, given the kind of activity we are talking about here, I think it is unlikely. But the blessing itself is an important first step. If it doesn't work, then it is still one required step chalked off. Which means we are closer to the exorcism. And, if it *does* work, then all the better... I suppose.'

Sarah narrowed her eyes. 'You don't sound like you want the blessing to be successful, David.'

'No, it isn't that. It would just be nice to get some verifiable evidence from the house.'

Sarah understood what he meant. In his book, David had told of some amazing events that had taken place during their investigation. However, the only 'proof' from it was his own word and testimony, as all the equipment had failed at the worst possible time. No video, no audio... no evidence. He'd had his most powerful experience ever in Perron Manor but had nothing to show for it.

This was a second chance for him.

'So,' George said, 'do we unpack everything now? It may take a while, so best to get started quickly, don't you think?'

'Yeah but... where are we all staying?' Jenn asked.

'I've been thinking about that,' David replied. 'It makes sense to use the beds already here, but I don't want anyone in a room on their own. So, I think we should double up.'

'Wait,' Ralph interrupted, 'does that mean sharing beds?'

'If everyone is okay with that,' David said.

'But there are seven of us,' Ann chipped in. 'That's an odd number.'

'True,' David began, 'but I thought it might be prudent if

the girls take the biggest room here and we try and squeeze another bed in.'

For Sarah, being forced to cram into a room with two other women she didn't know wasn't exactly appealing, but she'd been through worse during her time in the army. While there, she'd had to bunk up with a lot of people— both men and women—so this was hardly a deal-breaker. In truth, it was far preferable to sleeping alone.

'I guess we'll have to,' Jenn said. 'After all, our rooms will just be a place to get our heads down for the night. It's not like we'll be spending a lot of time in there.'

'So then why don't we pick out the rooms first before we go get our stuff?' Ann suggested.

'Seems sensible,' David said. 'In fact, I think a quick tour to get ourselves reacquainted with the house would be a good idea.' He then looked over to Sarah. 'Would you be okay with that?'

'Of course,' she replied. 'A tour sounds good.'

4

THE GROUP CARRIED out a lap of the ground floor first. For Sarah, it was a strange experience. It had only been a few weeks since she was last here, but in some ways, it felt like she had never been away. In other ways, however, it seemed as if a lifetime had passed.

The great hall was still impressive to see, with its high ceilings, antique dining-room table, and stone columns that ran down to a stone-tiled floor. There was an elegant, deep-green wallpaper to the walls as well as a plethora of oil paintings and a gold-framed mirror.

However, all Sarah could picture was the entities she had seen the last time she was in the room. The spirits of the dead: all pale, corpse-like, and distinctly demonic.

However, they were not as demonic as the thing that had killed her sister. The monster that *really* scared Sarah.

She knew it was still here in the house somewhere, hidden from them... but waiting. She could *feel* it. That creature was not just a ghost of the dead but something else entirely.

Something *more*.

'This is where a lot of people died in '82,' George announced to no one in particular. 'It was a massacre all over the house, but *especially* in here. Because this is where the chaos started.'

Sarah was aware of the events that took place back in 1982, and from what she understood 'massacre' was indeed the right word. It was strange to think her parents had been in the house when that had happened.

Chloe too, come to think of it, though her sister had remembered very little of that night.

They then moved on to the kitchen, which had been the hub for Sarah and her family. A place of laughter, food, drink, and bonding. Now it was silent. Sarah could practically hear her niece's babyish chattering and Chloe discussing her plans for their new home. Even Andrew's crappy jokes.

Next, Sarah found herself back down in the basement, and all the anxiety she was already feeling went into overdrive. It had never been a warm or welcoming place—the exact opposite, in fact—and the orange light above wasn't strong enough to illuminate the whole area, leaving large pockets of shadows around the perimeter. In addition, the ground consisted of uneven and dirty slabs, with the walls being thick stone blocks, some of which were streaked with watermarks. The biggest feature in the largely empty space, however, was the damn furnace.

Sarah would never forget that thing for as long as she lived. The first time she'd seen her brother-in-law start it up, the appliance had made a sound akin to a scream. They'd all thought it was just a quirk—a symptom of the furnace's age.

However, on the last night, Sarah had seen a man inside of it, practically burnt to a crisp. At the time, another entity

—a horrible old man in a tattered suit—had tried to throw poor little Emma inside while the furnace was ablaze. She remembered the nursery rhyme he sang as he did.

Ring-a-ring-a-roses.

Sarah had saved Emma. She'd found an inner reserve of courage, one she really wished she could tap into now. Because, while walking around the house she used to live in, Sarah felt like a lost little child.

Thankfully, their time down in the basement was brief, and Sarah suspected David had picked up on her discomfort despite her best efforts to hide it. They all moved upstairs, which was easier for Sarah to deal with. After looking into bedroom after bedroom, with one bleeding into the next to her, they finally agreed upon their accommodations for the next several days.

Sarah had insisted no one use the bedrooms that had previously been hers, her sister's, or Emma's—doing so just felt wrong. But the rest were fair game.

So, the three girls claimed a front corner room, one of the biggest in the house, complete with an en-suite. Ralph and Jamie were paired in a room adjacent, with David and George taking the other front corner room. While the boys had agreed to share beds, it would have been tough to squeeze three to a single bed in the girl's room. Luckily, Sarah was fine with sleeping on the floor. She pulled a mattress from an unused bed into the room—a full bed and frame would have fit, but would have been a lot of work— along with some covers. Hell, she'd slept in hastily dug foxholes before while in Afghanistan. This would be a cakewalk.

After the rooms were assigned, the group finally went up to the top story, which was just more of the same: bedroom after bedroom. However, there was one area in particular

David said he was interested to see, one he and his team hadn't been aware of back when they'd carried out their investigation.

The study.

As Sarah showed everyone around, she saw they were suitably impressed. Why wouldn't they be? The room contained a huge array of items and artefacts that were occult in nature: daggers, scrolls, sigils, even small animal bodies floating in a thick yellow liquid. Right up their alley.

'This is fucking unbelievable,' Ralph exclaimed.

'You didn't tell us about this place, David,' Jenn said with wide eyes. She turned to Sarah. 'How long has all this stuff been here?'

Sarah shrugged. 'Couldn't tell you exactly. It was locked off when we first moved in until we found the key. But I think it was here back in '82 at least. Probably before.'

George quickly spotted the somewhat faded pentagram on the floor. The one with a dark brown stain in it.

'What the fuck!' he exclaimed, pointing at the symbol.

'Weird, huh?' Sarah replied. It had freaked Chloe out when they'd first discovered this room as well. Despite talking about cleaning it up, they had never gotten around to it.

'It's more than weird,' George said. 'It's creepy as hell.'

David pulled out his phone and took a picture of it.

'Do you think this has something to do with what happened in '82?' Jenn asked David.

He shrugged in response. 'No idea. Possibly.'

'And what's that?' Ann asked before moving over towards a waist-high display case sitting central to the room. It had a glass top, and inside was a book that Sarah remembered all too well. It had previously drawn her interest to an almost unhealthy degree. Though why that was, exactly, she couldn't explain.

She also remembered the ledger, which sat on a writing table in the corner of the room. It had so far gone unnoticed by the others.

'It's just a book,' Sarah said. 'It isn't even written in English.'

David moved over beside Ann and put his hands on the lid of the case. '*Ianua Diaboli*,' he said, reading the title. He then looked over to Sarah and asked, 'May I?'

Sarah didn't really want him to, and her gut reaction was to tell him no. However, that was irrational, so she simply nodded her approval.

He lifted the lid and opened the book where it sat, staring at it in wonder. 'It's old,' he said. '*Really* old. And written in... Latin, I think.'

The others all gathered around as well and watched as David slowly worked through the pages.

'Funky drawings,' Ralph said while pointing to one of the sketches on the page. 'What the hell are they?'

'I think this is some kind of ritual book,' David said.

'Are you serious?' Ann asked, her mouth hanging open.

'I think so. I know a little Latin and can pick up some parts of it.' He then again looked to Sarah. 'Do you know where this came from?'

She shook her head. 'No. It was all here when we moved in.'

David's eyes drifted back down. 'I'll show this to Father Janosch as well. His Latin is much better than mine.' There was an obvious excitement in his voice. The room must have seemed like the find of a lifetime for him.

David then used his phone to take a few pictures of the book.

'How about we get set up?' Sarah asked. 'There will be plenty of time to look around here later.'

David seemed a little disappointed at the suggestion, but he slipped his phone back into his pocket. 'You're right,' he said. 'It would be good to at least have everything in the van unpacked before Father Janosch gets here.'

That brought the tour to an end, which Sarah was happy about. For the next hour, they unloaded the van and Sarah's car before starting to set up the equipment. Bags were dumped into the assigned rooms but were not unpacked. Sarah had decided to live out of her suitcase anyway, knowing they may well need to make a quick getaway.

They all gathered in the downstairs study accessed off the entrance lobby. It was not a room Sarah had spent a lot of time in. Looking at the walls, she saw a thick line of discolouration that ran up the full height of the room. It looked to her as if a bisecting wall had previously existed there at one point, separating the room into two spaces. Perhaps her Uncle Vincent's doing? There was a landline here as well, which Andrew had set up back when Sarah and her family had first moved in.

The computers had just been unpacked when the sound of a knocking on the front door drew the group's attention. Sarah felt a jolt of anxiety, and her mind instantly ran back to the night she and Chloe were terrorised by some unseen thing which constantly banged on the front door.

'That'll be Father Janosch,' David said.

'Of course,' Sarah added, feeling stupid and relieved in equal measure.

'Come on,' David said with a big smile. 'I'll introduce you.'

5

FATHER LUCA JANOSCH stood waiting outside the entrance door to the house. His leather satchel dangled from his left hand and his long coat was pulled tightly around him, covering up his black robes. However, he had deliberately left the front zipper low enough so that people could see his white clerical collar.

In truth, he didn't really want to be at the house, but had never been one to turn his back on people who requested his help. He just hoped this was another one of David's wild-goose chases.

There had been plenty of them over the years.

Despite David's heart being in the right place—and insisting he was impartial when investigating—Luca had seen the younger man take leaps of logic that were, perhaps, overeager and misguided.

But Luca had heard many stories about Perron Manor. And even if only a handful were true, then he'd be stepping back into a world he'd not been a part of since his days back in Romania.

He heard movement beyond the double-door before

him, and one leaf slowly opened. David was revealed first, wearing a big, friendly grin. There was a woman beside him, but not one of David's usual team. She had dark, wavy hair that hung just down past her shoulders, slightly tanned skin with a smattering of freckles, and piercing blue eyes.

Luca had a feeling he knew who this girl was, as David had briefed him on what was happening here. Also, Luca had heard the news around town as well, that Perron Manor had new owners, but one had died not long after moving in.

He assumed, therefore, that this was Sarah Pearson, the sister of the deceased Chloe Shaw. It had been Luca's own clergy that had carried out the funeral, though it was Father Roberts who had been in charge of the ceremony.

A terrible tragedy.

'Thank you for coming,' David said and shook Luca's hand before moving aside to let Luca enter.

'No problem at all,' Luca replied and stepped into the house. He turned to Miss Pearson and held out his hand to her. 'I'm truly sorry about the loss of your sister.'

Miss Pearson looked down at his outstretched hand for a moment. Eventually, she shook it as well, her grip firm and strong.

'Thank you,' she said. 'David tells me you're here to bless my house?'

'If that is okay with you,' he replied.

'It is. And if that doesn't work, then I understand we need to provide you with evidence that the house is...'

'Haunted,' he finished for her, nodding. 'That's right.'

'And you believe in stuff like that?'

'Ghosts?' he asked.

'Yeah. Because, if not, then you're gonna be kinda hard to convince, you know?'

Luca let out a chuckle. 'I see what you mean. But yes, I

do believe in things of that nature. Though... I think they are less common than some people think. *Much* less common.'

He hoped it wasn't too obvious he was thinking of David.

'You don't need to worry about that here,' David said, oblivious, and still wearing an excited grin. 'This place is like nothing you've ever seen before. I promise you that.'

'So, what do we need to do to get started with the blessing?' Sarah asked. He could sense her eagerness.

'Nothing really. I just... start.'

'Great,' she replied. 'Then let's get to it.'

6

DAVID AND SARAH accompanied Father Janosch around the house as the priest conducted the blessing. David had seen the ceremony before, but not in a house as large as Perron Manor.

He noted that Sarah had been a little curt with the priest and impatient to get things started. David sympathised, but her pushing could be a problem in the making. Even if successful, the whole process would likely not be quick. She needed to be patient.

Perhaps a delicately handled conversation was needed. But not now.

David was comfortable leaving the rest of the team to continue the set-up while he and Sarah again walked around the building, this time accompanied by Father Janosch. It was always an interesting experience watching the priest work, reciting passages from the gospel and sprinkling holy water from a flask.

David was interested to see if Father Janosch's rites invoked any anger or phenomena from the house.

He had known Father Janosch for a number of years,

after requesting the holy man bless other locations he had been investigating. The priest was always friendly and amenable, and during some of these investigations, David had found out a little of the priest's backstory, learning he had been born in Romania but had moved to England with his parents when very young. The man had, however, gone back to Romania for many years to work with the Church. David knew that *something* had happened over there that made the man amenable to the paranormal. It was something that troubled the priest, but not a topic he really spoke of in any great detail. All David knew was that it involved an exorcism at a Church in Hungary... and it had not gone well.

Father Janosch had the tiniest hint of a Romanian accent, likely picked up from his many years back in Romania as a young man.

At sixty-five years of age, he was in good physical condition, though he was quite a short man, standing at only five-foot-six. He had a pale complexion, short, brushed-back white hair, grey eyes, and a rather square face with a wide, letterbox mouth. His hands showed signs of ageing too, with pronounced veins and some liver spots on the back.

David noticed that as they progressed through the house, the priest's mood began to change. Especially after they ventured down into the basement.

'Interesting furnace,' he remarked as he splashed holy water on the ground.

'If you only knew,' David replied. 'Sarah has seen a spirit inside of it, when it was lit, no less.'

'Fascinating,' Father Janosch said. 'I have to say, the report you gave me on what happened here is quite astonishing.'

'Of our investigation, you mean? Well, what happened to Sarah's family here far outweighs my own experiences.'

'Shame you didn't manage to get any evidence during your investigation, though.'

'Tell me about it,' David replied. 'It would have been a game-changer for sure.'

'Let's hope you have better luck this time around.'

David felt Sarah's eyes fall on him. 'We will,' David replied with as much confidence as he could.

Father Janosch pulled his coat tighter around himself and continued around the basement.

'It's quite oppressive down here.'

'I noticed that as well,' David agreed. 'The whole house is the same, to an extent. You constantly feel like you are being watched.'

'But that isn't proof of phenomena,' the priest stated. 'Far from it.'

Sarah then cut in. 'I get the feeling you aren't one-hundred-percent sure you believe what we are telling you.'

Father Janosch stopped and turned to her. 'How so?'

'Just the tone of your voice,' she replied. 'I'm picking up on a little scepticism.'

'I can assure you I'm open-minded,' the priest replied, firmly. David felt the need to step in.

'Father Janosch is a believer, Sarah. He's seen things that not many people in this world have. Experienced the same things *you* have. He's here to help, I can promise you.'

Sarah held up her hand to quiet him and addressed the priest directly. 'I have no problem with you being sceptical about all of this, Father. In fact, I'd worry if you weren't. I imagine you deal with a lot of people who bend the truth when it comes to this kind of thing, so you need to weed out the crazies. I get it. But, at the same time, I know what I saw here. And I know my sister is trapped. So, if getting the house exorcised is the only way to free her, then that is what is going to happen. I'll walk to the fucking Vatican and drag the Pope here myself if I need to. Understand?'

David winced and he saw the priest's eyes widen in surprise. This wasn't something Sarah could bully her way through. Father Janosch would only take things forward to the Church if the evidence was indisputable.

'I sympathise with how you are feeling, Miss Pearson,' Father Janosch said in a kind voice. 'And I promise that I will judge any evidence I see impartially. *But*,' his tone took on a noticeable sternness, 'I will not lie to my superiors if I am not convinced myself of the validity of the claims. I hope that is clear?'

David stepped between the two. 'No need for things to get angry,' he said. 'We have our plan of action and we'll stick to it. We're all on the same side.'

Sarah kept her gaze on Father Janosch, her jaw set. She nodded, and Father Janosch did the same. 'Of course,' he said. 'I am just here to help.'

They didn't talk much more as they carried on around the rest of the house, and David made a note to have that conversation with Sarah sooner rather than later. She was grieving, he understood that, and so she could be forgiven for being short and agitated with people. However, everyone here was just trying to help, and David didn't want Sarah to push anyone away.

As they moved up to the top storey, and the last rooms to be blessed, David was eager to show Father Janosch the strange study. And, in particular, the book.

Once inside, David let the priest sprinkle his holy water and recite a passage, but could tell by the man's expression that he was surprised at what was in the room.

'Someone has quite the collection,' he eventually said.

'It belonged to a prior owner of the house,' Sarah told him.

'An Alfred Blackwater,' David confirmed. 'And it was then all passed down to his grandson, Marcus.'

After completing his blessing of the room, Father Janosch took his time inspecting the artefacts. He seemed troubled.

'I've not seen a collection like this before,' David said. 'I mean, I haven't had the opportunity to have a good look through it yet, but is it any wonder the stories of the house persist given all of *this* is sitting up here?'

Father Janosch took a moment before answering, looking through some of the books and journals that lined a shelf. He seemed much paler than he had downstairs.

'I... I honestly don't know what to think,' he said. 'I've actually heard of some of these books.'

'Well, you need to see this one in particular,' David said and guided the priest to the centre of the room where *Ianua Diaboli* sat in its case. The priest frowned as David opened the glass lid. 'My translation may be off,' David said, 'but isn't that Latin for *The Door to the Devil*?'

Father Janosch gave a small nod. 'Not far off. Translations aren't always straightforward, but I would wager it means *The Devil's Door*.' He then took hold of the book and lifted it up. '*The Devil's Door* is also a tome I have heard spoken of, but one I never thought was real.' He opened the book and started to go through the pages. As pale as he had looked before, David could have sworn he saw even more blood drain from the man's face. Before even getting to the halfway point, the priest closed the cover and dropped the book back in its case. He then laid his hands on the edges of the display unit to steady himself and looked up to Sarah.

'David tells me you saw many spirits in this house,' Father Janosch said. 'Not just one or two.'

'That's right,' Sarah replied.

'And something else as well... a demon?'

'I think that's what it was. Yes.'

David then cut in. 'It's my belief that the demon is the reason the spirits of the dead are trapped here. It is what's keeping them prisoner.'

Father Janosch was still staring over at Sarah. 'Can I ask —have you only seen the one demon here?'

That question gave David pause. Sarah nodded. 'I think so, yes.'

'There can only be one demon, surely,' David said. 'I didn't think more than one could ever co-exist in the same place.'

'I didn't either,' Father Janosch said, his voice weak. He again looked down to the book. 'Miss Pearson, how long were you and your family in the house before your sister died?'

'Not long,' she replied. 'About a month and a half.'

The priest nodded, but his brow furrowed. 'And during that time, did you ever personally feel... different?'

Sarah cocked her head to the side. 'Different how?'

'Like you weren't in control. Short-tempered. Angry.'

Sarah paused before shaking her head. 'No, not really. Don't get me wrong, the things that were happening stressed us all out, so I did fight with my sister more than I usually do. But it was nothing more than that.'

'And no one else in the house seemed different either?'

Again, there was a brief pause, before Sarah answered. 'No,' she said.

'I see.' Father Janosch then took a breath and straightened up. 'The blessing is done,' he declared. 'Now you will need to monitor the house and see if there are any further phenomena. I need to take my leave. However, David, you know where I am if you need me.'

'Erm... okay,' David said. He hadn't expected the man to be in such a rush to leave, as Father Janosch was generally quite social; he actually had to keep pace with the priest as they made their way back downstairs. They passed Jenn and George coming the other way on the stairs, each with small, mountable cameras in their arms. The pair moved aside to let the other three pass on their way down.

'You are more than welcome to stay a little while,' David offered.

'Most kind,' Father Janosch said as he stepped off the bottom stair and strode over to the entrance door. 'But I have things I need to attend to.'

Sarah opened the door for him, and David saw she was wearing a frown of confusion. Once Father Janosch stepped out over the threshold, he turned around and looked past both David and Sarah to the space behind them. He continued to stare beyond them as he spoke.

'Come to me with any evidence you have,' he said. 'But in the meantime, please be careful.' He then let his eyes settle onto Sarah. 'I mean that. If things start to get dangerous, don't force yourself to stay. You cannot help your sister if you end up just like her.'

He then turned and left. 'Wait,' David called after him. 'What spooked you so much, Father?'

'Nothing,' the older man shouted back, but he kept striding to his car. It did not take him long to start up the engine and disappear down the long driveway.

7

LUCA'S HANDS trembled as they gripped the steering wheel tightly. He had an urge to put his foot down and ignore the speed limit of the winding roads ahead, just so he could get back home that much quicker.

But no matter how frightened he was, he knew that flipping his car and killing himself, or skidding head-long into an oncoming car and killing other innocent souls, would help nothing.

He'd felt a little uncomfortable after first entering the house, noticing its heavy atmosphere.

However, an oppressive feeling alone was not evidence of an evil presence. Not in his experience. It was just the human mind reacting to an environment. If said environment or building had a reputation already, then it was only natural a person would feel uncomfortable inside.

Still, that discomfort had grown the longer he'd been in the house, especially down in the basement. Luca didn't claim to possess 'the gift,' as he called it, but the sensation of things watching from the shadows was palpable.

A reminder of Zsámbék Church.

But none of that had compared with finding the book upstairs. *Ianua Diaboli*—it was a title he hadn't heard in years, and a book he didn't believe even existed beyond folklore.

However, if that tome back at Perron Manor was genuine, then David Ritter and his team could be in a lot of danger.

Luca had been hesitant to divulge what he suspected to David, knowing it would serve nothing other than to heighten the younger man's interest in the house.

Miss Pearson and her family had been in the house for a month and a half before Chloe Shaw died. That wasn't a long time. Supernatural activity usually took much longer to manifest to people in a haunted location. So that was strange in itself. And then the level of phenomena she claimed to have taken place—full-bodied apparitions interacting with the living, and even the demonic showing themselves—should have, theoretically, taken years to manifest, if at all.

Luca had always assumed David's stories about his investigation at Perron Manor were embellished. But what if they weren't? What if there was a reason things happened so quickly there. *Ianua Diaboli* might explain that.

Luca couldn't believe the book being in the house was a coincidence, either. His mind raced to add everything up, remembering what David had told him regarding Sarah and her story.

During their stay, Sarah and her family had apparently started to experience things they couldn't explain. That activity grew and culminated the night Chloe died. They had been woken from their sleep by something, and Chloe had fallen down the stairs of the manor as they'd fled, breaking her neck. A terrible accident. However, not caused *directly* by anything supernatural. Which meant the entities inside, if real, were not physically able to hurt anyone as yet.

It didn't appear that anyone had been possessed during that time, if she was telling the truth, which was another good sign.

All of that meant that even if things picked back up in the house where they had left off three weeks ago, the team inside shouldn't be in any immediate danger. Even if the house was what he suspected it to be.

On top of it all was Miss Pearson's claim that she had seen her sister inside the house immediately after death. That was troubling, but not exactly unusual. Luca had heard many similar claims over the years after the loss of a loved one, and the people who made them usually thought they were being genuine. But, in reality, it was just a figment made up from a grieving mind.

Regardless, he would need to work fast.

His mind swam, jumping around from one thing to the next: in one moment it tried to decide if Perron Manor could indeed be a Devil's Door, and in the next he battled his guilt for running out on everyone, justifying it to himself that he still had time.

However, it was fear that had driven him away.

Luca had looked into many supernatural occurrences for the Church over the years, but only once had he been truly terrified. Zsámbék Church. That was because it wasn't just his life that had been in danger, but his very *soul*. And that scared him more than anything else he could imagine.

Perron Manor could pose the very same threat.

8

'Interesting start to the investigation,' Ralph said to Jenn. He was driving the van on the way to pick up food for the evening. Jenn was seated in the passenger seat next to him.

'Yeah,' she replied, looking out of the front window at the darkening skies. She felt a little tired as the adrenaline that had fuelled her for most of the day began to wear off. 'The priest didn't stick around for very long.'

'George said he practically ran out of the house.'

'Yeah, that's true,' Jenn confirmed. 'He just about knocked us over coming down the stairs. I think something spooked him.'

'Well, maybe that's a good thing and he'll take us seriously. Did David say what got the priest so freaked out?'

'Yeah, it was that book up on the top floor. Janosch took one look at it and apparently the blood drained from his face.'

'Crazy to think all that shit was up there back in 2014 when we were last here.'

'I was thinking the same,' Jenn replied. 'No wonder that part of the floor had been locked off.'

Jenn had been with David as part of his paranormal investigation team from the very beginning and was his longest-serving colleague. The work they carried out drove her and gave her purpose. Prior to Perron Manor, she'd had experiences that were truly unexplainable, at least to her. They made her believe that death was not the end. However, despite witnessing some amazing things, nothing had ever quite made her truly, one-hundred-percent certain.

But 2014 had changed that. Now she had no doubt *at all* that the paranormal was real. It was also more terrifying than she had ever thought possible.

'You feeling optimistic?' Ralph asked as they eventually pulled onto a main road with streetlights and houses lining either side. It felt like they were finally getting back to civilisation after having been stranded out in the middle of nowhere. The trip would be a quick one, just long enough to pick up the banquet of Indian food they had ordered and Sarah had been kind enough to pay for. In fact, she had insisted upon it.

'About the investigation?' Jenn asked. Ralph nodded. 'I guess,' she said. 'If I'm being honest, I'm nervous about what we'll find.'

'Me too,' Ralph admitted. 'Truth be told, I almost backed out.'

Jenn chuckled. 'You aren't alone. George and Jamie told me the same. I think Ann is hesitant as well.'

'Our psychic?' Ralph asked with a big smile and a voice thick with sarcasm. 'What does she have to be scared of?'

Jenn laughed again. 'That woman is about as psychic as I am.'

'David believes it.'

'David can be an idiot at times. Anyway, I'm surprised *you* were thinking of bailing out. How big are you... like, six-four or something? And you're built like a fridge.'

Ralph shrugged and a look of slight embarrassment washed over his face. 'I don't think a fridge would do much good against what we saw there.'

'No,' Jenn admitted. 'I suppose you're right.'

'You ever think about that night?' he asked.

'All the time,' she said.

'Me too. It still scares the shit out of me. I mean, we found what we desperately wanted to find, but then... I dunno. It just left me with a lot more fear than excitement.'

Jenn turned her head to look at him. 'So why come back? No one would have thought any less of you if you didn't.'

'Pride, I guess. And the fact that I still need to know. Despite what we saw, do you *really* feel like you understand any of it any better? We have our little toys and we live for the snippets of evidence we get, but really we're just fumbling in the dark. It would be nice to learn a little more.'

Jenn understood that. The lust for knowledge—to have a definitive answer for what lay after death—was what drove her too. It had been that way ever since she was twelve and had woken up one night to see her recently deceased 'Nana' standing at the end of her bed.

Her parents had insisted it had just been a dream. Maybe they were right. But the experience lit something inside of Jenn.

All of the team had had similar experiences, something that had sparked their interest in what most people generally dismissed. Especially David, whose own story was tied directly to Perron Manor itself.

'What do you make of the client?' Ralph went on to ask.

'Sarah? She seems okay. I like her.'

'She's pretty intense, huh.'

'Maybe that's why I like her. She used to be in the army, you know.'

Ralph turned to look at her. 'I actually had no idea.'

'Yeah,' Jenn said, smiling. 'So I'd watch what you say to her.'

Ralph smiled and gave an exaggerated salute. 'Will do. But do you believe what she says?'

'About the house? Why would I not?'

'No... I mean about her sister.'

Jenn paused. She knew what Ralph was referring to—that Chloe Shaw had reappeared immediately after her death. Even for someone who believed in the paranormal... that was a stretch. Could a spirit really show itself so quickly after its body had died?

'I'm not sure what to make of it,' she admitted. 'But the way I see it, if we go in there and get the exorcism done, then everyone is happy. Whether the poor girl saw her sister or not, it should still give her some kind of peace.'

'I guess that's as good a way to look at it as any,' Ralph replied. 'Hell, we're even getting paid this time. She must be desperate.'

'The money will certainly help out,' Jenn said. 'The company I work for might make me take some unpaid leave as I'm nearly out of personal days.'

'I'm going to be in and out of the investigation,' Ralph said. 'Work is busy, so I'll need to spend some time away if things run on too long. Plus, things are getting more serious with Helen, so I need to make sure I spend time with her.'

Jenn could understand Ralph's need to balance his life with what they did. It wasn't a full-time job for any of them, including David. They all had their own responsibilities to fulfill. Ralph was a self-employed groundworker, she herself had a warehouse job, and David and George were in IT. Jamie and Ann were the only two who didn't have full-time employment.

Ralph pointed up ahead. 'I think that's the restaurant.'

Jenn gazed hopefully out into the night as her stomach started to growl. She saw a cluster of buildings about half a mile ahead, washed in pink and purple neon light. The sign above the door proved Ralph correct.

'Thank God,' Jenn said as they approached. 'I could eat a horse.'

'Gonna have to make do with chicken and lamb,' Ralph joked.

Jenn let out a chuckle. 'I guess that will work. Nice to have a feast like this together. We normally pick at sandwiches during our investigations, then sit up all night in the cold.'

Ralph pulled to a stop. 'Yeah, I was thinking the same. It'll be nice to have a little bit of comfort for once.'

Jenn got out of the car. 'Keep the engine running,' she said, feeling optimistic about the job ahead. 'I'll be back in a flash.'

9

THE GROUP HAD GATHERED in the great hall, where they sat around the long table to partake in the banquet Jenn and Ralph had brought back. David had suggested that Sarah take a seat at the head of the table, but frankly, she didn't want the attention, so she insisted that David take it. Jenn, Ralph, and George were on one side of him with Jamie, Ann, and Sarah on the other. Sarah noticed that most of the team had handheld cameras with them, all set on the table.

Best to be prepared, she thought.

The food laid out was a mixture of chicken, lamb, and prawn dishes, accompanied by different types of rice, naan, popadoms, seekh kababs, and more. The normally stuffy odours of the hall were replaced with mouthwatering smells of onion, spices, cinnamon, and charcoaled chicken.

Everyone dug in, loading their plates with a mixture of the different foods on offer. Jenn and Ralph had also picked up some alcohol from the restaurant: some had beers and wine, though Sarah and Ann stuck with water. In truth, Sarah wanted a drink, but she wasn't sure she'd be able to stop after just one or two. Not with the way she was feeling.

Plus, she desperately wanted to keep her wits about her.

Despite her paying for it, the meal felt wrong to Sarah. There was a celebratory atmosphere between David's team as they sat chatting and went over old war stories. Though not quite a party, the atmosphere was close to it.

However, Sarah kept those feelings to herself and continued to eat. After all, she needed their help.

'Remember that place in County Durham?' George asked with a smile.

'Ah yeah, Birkley Close,' Jamie replied. 'That EVP we got... still freaks me out listening to it.'

'The voice definitely sounded like a child,' Jenn said.

'It *was* a child,' Ann confirmed. 'It communicated to us through me, remember?'

David nodded. 'That's right. It was really something to see.'

Sarah frowned. Did that mean Ann was a medium? She cast her eyes about and saw that Jenn and Ralph shared a look between each other, and Jenn rolled her eyes before giving a slight shake of the head.

That was interesting to note.

Sarah popped a piece of chicken into her mouth. Heat radiated from the rich, brown vindaloo sauce covering the meat. The intense warmth was a welcome sensation, and it was only intensified after she tore off and devoured a piece of chili-infused naan.

In her view, if the food wasn't spicy enough to melt your teeth fillings, it wasn't real Indian food. It was something Chloe had always disagreed with, as her pallet had always been more pedestrian.

The thought of her sister immediately made Sarah wonder if Chloe was with them now, watching them. If so, was she still in pain and torment?

She glanced over at the rear double-door that looked out over the courtyard. More memories from her recent-past flooded back, where Chloe had insisted she'd seen a man that looked like a monk, staring back in from outside. Sarah shuddered.

Over the course of the day the team had set up all of their equipment, a process made easier because of their last visit. They knew roughly where all cameras and sensors were to be positioned, and they had also shown Sarah where everything was. In addition, the group had demonstrated the computer equipment in their headquarters, so she now knew roughly how to cycle between camera views. They'd taught her how to work some of the EVP recording equipment, heat sensors, and motion detectors.

It was all fancy stuff, and Sarah just hoped they could get something usable that would convince Father Janosch.

She was worried about what had happened to the team's evidence the last time they were here. She'd read David's book, which covered that investigation, and in it he claimed the equipment had all failed at the crucial time. Either he was full of it, or more likely the house had decided not to let David have his proof.

If that was the case, what was to say this time would be any different?

Perhaps the only solution was to get Father Janosch back here so he could experience Perron Manor for himself.

'Sarah?' Jenn asked, pulling Sarah away from her thoughts.

She looked up. 'Yeah?'

'We've gotten a brief overview from David on the things you experienced here. But it might be a good idea to go over some specifics, if you don't mind?'

'Sure,' Sarah replied. She was thankful the topic of

conversation was being brought back to the job at hand. 'What exactly do you want to know?'

'Well,' Jenn replied, 'I suppose the best thing to focus on is going over some of the things you and your family saw. And *where* exactly you saw them. I know on your last night the basement played a large role, so we'll concentrate a lot of our efforts down there. But beyond that, were there any other hotspots?'

Sarah thought about the question. The basement was probably the area with the most activity. It was also where one of those fucking ghosts almost threw her niece into the lit furnace. The entrance lobby played a part as well, since that was where Chloe had died. Sarah ran through the events in her head to think of any other locations where things happened.

'Chloe had some experiences in this very hall. She saw something standing just outside that door.' Sarah pointed to the rear, glazed door. 'And she saw something inside the room with her as well. She also claimed to have seen a woman in my room. An old hag, as she put it, who was crouched on my bed while I was asleep.'

'Creepy,' Ralph chimed in.

'I didn't see it myself,' Sarah told him, 'but it really creeped Chloe out. In truth, the last night was the only time I actually witnessed the things she had been talking about.'

'So everything was really focused on Chloe?' Jenn asked.

Sarah nodded. 'Yeah, I'd say that's accurate. I think the house focused on her because she got away back in '82... but now it has her.'

Jenn gave Sarah a sad smile. 'I can't imagine what you're going through,' she said.

There was an awkward silence between them all. It was

the familiar, uncomfortable air that Sarah had noticed from people when they spoke to her about Chloe. She decided to press on. 'There is the entrance lobby, of course' she said. 'That's where Chloe died.'

Jenn leaned forward in her seat. 'And what exactly did you see in there, if you don't mind me asking? I know you were all running when Chloe tripped and fell, but I didn't realise there were entities in the area with you at the time.'

Sarah paused. She couldn't tell them the whole truth of what happened—where a demon had thrown her out of the house and then snapped her sister's neck. Sarah had already started the lie of her sister's death being an accident, and needed to continue it so as to not scare away the team.

'We were running from... ghosts,' Sarah said. 'There were scores of them, just standing watching us in the corridors and coming out of rooms. So we kept running as fast as we could.'

Sarah felt a pang of guilt in her gut for concealing just how dangerous the house was.

She knew it wasn't right. But she also needed to save her sister, and Sarah would happily damn her own soul to make that happen.

'Nothing in the study upstairs?' David asked. 'The one with the artefacts?'

Sarah considered the question, then shook her head. 'Not that I'm aware of.'

'Well, if everyone agrees,' Jenn began, 'I think we focus on the areas where there has been activity recently. We know where we saw things back in 2014, but with Sarah's experiences being more recent, I think we have to focus on the basement, the entrance lobby, Chloe's bedroom, and this hall,' she said as she gestured around the space they sat in.

'Makes sense,' David agreed. The others gave nods of confirmation as well. Sarah liked what she'd seen of Jenn; the woman seemed smart, straightforward, and practical.

'Sounds like a good plan,' Jamie said. He then looked over to Sarah. 'I know you weren't here back in '82 when all those people died, but did your parents or sister ever tell you anything about that weekend?'

Sarah shook her head. 'Not really. Chloe couldn't remember any of it, and my parents always avoided the topic whenever it was brought up. So you guys probably know more than me.'

'From what I've heard, you were lucky you weren't around,' Ann said. 'It was horrific.'

'Well, I didn't come along until the following July,' Sarah said. 'So I'm happy to have missed all the fun.'

'Understood,' Jamie replied. 'I've just always felt that weekend was important. It was the biggest known supernatural event in the house's history, after all. Any new insight might have helped us shape our investigation.'

Sarah just shrugged. 'Afraid I can't help you.'

Everyone suddenly stopped talking as the sound of thudding footsteps from the floor above them echoed. The fast, stomping footfalls directly overhead were soon followed by the sound of a door slamming shut.

Sarah's body locked up, and she looked over to the others with wide eyes. They all seemed equally shocked.

'Shit!' Ralph exclaimed. Nobody moved for the next few moments. Not until David suddenly slid back his chair.

'Let's go,' he commanded. 'Everyone upstairs now!'

Everyone leapt into action, springing to their feet and grabbing their cameras. The mood changed in an instant, and Sarah could sense the nervous anticipation and excitement radiate from the team.

They all quickly filtered out of the great hall and ran towards the stairs, Sarah bringing up the rear.

10

DAVID LED the way as everyone raced up the stairs. He had his handheld camera pointing ahead, trying to keep it as steady as possible just in case it picked something up.

His heart was racing. The footsteps and slamming door had been unmistakable.

With the sounds coming from directly above the great hall, David knew which direction he needed to head.

Once they were up on the mid-floor, David led them to where he thought they needed to be, which was close to the stairs that led up to the top storey. Those stairs were flanked on either side by small rooms. He figured it *had* to have been one of those doors that had slammed.

David felt a swell of exhilaration mixed in with the nerves, realising they had a camera mounted close by that had likely picked up what had happened. He just hoped the camera was running okay and everything had been recorded.

If so, they may have already captured their first compelling piece of evidence.

The doors to both rooms were closed, and the stairs

between them that ran up to the floor above were shrouded in darkness. The group stood in silence... waiting and listening. The narrow corridor had dark oak panelling to the bottom half of the walls and cream wallpaper above. The ceilings were high with ornate coving, and the lighting was cast by iron chandeliers.

David pointed his handheld camera up the steep stairwell, but couldn't make much out through the viewfinder. It was just too dark.

'Okay,' he said to his team. 'Given the great hall is directly below us, the slamming door had to be one of these two. Hopefully, we have caught the whole thing on that camera there.' He pointed to the end of the corridor, where the wireless camera was fixed to a wall bracket and pointed back towards them. David then turned to the first storage room, the one just to his left.

'Let's check it out,' he said and took a step towards the heavy oak door. David reached out a hand and slowly opened it. The door swung inwards, and he held his camera up. The room inside wasn't very big at all, about four feet by four feet, and the back wall was lined floor to ceiling with bare shelves.

A storage room.

He could see most of the room thanks to the light from the corridor outside, but still reached a hand inside and found the light switch. The extra light revealed nothing, however, as the room was totally empty. He let the others peek their heads inside to see as he moved on to the next door.

In truth, David didn't expect to see anything. Not now. He felt the activity they'd heard was just the house warming up, and it would likely be all they encountered for a while. That was how these things tended to work: little bursts of activity that were sparse at first, but that sometimes grew into something more substantial.

The second room was identical to the first, and just as empty.

'We need to go check the footage,' Jenn said after everyone had looked into the second room for themselves.

She was right, but David couldn't help but again look up those stairs that led to the floor above, and how they vanished into darkness at the halfway point. As he looked, an awful sensation came over him that something was staring right back.

'Agreed,' he eventually said in response to Jenn. 'Let's go.'

'Not to be that guy,' Ralph started, 'because I'm as excited as the rest of us to look at the footage. But we have a hell of a meal waiting for us downstairs that's just going to get cold.'

David turned to Ralph with a look of bewilderment. The others stared at him as well, all sharing the same expression. Ralph's cheeks flushed red and he held up his hands.

'Fair enough,' he said. 'We check the camera feeds first, *then* we can eat the cold food.'

11

SARAH STOOD over the shoulder of David, who was seated at the computer in the room designated as their headquarters. The other team members were present as well.

David pulled up the camera view from upstairs that focused on the corridor and the two storage room doors. It also showed the first few steps of the stairs that led up to the top storey.

The image on the laptop screen was in colour, though the reds of the carpets and dark browns of the oak panelling to the walls were washed out. The video feed wasn't high definition, either, with a slight grainy quality to it.

'The noises we heard happened about ten minutes ago,' David said and rewound the footage. As the feed skipped backwards, they all saw the moment where the door had closed, though in reverse it looked like it opened.

'There,' Jenn said, excitement in her voice. 'We caught it!'

But David kept going back, and Sarah soon saw why.

'I knew it,' David said as he paused the video. 'I was certain both doors up there were closed when we looked around earlier. So something opened the door first, then slammed it shut.' He started the footage again, playing it forward at normal speed and turning up the volume to full.

All Sarah could initially hear was some faint feedback and a slight crackle. Eventually, however, the door to the storage room nearest the camera slowly drifted open with an audible creak.

Sarah felt a tingle run up her spine.

The video kept playing for a minute longer before they all heard it, loud enough through the tinny speakers of the laptop that Ann jumped. The thudding footsteps they'd heard from downstairs thundered down the corridor over to the open door, which was promptly slammed shut.

'Did anyone else see that?' Sarah asked.

'Of course,' George replied, 'how could we miss it?'

Sarah shook her head. 'No, I'm not talking about the door closing. David, can you rewind that bit again, to just before the footsteps.'

David did as she asked, then played the video back. Yet again, the heavy running of some invisible person was audible from the laptop.

Only, they weren't quite invisible. Sarah put a finger close to the screen. 'There, do you see it?'

David leaned forward and squinted his eyes. He rewound and played it again.

'I see it!' he then exclaimed. Everyone else leaned in close.

It was a faint shadow of a humanoid shape, and translucent enough to be almost undetectable. It moved quickly and disappeared inside of the storage room moments before the door was closed.

'Oh wow,' Jenn said as David played it yet again.

'Definitely looks like a person,' Ralph added, then turned his head to Sarah. 'Nice catch.'

She smiled, feeling pleased with herself.

'I agree,' David said. 'I think we really have something here.'

'So then let's call that priest!' Sarah suggested. 'We can get him back here to see this.'

'Well,' David started, 'we need a bit more. Don't get me wrong, this is a hell of a start, but for an exorcism we really need the evidence to be overwhelming.'

'And this isn't?'

'Not quite. Like I said, it's great, and something to really build off. I *will* call Janosch and give him an update tomorrow, but let's see what happens tonight. Who knows, we might even get more.'

Sarah felt herself deflate. Just what did the Church need as proof, a personalised fucking message from a ghost? She sighed. 'Fine.'

David reached up from his seated position and put what was supposed to be a comforting hand on her forearm. As he did, Sarah had to resist the urge to flinch away.

'I know it's hard to be patient,' he said. 'Hell, it's bad enough for us, so I can't even imagine how impatient you must be feeling. But if we don't do everything right, then it will just delay things in the long run. The last thing we need is the Church to look at what we send and just dismiss it. This,' he pointed at the screen, 'is only one incident. We need to give them—and pardon my French here—a *shitload* more of the same.'

Sarah nodded. He was right, but that didn't make having to wait any easier.

Everyone watched the video again a few more times, following it through to when they all appeared on camera to investigate the slamming door, just to see if there was anything else of note.

There was not.

Eventually, they all went back down to the great hall to pick through the remains of the cold food. It was hardly the tasty feast it had started out as, but everyone needed the energy. A little after ten, David suggested they all turn in, since it had been a busy day and he wanted everyone well-rested. They could begin again in earnest the following day.

Sarah readied herself for bed with her two new room-mates without saying much. The lights went out, and she pulled the duvet tightly around herself. She then fell asleep thinking about Chloe.

12

JENN'S EYES FLUTTERED OPEN, and she was met with darkness. She felt tired, like she hadn't gotten a full night's sleep.

She blinked and let her vision focus, taking in the details of the bedroom—the window on the far wall with its heavy blue curtains pulled closed. A dresser. A side table where her phone and a nightlight lay.

It was cold in the room as well, even under the covers.

Jenn was lying on her side, facing the far wall, but she could hear Ann's gentle snoring from directly behind her. Jenn also felt Ann's cold foot on her leg. She kicked it away and groaned, leaning over to check her phone. The screen lit up and showed it was just after three in the morning.

Why the hell have I woken up so early? And why the fuck is it so cold?

She rolled to her back and pulled the duvet tighter around herself. Then, she looked down to the foot of her bed.

Jenn's breath caught in her throat.

She could see part of someone crouched over where Sarah lay, though she was just able to make out the head and shoulders, the rest of the body disappearing below the edge of her bed.

It was hard to make out in the dark, and the form was like a shadow, almost translucent.

Jenn fought through her fear and forced her body to move. As she did, the head that had been looking down quickly spun to face her.

In a panic, Jenn quickly leaned over and switched on the nightlight. It kicked out a dull orange glow that, while not strong enough to completely illuminate the room, was enough to let Jenn see.

There was nothing there. Nothing at the end of the bed sitting atop Sarah, who now began to stir, along with Ann.

'What's going on?' Ann asked wearily as she sat up, eyes squinting and her black hair a wild mess. Jenn saw Sarah sit up as well and look over the frame of the bed, confusion evident on her tired face.

'I...' Jenn trailed off. For a moment, she was unsure if she should share the experience. What if it was nothing? She was in the game to get *true* evidence of the afterlife, not confused accounts that could well have been the remnants of a dream.

'Well?' Ann pressed. Jenn decided it was best to share regardless, just in case.

'There was something crouched over Sarah,' she said.

Ann then sat upright.

'There was what?' Sarah asked in shock.

'A shadow, a faint one, like we saw on the video feed earlier. It was just crouched over you, but when I put on the light, it vanished.'

Sarah looked around. 'I can't see anything.' She then hugged herself. 'It's fucking cold, though.'

'The whole room feels cold,' Ann added. 'Which is a sign of activity.'

That was true, however Jenn actually felt like the room was warming up a little compared to when she had first woken up.

'But how do we know for certain it *was* something?' Sarah asked. 'How do we prove it?'

Jenn shrugged. 'I'm not sure we can. There are cameras in the corridors outside, so we can check those in the morning to see if anything has been picked up. But in here, we don't have anything recording us.'

'But why?' Sarah asked. 'We need to get everything.'

'It's a privacy issue,' Jenn said. 'David is pretty strict on that. He isn't comfortable with having video footage of us sleeping or changing clothes. He says it isn't right.'

'And he has a point,' Ann added. 'I wouldn't be comfortable being naked on camera. That's not what I signed up for. Imagine if the footage got leaked.'

'I don't think it would be a national scandal, Ann,' Jenn replied, though she knew Ann wasn't exactly being unreasonable.

Sarah shook her head and looked exasperated. 'Are you serious? We could be missing way too much. I'm going to speak to David in the morning.'

'I'm *not* being recorded while I sleep,' Ann insisted.

'Then go home!' Sarah shot back. Ann looked insulted, her eyes wide, but instead of firing back she just sat in silence, sulking. They all stayed that way for a little while, waiting for something to happen.

Eventually, Ann lay down and angrily pulled the covers over herself. It was clear she was still annoyed at Sarah's comments.

Sarah cast Jenn a look, as if asking 'is she for real?' She

then shook her head and lay down herself. 'You can switch off the light when you're ready, Jenn,' she said. 'I guess we can talk about this more tomorrow.'

Jenn did as she was asked, smiling a little at Ann having thrown a tantrum. It was nice to see the princess brought down a peg or two, even if Jenn didn't wholly disagree with her in principle.

While trying to get back to sleep, Jenn kept glancing down to the edge of the bed to see if the shadow had returned. She remembered how it had turned to face her just a moment before it vanished. It sent a chill up her spine.

Perhaps Sarah had a point. Could they really let modesty get in the way of capturing indisputable evidence?

13

'Nope,' David said. 'I'm not seeing anything.'

Sarah sighed in disappointment.

The team were again in HQ, poring over the computer monitors. The first thing that morning, Sarah had knocked on David and George's bedroom door, and then told them what had happened the previous night. David's eyes lit up. Everyone was quickly rounded up and brought downstairs, still in their sleeping clothes and robes.

They checked the footage outside the girls' bedroom around the time of the incident but came up short. Whatever had happened inside the room had been isolated.

'Damn it,' Sarah said. 'How much is Jenn's experience worth to Janosch without evidence?'

David looked up at her from his seat. 'He may well believe her,' he said, 'but it won't hold too much water on its own. However, we will document it and add it to everything else.'

That wasn't good enough for Sarah. Two things of note had happened since they'd arrived yesterday, but only one had been caught. Batting at a fifty-percent success rate was going to make the whole process take much longer.

'We need cameras in the bedrooms,' Sarah said.

'We don't have enough for all the bedrooms,' David said. 'We already have them in a few, your sister and your niece's for example, as well as your old room, but we'd run out pretty quick if we tried to monitor every bedroom.'

'No,' Sarah said. 'I meant the bedrooms we're using.'

David paused, then shook his head. 'We can't do that. People should be allowed their privacy.'

'What does it matter?' Sarah pressed. 'I mean really, is anyone here going to use any of the footage for anything other than proof? It's not like videos of us sleeping are going to get leaked online like some seedy sex tape. It's nothing. Plus it just seems stupid not to monitor ourselves while we sleep. Everything here seems to happen late at night, often in the rooms that are in use. Those things focus on *us*.'

'We all have handheld cameras,' David argued. 'Those can be used.'

'But look what happened last night,' Sarah countered. 'There was no time to get the camera before whatever the hell it was disappeared.'

'I'm not comfortable being recorded like that, David,' Ann cut in. Sarah gritted her teeth but took a calming breath.

'I understand,' David said. 'I would never ask you to do anything you aren't comfortable with.'

'Then switch rooms,' Sarah insisted. 'Hell, I'll go sleep in a room on my own.'

'That isn't happening,' David stated. 'We can't get reckless... or impatient.'

'Actually,' Ralph said, sounding hesitant, 'I think Sarah makes a good point.' Everyone turned to him, and Sarah felt a small pang of relief. *Finally, some back-up.* 'We could be missing a hell of a lot. I get what Ann is saying, but let's face it, it isn't like we're waltzing naked around our rooms all the time. And we obviously wouldn't record bathrooms. So... is it really such a big deal?'

David looked around the group. 'How does everyone else feel about it?'

There were a few nonchalant shrugs before George chimed in. 'I'd be fine with it. We can just get dressed in the bathrooms if we need to, like Ralph says.'

'I'm okay with it, too,' Jenn added.

Jamie then chipped in. 'Me too, I guess.'

Ann threw her arms up in the air. 'David, no!'

However, Sarah had a solution.

'Look, given that shadow was close to *me* last night, it stands to reason to monitor the room I'm in. So, if anyone is game, I'll share a bedroom with someone else, and Ann and Jenn can stay where they are... without being watched.'

'But that would mean bunking up with a guy,' David said.

'I know, but that isn't a big deal. For God's sake, when I was in the army I bunked with men all the time. I think *you're* making a bigger issue out of it than it really is.'

David paused and chewed at his lower lip. 'I guess that would be okay, as long as you have no issue with it?'

'I don't,' Sarah insisted.

Then Jenn cut in. 'I have no problem being filmed. I'm happy to share a room with Sarah for this.'

Ann's eyes went wide. 'And leave me on my own? Because I am *not* sharing a room with one of the boys. I'm sorry, but *I* wasn't in the army, and I'm not comfortable with it.'

'Sleep on your own, then,' Jenn replied with a grin.

'Enough,' David said, raising a hand into the air. He again looked up to Sarah. 'If you're okay with it, I'll share a room with you. We can pull another bed into one of the rooms and I'll take that.'

Sarah smiled. 'Works for me. And we'll get a camera set up?'

'Yes,' David said. 'But we'll do that after breakfast. I'm starving, and right now I need coffee.'

Sarah was happy with that, and she was pleased David had finally seen sense. It would hopefully move things on at a much quicker pace.

While Sarah hadn't seen what Jenn had, the fact the shadow was over *her* meant she was potentially a target for the things in this house—much like her sister had been.

However, Sarah had another theory about that shadow. Maybe it was the same one they had seen running down the hall. It was entirely possible that *this* entity was not malicious.

Perhaps it was Chloe.

14

'VERY INTERESTING,' Luca said into the phone pressed against his cheek, trying to block the concern from his voice.

He had blessed the house only yesterday. Now, if David was to be believed, there had been more activity already.

Luca was in his study and seated at the pine desk, which held his laptop. The study was his place of refuge—somewhere he could hide away, close the door, and block out the world. It wasn't a huge room, and that only helped convey a welcome sense of solitude. The window beside him gave a view out over the rear gardens of the clergy house, which had a neatly trimmed lawn and high conifer trees around the perimeter. A bookshelf sat behind him, packed with reference books and scripture, some of which were devoted to a subject on which he had become a reluctant specialist.

'We caught something on video,' David said, 'but missed the incident in the girls' bedroom last night. However, I'm very confident we'll see more soon. Can I ask, is there any way you can forewarn your superiors, so they know what's coming? It might speed things up, and our client is quite... impatient, as you can imagine.'

'I appreciate that,' Luca replied. 'But there really is no rushing these things, unfortunately. We will have to go through the appropriate channels, but only when we have a strong enough case.'

'Fair enough. I had to ask.'

'I understand. While I have you, I would be interested in looking at the book again, if that is okay. The... *Ianua Diaboli.*'

'Of course,' David replied eagerly. 'When can you come over?'

Luca paused for a moment, searching for the best way to frame his words. 'Well, it might be beneficial if you actually bring it to me. I think it would be easier to study it that way. I'd therefore be able to spend a bit more time with it, you know?'

That was an exaggeration at best. *You're afraid, Luca. You know you are.*

It was David's turn to pause. 'Well... I'd need to check with the client first. It's her book, after all, but I think she would be okay with it.'

'Could you find out and let me know?'

'Sure. Is there something interesting about that book, Father? Anything I need to be aware of?'

'Not really,' Luca said. *Is it really a lie if I'm protecting someone?* Luca hoped not, because that was his only justification. 'However, its age and subject matter are of great interest. That book might even help make the Church take notice of our situation.'

'There are tons of rare artefacts up there,' David said. 'We could catalogue them all if need be. Would that help?'

'Well, let's look at them after I've finished with the book. One step at a time.'

The other things in that study might indeed be valuable, and significant, but Luca could not look past *Ianua Diaboli* —if, of course, it was the real deal.

He sincerely hoped it wasn't.

15

DAVID HUNG up the phone and scratched his chin. The conversation with Father Janosch had been interesting, and thrown up something of a curveball. Perhaps it was an opportunity, as Father Janosch had said; a reason for the Church to take a closer look.

The priest had indicated the book was of interest, but only because of its historical significance. However, David got the feeling Father Janosch may have been hiding something, which made him want to check out the book again.

He slipped his phone into his pocket and stood up from the ornate lounge chair he had been sitting on in the library. The ground-floor room was beautiful, with the walls filled with bookshelves that almost touched the high ceilings. Each shelf was neatly stacked with thick books. The space had a musty smell of old leather, and the tall window that looked out over the front grounds let in plenty of natural daylight, making the space feel light and airy... if a little dusty.

It was a little after midday, and while the others were finishing lunch in the great hall, he had left them to make the call. He quickly returned to them. As he entered the hall, Sarah looked up.

'Well,' she asked, 'what did he say?'

'He was interested to hear our experiences,' David replied and walked over to the table. All eyes were on him. He took a seat and felt a small pull in his back, a resulting twinge from when he and Sarah had earlier rearranged the bedroom they would share.

'And...?' Sarah asked.

'We have to carry on as we were, like I thought,' David replied. He saw Sarah's shoulders drop. He understood her disappointment, but it was what he had been anticipating before making the call—they simply didn't have enough yet.

Sarah took a deep breath. 'Okay. We carry on as we are. So what's next?'

'Well, before we get to that,' David said. 'There was something that came up in the conversation that was interesting. The book upstairs, in that weird study... Father Janosch would like to study it?'

Sarah frowned. 'Why?'

He shrugged. 'I'm not certain. He said it could be valuable.'

'Valuable?' Sarah asked. He saw her jaw clench. 'I'm sorry, but we have more pressing matters than finding out how much an old book is worth. What... is he planning to sell it on eBay and make a little money or something?'

David held up his hands. 'Sarah, it's nothing like that,' he said. 'Given what that book deals with, and also finding it in a house like this... he says it warrants investigation, and that it might help make the Church take notice of what we're doing here. I got the impression—though he didn't say it directly—that there's more to it than just monetary value.

And think about it... if it interests the Church, then you have a bargaining chip.'

A look of realisation washed over her. 'I see,' she replied. 'Clever. Okay, he can come here and have a look. But only for a few hours. If he wants to see more, we need this place exorcised first.'

'There may be a problem with that,' David said.

'Which is?'

'He didn't want to come to the house to study it. Said he'd prefer we take the book to him so he'd have more time with it. Apparently it would be easier for him to study in his own home.'

Sarah let out a humourless laugh. 'I bet it would be. But then I'd never see it again.'

'He isn't a thief, Sarah,' David stated. 'He's a *priest*.'

'Let's not pretend that those things are mutually exclusive,' she shot back.

David shook his head. 'We can trust him. Father Janosch is a good guy. He's on our side.'

'Maybe you think so, but I don't know him from Adam. And I *certainly* don't trust him enough to loan him my stuff. Look, it's my book, and my decision. If he wants to study it, he does it here.'

She folded her arms across her chest, and though David wanted to try to make her see reason, he knew her mind would not be swayed. Besides, having Father Janosch spend some time here certainly wouldn't hurt their investigation.

'Fine,' David said. 'I'll speak to him again and let him know.'

'Great. So... what's next for today?' she asked.

16

WITH THE NIGHT-VISION MODE ENGAGED, Jenn looked through the viewfinder of her camera. It was focused on Ann. The tall, raven-haired woman stood with her eyes closed and arms held out to her sides, attempting to contact the dead.

That woman is about as psychic as a doorstop. Why is David taken in by her bullshit?

It was approaching mid-afternoon and they were down in the basement. All of the lights were off, and the only source of illumination was the two bright beams from the torches Ralph and George carried.

'I'm getting something,' Ann said, cocking her head to the side.

'What?' David asked eagerly.

Ann was standing in the middle of everyone as they formed a crude circle around her. There was a chill to the air and a musty, moldy smell.

They had been down there in the dark for ten minutes, watching Ann through their viewfinders as she paced around, looking off into the shadows like she could see something the rest of them couldn't.

'Over there,' she said and pointed to a corner of the room. Ralph and George cast their torchlights over to where she was pointing, but all Jenn could see was the point where the two stone walls met. Nothing else. 'I feel a presence,' Ann went on. 'A child, I think.'

Jenn had to force herself not to roll her eyes.

It's always a fucking child with Ann.

That was her go-to. Jenn knew why: the ghost of a dead child would always pull at the heartstrings, so it helped keep any scepticism in check the others may have. Jenn fully expected the child would be a girl.

'It's a little girl,' Ann added.

Fucking bingo!

'Is she aware of our presence?' David asked.

'She is,' Ann confirmed with a slow nod. 'She's curious as well.' Ann then took a step forward and addressed the empty corner in soothing tones. 'Don't be scared, little one; we aren't here to hurt you. Do you have a message for us?' Ann cocked her head to the side as if listening.

After her pause continued for too long, David asked, 'Is she saying anything?'

Ann held up a finger to silence their leader. She then gave a slow nod. 'She says we have to be careful. There is something here that means to do us harm.'

'Some*thing*?' David asked. 'Not some*one*?'

'That's right. She was very specific about that.'

'The demon. It has to be.'

'I agree,' Ann said.

David shook his head in awe. 'That is amazing.'

Jenn gritted her teeth together. It was *not* amazing in the slightest. They all knew about the demon here already, because they'd *seen* it in 2014, and this non-incident had provided nothing in the way of true evidence.

This was the kind of bullshit nonsense that was far too easy to dismiss, and it made them all look like idiots or charlatans.

But Jenn knew she had to push through. For whatever reason, David believed in what Ann said and what she claimed she brought to the table.

Away from that nonsense, however, Jenn was convinced they were doing good work with their investigation. And *that* was the important thing to her. So she just had to accept Ann as she was, at least for now.

'Is she saying anything else?' Ralph asked. Jenn could hear the faintest touch of exasperation in his voice.

'She's just saying the same thing again: that we need to be careful. Wait... now she's saying she needs to leave us.'

Thank God.

'Can't you ask her to stay?' David asked.

'I'm afraid she's already gone,' Ann replied, before adding, 'travel safe, little one.'

They spent another ten minutes waiting for something else to happen before Ann eventually said, 'There is nothing down here with us anymore. I can't feel anything.'

And, instead of trying something else, David took that as evidence enough to leave the location. 'Let's head upstairs,' he said. 'I think it would be a good idea to try some vigils. We'll split up into teams and spread out.'

Everyone started to head out, and Jenn checked the battery on her camera as she walked. It was then she felt a cold hand grab hold of her shoulder. Jenn assumed it was Jamie, who had been standing close to her.

As she raised her head, she lifted the camera up as well, and as she did she saw through her viewfinder that the

other six members of the team were all in front of her...
including Jamie.

She was bringing up the rear alone.

The cold hand clamped tighter and Jenn's body stiffened
in fright. Her breath caught in her chest. She wanted to turn
round and face whatever was behind her, but she struggled
to move. The others carried on trudging over to the steps.

'Guys...' she managed to squeak out, but no one heard. A
foul, rotting smell flowed from behind her. Jenn began to
shake. There was no question she was in the middle of an
encounter, but fear had seized her, and she was terrified at
the thought of turning around.

Instead, she held the camera out before her with one
hand and slowly rotated it towards herself, flipping the
viewfinder as she did. In the small screen, illuminated with
the blue hue of night vision, she could see herself come into
focus. Her eyes were wide and pupils were like pin-pricks.
She studied her shoulder on the image before her but could
see nothing. It was then she noticed she could no longer feel
the cold touch.

'Guys!' Jenn shouted as she found her voice. She was
suddenly blinded by torchlight as the others turned to
face her.

'What is it?' Ralph asked, quickly lowering his beam
from her eyes. Jenn momentarily saw stars and swirling
motes. She blinked quickly to clear her vision.

'I felt something,' she said. 'A hand... on my shoulder.
I'm sure of it.'

A moment of stunned silence was quickly broken by the
sound of running feet over the stone ground. Everyone
came over and crowded around Jenn.

'Can you still feel it?' Sarah asked.

Jenn shook her head and finally felt her body relax. 'No,'

she said, rotating her arm at the shoulder a couple of times. The two torch beams flicked around the room but no one could find anything.

'George, go put on the main light,' David ordered. 'Quickly.'

George did as instructed and trotted over to the steps that led up to the floor above. The switch was situated on the wall just next to them, and he flicked it on.

The lights slowly blinked to life, giving off a brief strobe effect as they powered up. The team searched the basement but came up short.

'Are you certain about what you felt?' David asked.

'One hundred percent,' Jenn stated.

David then turned to Ann. 'I thought you said that whoever was down here had left?'

Jenn had to stop from shaking her head in disbelief. *Get a clue, David.*

'I thought they had,' Ann replied. 'But someone else must have come through just as we were leaving.'

Jenn ignored their conversation and pulled up her camera, skipping back through the footage to when she had felt the hand. She played the footage back, but all Jenn could see on the screen was her own terrified face. And behind that was only darkness.

No... wait.

There *was* something else there: two small glinting objects, which could easily have been floating dust particles if not for them being perfectly parallel. Jenn paused the footage and went into the settings menu of the camera. She started to increase the contrast, washing more light into the image. Click by click, the blacks behind Jenn on screen were forced back and replaced by a dull blue, making more and more of the space behind her visible. When the contrast was turned up to its fullest Jenn could make out the far wall behind her, as well as the black form of the furnace.

There was something else, too—something she could see more clearly now: a man standing flat against the wall.

Though the image was grainy and pixilated, he looked to be wearing dark robes. His face was a blank stare and his eyes glinted like reflecting pennies.

'Holy shit!'

17

THE EVIDENCE SEEMED to be falling into their laps.

First was the shadow moving across the hallway, and now the footage from the basement, of something standing behind Jenn. While neither piece of evidence was completely clear, in Sarah's mind both were undeniable.

And on top of that, there had been the experience during the night.

The house is still alive.

David had warned Sarah that things might be slow to pick up because the building had been empty for three weeks. Spirits and demons drew on the energy of the living. It fuelled them and allowed them to make themselves known.

However, in the space of a single day, it seemed like the house hadn't missed a step at all.

David had given everyone some free time before they ate, so people had paired up and gone off to different rooms to conduct some vigils. From what Sarah could tell, a vigil just consisted of sitting in a room and asking the spirits to show themselves.

However, Sarah was interested to see what David was up to. He had disappeared off somewhere on his own.

After searching the ground and middle floors and not finding him, Sarah then moved up to the top storey. She circled the corridor and made her way to where she suspected he was: the study.

As she turned the corner to the room, she saw the door was open and a light was on inside. While it wasn't dark out just yet, daylight was beginning to wane.

She poked her head inside the room and saw David was in the centre, and he had *Ianua Diaboli* out and resting on top of the cabinet's glass display lid. The book was open and David was scribbling something down into a small notebook that lay on the case as well.

'Hiding away?' Sarah asked, and David jumped in fright.

'Jesus,' he exclaimed, holding a hand over his chest. 'You just about gave me a bloody heart attack.'

'Sorry,' Sarah said, though the chuckle that followed probably showed her lack of sincerity. 'Are you supposed to be up here on your own? I thought we were always meant to be in pairs at least.'

'Fair point,' David replied. He then took a deep breath and lowered his hand from his chest. 'I figure with it still being daytime I should be okay for a little while.'

'Interested in my book?' Sarah asked, nodding to the artefact he was studying.

'A little,' he replied. 'I'm curious as to why Father Janosch is so focused on it.'

'Did you call him back?'

David nodded. 'I did, though couldn't get hold of him. I left a message saying he would need to come down here if he wanted to study the book.'

Sarah made her way over to David. She didn't like the

study the first time she had seen it, but the longer she stayed, the more Sarah found herself spending time up here, always drawn back to *Ianua Diaboli*. She couldn't explain why, but there was something alluring about the book.

'If he's interested enough, he'll come around,' Sarah said. And she dearly hoped that he *was* interested enough, though she was prepared to use every dirty trick she had at her disposal to get this fucking exorcism finally underway.

'I also mentioned what happened last night, and about the footage we got down in the basement, too. I said that things really seem to be ramping up already.'

'Things haven't taken long to get going,' Sarah said, looking down at the book.

'No, they really haven't. Which is both good and bad.'

Sarah blinked, then lifted her head to him. 'Bad? How do you mean?'

'Well, I mean it could be a sign that things are going to become dangerous. I've never had so much activity in such a small space of time before. Well, not since I was last here.'

'But that's a good thing!' Sarah said. 'That means we will get our evidence much quicker.'

'Or everything gets out of hand and someone gets hurt,' he replied. 'Remember, things don't tend to end well for people in Perron Manor: the events in 1982, for example. And my own investigation in 2014 got a little dangerous at the end. Then, of course...' he trailed off.

'Then my sister died.'

He gave a sad nod. 'Exactly. Sorry, I don't bring it up to upset you, just to a make a point.'

'Which is?'

'That we have to be careful here,' David replied.

'I get that. And I'm with you. We'll be careful.' There was

a brief look of hesitation on David's face, and he sighed. 'Something wrong?' she asked.

'I... I don't quite know how to put this, but I think we do need to have a talk.'

Sarah smiled. 'David, are you breaking up with me?'

He frowned. 'What do you mean?'

She just chuckled. 'That's pretty much how every break-up speech starts. '*We need to have a talk.*''

'Oh, I wouldn't know about... I mean, that isn't what I'm getting at. Look, I know it's hard for you, but I just think you need to be a little bit more patient with how things are going. And a little more patient with the people here.'

'I *am* being patient,' Sarah insisted, her smile falling away. 'I've been nothing *but* patient since we got here.'

'Sarah... come on. I'm not trying to start a fight, but pushing Father Janosch like you did, insisting on the camera in the bedroom despite Ann being uncomfortable, and getting annoyed when we don't get every little thing recorded...'

'Every little thing? David, according to Jenn there was something sitting on me last night. That's a pretty fucking *big* thing.'

'I know,' he said, holding up his hands. 'I just mean... this whole process is going to take time. I know that must be killing you, but there's no way around it. I just need you to go a little easier on everyone. They're giving up their free time, after all. And Father Janosch will do all he can for us, I know it.'

'And I'm grateful,' she said, her voice cold as ice.

But David just pointed to her hands, which were down by her sides and clenched into fists. 'Really? Look at how angry you're getting now.'

Sarah looked down and lifted her hands. The fingers

had started to turn white, and her palms stung as her nails dug into the tender skin.

Perhaps David had a point. Sarah relaxed her hands and lowered them. She took a breath. 'Maybe you have a point.'

He gave Sarah a mournful smile. 'Again, I don't want to dismiss what you're going through with the death of your sister, and I don't blame you at all for being anxious. Just... please remember that everyone here is trying to help.'

'I get it,' Sarah said, meaning it this time. 'I guess I have been a little forceful. It's just, when I saw Chloe up in that window... she wasn't herself. She was *wrong*. All twisted up and rotting. She looked like she was in pain, and she was begging for my help. I just know she's suffering. I think all the spirits of the dead trapped here are going through the same thing. It's killing me knowing Chloe is trapped in that purgatory and I can't help her.'

'I get that,' he said. There was a look on his face she had never seen before. Serious, sad, even a little angry. 'I get that more than you...' He shook his head and went on. 'Never mind. Look, we'll free her, Sarah, I promise. We'll free *all* of them.'

Sarah smiled at him. 'Thank you. And I'll try harder to be a little more patient.' She then looked down to the book. 'Find anything interesting?'

David nodded. 'Plenty... I think. My Latin isn't great, but it seems to be a book of rituals, curses, rites, ceremonies, and God knows what else.'

'Sounds ominous,' Sarah said.

'Maybe. But the interesting thing about it is the constant reference to something called a Devil's Door, or Door to the Devil, and other variants on that.'

'And you don't know what a Devil's Door is, I take it?'

David shook his head. 'Not something I've ever heard of.

Father Janosch seemed to know. I got the impression this book spooked him. He practically ran out of the house after seeing it.'

'I think we may need to have a talk with Father Janosch,' Sarah said. 'Sounds like he's holding out on us.'

'Agreed. I do think he's on our side, but I'd really like to know the full story about the book.'

Then something clicked in Sarah's mind. *The ledger!*

Sitting in the corner of the study was an antique writing desk that held a ledger with a brown leather cover. Sarah remembered looking through it weeks ago and realising what it contained: transcriptions of *Ianua Diaboli.*

'What are you smiling at?' David asked.

'I think I have a way to find out more about the book.'

18

'WHERE ARE YOU GOING?' Jamie asked Ann as she got to her feet.

Ann turned back to him. 'I need to spend a penny.'

Jamie frowned in confusion. 'Spend a what?' Ann rolled her eyes.

Do I need to spell it out for you?

Thankfully, Jenn did it for her. 'She needs to go pee,' Jenn clarified with a chuckle.

The three of them were up in one of the mid-floor bedrooms carrying out a vigil. They all had their cameras with them, and Jenn also had an audio recorder as well as a device that detected any sudden changes in temperature. They had been in the room for close to an hour with no activity.

Ann was certain the room had nothing to offer and had told the other two they should all move on; she could feel no presence in the room. However, Jenn wouldn't listen... just like always. She said she wanted to be thorough.

'Oh,' Jamie said in response to Jenn's clarification. He then looked up to Ann. 'Should you really go alone?'

Ann appreciated his concern for her, it was sweet, but she didn't need babysitting. However, they'd picked one of the few rooms without an en-suite, meaning she'd have to find a toilet elsewhere. 'I'll be fine, Jamie,' she said. 'My room's just down the corridor.'

'Just go to the main toilet across the hall,' he said.

'No,' Ann replied, shaking her head. 'It's cold as hell in there.'

Jamie looked as if he had more to say, but relented. 'Okay,' he said. 'Just be careful. And shout if you see anything. We should be able to hear you from here.'

Ann smiled. 'I will.'

It was nice that he always looked out for her. Jamie was cute as well, and at least he believed in her abilities—unlike some of the others, who Ann felt were just jealous.

She left the room and strode down the corridor, back to the room she was sharing with Jenn. Sarah had moved over to David's room now, so Ann's bedroom felt bigger without that extra mattress crammed inside. It was still messy, however, and most of that was her fault. Her case was open beside her bed, and her dark clothes were strewn about the floor. She knew she wasn't the tidiest, but what did that matter when they were living out of suitcases?

The room smelled funky, and she wondered if perhaps there was some standing water in the radiator or pipes. She had some incense with her that she'd wanted to light, but Jenn had objected, saying that she hated the smell, and also that she didn't want it burning if they were out of the room with no one to watch it. It was a fire hazard, apparently.

Ann was certain the woman just wanted to disagree with her on principle. If Ann claimed the sky was blue, Jenn would argue it was pink.

Ann walked through into the en-suite, which was

smaller than the main toilet on the floor, but more cosy and with a nicer décor.

The floor was tiled white, as were the walls. However, there was a thin band of turquoise tiling halfway up the walls which broke up the expanse of whiteness. A thick blue rug lay next to a cast-iron bath, and there was also a beautiful, old vanity unit and sink sitting below a large mirror. There were no windows in the room, but the small chandelier fixed to the ceiling was sufficient to fully light the space.

Ann gently swung the door closed behind her and heard it catch on the latch. She took a quick look in the mirror to check her hair, then walked over to the toilet.

A slow creaking sound made Ann turn, and she saw the door drift open.

She frowned, feeling her heart quicken. However, she soon caught herself. *You didn't fully close the door, so it obviously just blew open. Nothing to be scared of.*

She closed the door fully this time and waited, just to make sure it stayed closed. When satisfied, she then went to answer the call of nature, and after that stood to wash her hands in the sink. Ann again heard the click of the latch, and the long, drawn-out creak as the door slowly swung open.

Ann froze.

There was no way a simple draft could have opened the door again this time. *Could it?* She watched with bated breath as the door opened, revealing the bedroom behind. Ann expected to see someone standing on the other side—human or otherwise—but nothing was there. The bedroom appeared to be completely empty.

'Hello?' she croaked out, her throat feeling tight. Nothing.

Not knowing what else to do, and feeling a creeping

dread climb up from her gut, Ann kicked out a booted foot to shove the door closed.

She waited. The door remained closed.

Ann finished washing her hands and turned off the tap. While towelling off, and facing away from the entrance to the room, she heard the ominous click of the latch again, as well as the drawn-out creak.

Feeling that sense of dread rise farther, Ann reluctantly turned her head to see the door opening yet again, as if it were taunting her.

But again, there was no one on the other side.

What the fuck is going on?

'Is there something you want to tell me?' she asked, deciding direct communication with the entity was the most appropriate course of action—because there *was* something here with her now, she had no doubt about that.

Ann just hoped it wasn't malicious in nature. Perhaps a benevolent spirit wanted to make itself known. Maybe even Sarah's sister.

'Chloe... is that you?'

Again, nothing. Just an unbearable silence. Ann thought about what to do next as her anxiety levels rose. Closing the door to see if it opened again was an option, or she could just try and leave to go get the others.

If Ann was honest with herself, the experience was unnerving her.

Another option would be to just scream. That would get the others to come. But how could she live that down? She could just imagine Jenn's smug face at seeing Ann so scared.

She then cursed herself for leaving the handheld camera back in the bedroom with the others. This was the *exact* reason David always insisted they take the cameras everywhere they went.

However... Ann did have her smartphone, which she could record video on. Sensing a chance to capture some evidence all on her own, and maybe prove to Jenn that she was a valued member of the team, Ann pulled out her phone and set it to record. She initially filmed herself as she spoke into the camera.

'This is Ann Tate, and I am in one of the mid-floor bedroom en-suites in Perron Manor. While in here, the door to the room has been consistently opening of its own accord. It has happened three times now, so I'm going to try again.'

She then hit a button to flip the camera view so that it now looked ahead, rather than back at herself. She took a breath, then stepped forward and closed the door again. Then... she waited.

Seconds went by, then a minute. Nothing. After waiting for close to four minutes, Ann was ready to give up. Perhaps her visitor had left her.

However, just before she put her phone away, the door opened again. This time much quicker than before.

Yet again, there was nothing on the other side.

'See,' Ann said for the benefit of the recording. 'That is the fourth time, and no one is here to open the door.'

She started to walk into the bedroom, wanting to film the room to prove it was indeed empty. However, as soon as she took a step forward the door quickly slammed shut, hard enough that it reverberated in the frame.

Ann let out a gasp and backed up again. Whereas before she had felt unnerved, now she was outright scared. Through the fear, however, she managed to keep her recording going, determined to come through for the team and prove her worth.

But Ann knew she needed to be out of that room. She

reached forward and grabbed the brass door knob, trying to twist it. It didn't budge.

She tried again and shook it as hard as she could, growing desperate.

'Come on,' she pleaded, now terrified. Ann was trapped in the room and the temperature in there suddenly plummeted.

She continued to try to force the door. 'Please,' she cried, pulling and twisting again and again.

Finally, the door freed up and swung inwards, and as it did Ann lost her footing and fell to the floor, dropping the phone in the process.

She hit her back hard on the tiled floor. After letting out a groan, she rolled to her front and scrambled over to retrieve the phone, which had bounced and skidded off to her side, facing up.

Ann then ran from the room, the air around her still ice-cold. As she ran, she had a horrible feeling some unseen force would stop her and drag her back inside.

Thankfully, her escape was unhindered, and she thundered down the corridor and into the bedroom where she had left Jenn and Jamie. They both looked up to her in surprise.

'What happened?' he asked with a concerned frown.

'Something... something trapped me, in the bathroom,' Ann managed to wheeze out, lost for breath after sprinting for her life. The others quickly sprang to their feet.

'What do you mean?' Jenn asked. Ann took a moment to regain her composure.

'Something had me trapped!' Ann went over the full story, the words tumbling out of her without pausing for breath. When she finished, Jamie was wide-eyed in shock.

'Let me see the video,' Jenn said. 'We might have more evidence there.'

Ann was annoyed Jenn was more concerned with what was on the video rather than Ann's safety. Regardless, she pulled out her phone and played the footage for them.

They watched Ann on the playback telling who she was, where she was, and what had just happened. The view flipped to point ahead and Ann closed the door. Minutes passed by and eventually the door was thrust open again.

'Jesus,' Jamie said. 'That's incredible.'

'It is,' Jenn agreed. 'But it could have been opened from the other side, by someone out of the shot.'

'Jenn!' Ann snapped. 'I can't believe you think I'd fake this. Who the hell else was there with me to even open it?'

'That isn't what I mean,' Jenn said, shaking her head. 'I know you're telling the truth. But to someone looking from the outside in, who would want to debunk our evidence, that's exactly what they would say.'

The door on the video then slammed shut.

'No way you can fake that,' Jamie said. 'The door was open and no one reached in to grab the handle.'

Jenn nodded with a smile. 'I agree. That part is indisputable, I'd say.'

Ann felt relieved.

'Must have been terrifying,' Jamie said as they watched the rest of the footage. He laid a hand on Ann's shoulder. She smiled at him, appreciating the gesture.

'It was a little,' she admitted.

The video footage then shook and jostled as Ann dropped the phone. It came to a stop facing the ceiling, but picked up quite a bit of the room in the frame. Everyone drew in a breath before Ann's hand appeared on screen and snatched up the phone.

Something had been in the shot.

Ann looked first to Jamie, then to Jenn, as the footage played out.

How did I miss that?

Ann realised she was shaking.

'Did you see it?' Jamie questioned, pointing to the screen.

They both nodded. Jenn then asked, 'Did you notice anything in the room with you at the time?'

Ann shook her head.

'No... but I didn't look behind myself when I was in there. Was... was *it* there the whole time, do you think?'

'No idea,' Jenn replied.

'Play it back,' Jamie said. 'We need to see it again, then tell the others.'

Ann rewound to the point she was trying to force the door open. The footage started again. They watched as the door released and the phone fell. When it came to a stop, and the spinning picture finally settled, Ann hit pause.

On the still image, a dark, slightly blurred figure was standing against the far wall of the bathroom. His hands were down by his sides, and the man with the pale face wore an expressionless gaze. He looked to be wearing a dark suit and had black, brushed back-hair. There was a gash of red across his throat.

'Holy shit,' Jenn muttered. 'We need to show the others.'

19

'FASCINATING,' David said as he looked at the image on Ann's phone.

Everyone was back in HQ again after being called by Ann, who had insisted there was something important the whole group needed to see.

David had been up in the study with Sarah. She'd been about to show him a ledger she claimed would shed more light on *Ianua Diaboli*.

However, before they managed to look at the book, Ann had shouted up the stairs for them.

'Let me see that,' Sarah insisted, leaning closer to the phone. Her eyes grew wide. 'I think I recognise him,' she said, pointing at the man on screen.

David turned to her. 'Recognise how?'

'I think we saw him one time in the house—me and Chloe. I'm certain of it. I recognise the wound across his throat, and I'm sure he even spoke to us.'

'What did he say?' Ralph asked.

Sarah squinted her eyes in thought. Then, however, she

shook her head. 'I can't remember exactly. But it was aimed at Chloe. Like he knew her, somehow.'

'How could he...' David started to say, then trailed off. Something clicked in his mind. 'Wait.'

He walked over to one of his many backpacks that were stored in a corner of the room, and pulled out an old scrapbook with a ring binder. David had used this to collect cutouts and notes when researching Perron Manor to write his own book.

Within the scrapbook were a variety of cuttings from newspaper articles glued onto the pages—not originals, but photocopies that he'd made at the local library and historical centres. He flicked through to the page he was looking for: an article about the formerly abandoned house finally being bought again. There was a picture of the new owner.

Marcus Blackwater.

David set the scrapbook down on a desk and asked Ann to put her phone down next to it, which she did.

'What do you think?' David asked. 'Same guy?'

'Holy shit,' Ralph exclaimed. 'It could be!'

The image from the phone wasn't perfectly focused or clear, so exact details were difficult to make out. However, there was definitely a likeness: the hair, the facial structure, and the dark clothes.

'If it is Marcus Blackwater,' David said to Sarah, 'then it would explain how he knew Chloe. She was living here when he died, right?'

Sarah nodded. 'Yeah, that's right.'

'*And* he cut his throat,' David added, pointing to the neck wound of the man on the phone screen.

'This is unreal,' Jenn cut in. 'Are we saying Ann may have captured footage of Marcus Blackwater?'

'I think so,' David replied. 'And if we have identified one

of these spirits, maybe it will be more compelling to the Church.' He turned to Ann. 'Way to go, kid.'

'Yeah,' Jamie added. 'Nice work.'

Ann beamed with pride.

It must have been a terrifying ordeal, but she had come through it with something tangible for them to use. David was proud of her.

'We need to get the video from the phone and onto our system,' George said. 'Ideally as soon as possible so we can get it properly logged.' He then dug through a bag of his own and pulled out a white connector cable. 'May I?' he asked Ann.

'Of course.'

George got to work transferring the data. As he did, David felt a hand touch his elbow. He turned to see Sarah signalling for him to step away with her. They both moved over to the corner of the room.

'Has Father Janosch called you back yet?'

David shook his head. 'Not yet. I'm guessing he's just busy.'

'Okay,' Sarah said with a sigh. 'Still, things seem to be progressing pretty quickly, huh?'

'You can say that again. I'm not making any promises, but I wouldn't be surprised if we have all we need soon.'

'So what's the plan for tonight? I think it would be prudent to try and capitalise on the momentum.'

'I agree,' David said. 'Jenn and I were discussing this earlier. We have something with us, called a Demon Board—'

'I remember that from your book,' Sarah cut in. 'You used it down in the basement during your last investigation. Didn't it spark a lot of activity?'

David nodded. 'Probably too much. So I was considering

using it tonight, but honestly I think we should hold off on that for now.'

'But why, if it's the best way to get results?'

'Because the way things are going, I don't want to push too hard and put us in danger,' David explained. 'And I think the Demon Board could do just that. Let's think of it as a last resort.'

He hoped Sarah understood and she was able to rein in her enthusiasm. Thankfully, she smiled and nodded. 'That makes sense. So, if not the Demon Board, then what?'

'Well,' he began, 'we talked about carrying out more vigils. At night I think we might get more activity from them. So, we'll split into two groups and see what happens. You up for a late night?'

Sarah smiled. 'Sounds good to me.'

20

IT HAD BEEN a hectic day for Luca, but he'd had only one thing on his mind throughout it all.

The book.

Sarah Pearson's refusal to let him take it was an annoyance. No, it was more than that, since it meant he had to go back.

Luca had received David's voicemail not long after it had been left. However, he'd wanted to consult someone higher up the chain of command for advice before replying. So, he'd sent an email to the Bishop of Newcastle. Normally, it would have taken a few days to garner any kind of response, because the Bishop was a busy man.

After sitting back down at his desk in his study, following a community event which ran on longer than it should, Luca checked his email. There was a response from the Bishop, and it was not from his normal email address, but a private one.

· · ·

I escalated your concerns and the response back to me was almost immediate. You are to determine if the book is indeed genuine. Also, you are to investigate the house to validate the owner's claims. If true, and if the house is what you believe it to be, then we must act quickly.

All of your other responsibilities are to be delegated. This is your sole concern until resolved.

Please update us daily with reports on your findings. And be careful.

Regards,

Bishop Turnbull.

Luca leaned back in his chair and let out a sigh. He brought a shaking hand up to his face and rubbed his mouth, which suddenly felt dry. The instruction to investigate was expected, but the speed at which he had received it was not.

That likely meant someone higher up knew what a Devil's Door truly was and had taken notice.

Luca considered his next step, and knew he should really call David straight away and arrange to go back to the house. But that could wait for tonight. He got up from his seat and walked into his lounge, pouring himself a large measure of single-malt whiskey. Luca downed it in one mouthful, then poured himself another.

21

DAVID READIED HIMSELF FOR BED, feeling utterly exhausted. The vigils had run late into the night and proven uneventful.

The cameras had been positioned and were rolling, one mounted up in one corner that covered most of the room, and another on top of a wardrobe that focused on Sarah's bed. After all, she was the likely focus of any activity that might occur.

Sarah took her sleeping clothes out of her suitcase and started to pull off her t-shirt. David immediately turned around, feeling himself blush.

'You can use the en-suite to change,' he suggested.

He heard her chuckle. 'Would that make you feel more comfortable?'

'Well... I was thinking more about you.'

'I bunked with lots of guys in the army, David. I honestly don't care.'

He turned back to see Sarah standing in her bra and immediately looked away again.

'I know, but that was... I mean, this is...'

She laughed again. 'It's fine, I'll spare your blushes and change in the bathroom. I need to brush my teeth anyway.'

Sarah then gathered up her stuff and walked into the en-suite, casting David a sly grin as she did. She was clearly less reserved than he was. He wondered if he had been too quick in agreeing to share a room with her.

While Sarah was in the bathroom David quickly changed into some jogging bottoms and a t-shirt. As he was putting his old clothes back into one of his bags, he noticed the compact mirror he'd packed for the trip. It was something of a good-luck charm.

Katie's.

He lifted the mirror from the brown leather bag and held it. In truth, it was more than just a good-luck charm. He'd learned over time that mirrors could play a large part in investigations. Often, you could see things in them that you couldn't otherwise. Shadows, orbs, outlines of people: it was like the reflective surface bounced back an image of what was *really* there, not just what the naked eye could see.

The mirror was a compact one, sitting roughly the size of his palm and circular in shape. The lid was brass and had a raised pattern of swirling leaves that came together at the centre. It was old, a hand-me-down, and clicked open via a small button on the side. He pressed it, causing the lid to release and open a little, allowing his thumb to push it the rest of the way and reveal the reflective surface beneath. He saw his own face looking back.

David was reminded of some of the details Sarah had shared from her time in the house, such as when Chloe saw a woman in a reflection, sitting above Sarah while she slept.

Or the reflection Chloe had seen in the downstairs rear door, moments before a ghostly man made himself known.

It was something to think about, and David resolved to

keep the mirror with him during their next vigil or investigative session.

He set the mirror back in his bag, slotting it in next to a first-aid kit that he'd also brought with him. He did that for every investigation.

Can't be too careful.

He was trained in first aid, something he felt was important when he'd decided to make the investigations a regular thing, Fortunately, those skills had yet to be called into use.

David sat on his bed waiting for his turn to use the bathroom. He looked up at the camera mounted in the corner, wondering if it would get anything of interest during the night. The investigation had started well with lots of activity, but the latest vigils were a bust. He hoped there was more to come from the house.

His mind wandered, again casting back to the investigation in 2014, and to the message he'd received from that ghostly voice. '*Return here. Help another in need.*'

He was finally back, and he hoped the meaning of that message would reveal itself.

It was also bothering David that Father Janosch hadn't gotten back to him yet. The priest was normally quick to reply, so David decided to try and contact him again the following day.

He was also aware he hadn't had the chance to follow up on what Sarah was going to show him up in the study: a ledger that would apparently shed more light on the book in the display case. The excitement of the day had pushed that particular issue down the list of priorities, but David made a mental note to speak to Sarah about it the following day.

Eventually, Sarah emerged from the en-suite and walked over to her bed, wearing only a vest top and some pyjama shorts. David again felt the need to avert his eyes as she sat on her bed and started to flick through her phone.

'I'll go use the bathroom now,' he said and got up.

'Uh-huh,' she replied, still looking at her phone. David left her to it and went into the bathroom.

It was close to one in the morning. Late-night sessions were required, but so was getting enough rest so they could stay alert. It was a fine act to balance. However, there was no time limit to their investigation here, so there was no reason to push themselves to exhaustion.

David finished up with using the toilet and brushing his teeth, then started to wash his face in the sink. He scrubbed his skin with a washcloth and soapy water, keeping his eyes screwed shut.

As he scrubbed, David started to feel a cold sensation wash over him from his left and roll over his cheek like a sour-smelling breath.

David paused, though his eyes were still closed tightly. Had it just been in his mind? The sensation had quickly passed, as had the smell, and all David could hear was the running of the tap.

After a few moments of nothing else, David dunked his hands into the full sink.

Something grabbed his wrist.

The grip was so strong and cold David let out a gasp. He instinctively opened his eyes and pulled his arm away. The soap stung as it seeped between his lids and David blinked quickly.

His hand was now free, with nothing grabbing his wrist any longer. Though his vision was blurry, David couldn't see anyone around him. He quickly rinsed his hands and splashed water on his face, washing away the last of the soap. With clear vision, he looked around again.

Nothing.

He brought up his arm and looked at his wrist. There was a noticeable red mark around it, with three distinct lines. He rubbed at his skin, trying to rid himself of the lingering cold.

David waited to see if anything else happened. His heart rate had quickened and his adrenaline levels had risen as well. He felt on edge. The sensation was something he was used to during investigations when things were happening, and it was controllable. He took deep breaths.

'Hello,' he said, hoping to draw out whatever was in here with him. Then he cursed himself: both his handheld camera and his phone were in the bedroom. Though he'd only expected to be in the bathroom for a couple of minutes, it was still a novice mistake.

A knock on the door made him jump.

'Did you say something?' Sarah called from the other room.

David didn't respond; instead, he just walked to the door and opened it, seeing Sarah standing on the other side.

'You okay?' she asked with a frown.

He nodded. 'Yeah. Just... something grabbed my arm, I think.'

'Really?' Sarah asked, eyes going wide. She then looked past him into the bathroom.

'There isn't anything here that I can see,' David said. 'It was just a quick experience. Over as soon as it happened. But look...' He held up his arm again.

Sarah squinted and leaned her face forward. Then a look of surprise came over her. She grabbed his forearm. 'Holy shit, look at the marks! They look like fingers.'

'That's what I thought. Only three of them, though.'

'Did you see anything?'

David shook his head. 'I was in the middle of washing my face, so I had my eyes closed. There was nothing around me when I opened them, though.'

He then moved fully into the bedroom with Sarah, closing the door to the en-suite behind him. Sleep would not come easy now, but they had to try. The cameras were running, so there wasn't much else they could do. And besides, if Jenn had been correct about what she'd seen the previous night, then an entity had come to visit Sarah while she slept. Perhaps tonight would see a repeat performance.

David switched off the main light, leaving only Sarah's nightlight on, and they both got into bed.

'Goodnight, Sarah,' David said as he lay down and pulled the duvet up over himself.

'Goodnight,' she replied, switching off her nightlight and plunging the room into darkness.

It was eerily quiet, and David could hear only the sound of Sarah's breathing. Though he didn't know why, he felt the need to speak to her rather than just rolling over and going to sleep. He wanted to make sure she was okay and felt safe. In reality, he knew she was tougher than he was; when it came to the spirit world, though, bravery and toughness could not replace experience.

In the end, he stayed silent and tried to focus on falling asleep.

~

'*Kill him.*'

David blinked himself awake, his mind in a state of confusion at being pulled from sleep.

'*Kill him.*'

The room was cold and dark, and everything was quiet...

except for the voice he'd heard. It was a horrible, low, hoarse whisper, but he couldn't be sure if it was real or just a remnant of his dreams.

David rolled over and saw something standing over him, and immediately let out a cry of fright.

There was a woman, completely naked, standing motionless in the dark just next to his bed.

Sarah.

She had her eyes closed and her face was expressionless, but her head was tilted down towards him.

'Sarah?' David whispered. No response. He quickly came to the conclusion that she was asleep. Which made him wonder if it was *she* who had uttered 'kill him,' but in her sleep. He sat up and looked beyond her and around the room, to see if there was anything else present. But he could see nothing.

He turned back to Sarah, who must have been freezing, considering the temperature in the room. He had no idea why the hell she was naked, but quickly got out of bed and walked past her, grabbing her duvet up from the bed and making a mental note to ask her in the morning if sleep-walking was a common thing. When he turned back around with the thick quilt gathered up in his arms, he saw that Sarah had turned to face him.

She was still motionless, still asleep, but she had silently turned her body in his direction while he wasn't looking. Which was... strange. A creeping feeling of unease worked its way up David's spine.

Was it she who had uttered those words?
Kill him.

It was hard not to take in her full, naked body, even though it made him uncomfortable. It was just... there. And she was undeniably an attractive woman. David quickly walked over to Sarah and dropped the duvet around her, wrapping it tightly around her front.

'Sarah?' he said. He kept his voice even and gentle. She didn't move or acknowledge him. David didn't want to shake her awake, so he tried something else instead. He took hold of her hand and attempted to lead Sarah back to bed. Thankfully, she came with him, and David guided her down to a lying position on her mattress and dropped the quilt back over her, covering her naked body completely.

He then moved back over to his own bed. The room had a cold bite to it so he quickly hopped under the covers. He then looked back over to Sarah with a feeling of trepidation, half expecting to see her sitting up again, facing him.

But she was just as he'd left her: lying down and unmoving, except for the slow rise and fall of her chest.

David checked his watch which was next to his bed. It was close to three-thirty, which was something to remember. It would help him determine what time to focus on the next day when reviewing the camera's footage. Hopefully, it would make for interesting viewing.

22

THE SMELL OF COOKING EGGS, frying bacon, and sizzling sausages filled the kitchen, making Sarah's stomach grumble in anticipation. She was ravenous.

The team were all sitting around the kitchen table sipping tea, coffee, and orange juice while Ralph cooked a traditional English breakfast.

'Can't hunt ghosts on an empty stomach,' he'd insisted.

While the group had brought some supplies and food, it wouldn't last them long, and Sarah knew she would need to fund a shopping trip soon to stock up.

The kitchen was full of noise and activity as the seven of them chatted and laughed. The room felt alive, like it had when Sarah lived in the house with Chloe, Emma, and Andrew. It was a nice feeling and lent a little warmth to Perron Manor, which had so far felt cold and unwelcoming.

It was just after nine in the morning, and Sarah was still wrestling with what David had told her, about how she had been standing over his bed in the night.

Her mind ran back to a few weeks ago, where her sister Chloe had told her she'd done the same thing.

The team hadn't checked the footage of the previous night yet, but Sarah was interested to see what it would show. It would be interesting to see her sleepwalking in action, as she had no memory of it happening.

Jenn got up and moved over to one of the sets of drawers, then began digging through them.

'What are you looking for?' Sarah asked her.

'Some mats and coasters,' she said. 'Don't want to leave marks on the table.' She moved onto the second drawer down in the set. 'Do you have any? I can see candles and matches here, so we are set for a blackout.'

'It's fine,' Sarah insisted. 'Don't worry about it.'

Through the noise of chatter and cooking, Sarah thought she heard something else. A knocking.

She tilted her head to try and focus in on the sound. She soon heard it again. It was coming from the front door.

Then she heard the doorbell, which carried over the din in the room and made everyone stop talking.

Sarah got to her feet.

'Are we expecting someone?' she asked David, who was standing against the kitchen units with his mug of coffee.

He shook his head and frowned. 'Not that I know of,' he replied and followed her out of the room.

Sarah and David made their way to the entrance lobby and, through the glass in the door, saw the shape of someone standing outside. Sarah cast David a confused look before she pulled open the door.

Father Janosch stood outside.

'Father!' David said in surprise.

The priest gave a smile. 'Good morning to you both,' he said.

'I... I left you a message,' David went on. 'I wasn't sure if you got it.'

Father Janosch's expression grew serious and he took a moment before answering. 'I did,' he confirmed. 'But I was just so busy yesterday that I didn't really have the chance to call you back, not until the hour was late, anyway. So... I thought I would come by this morning instead. I hope I'm not intruding at all?'

Sarah wasn't a mind-reader, but she knew when someone wasn't being completely honest, and Father Janosch's story didn't exactly sound genuine.

'It's no trouble,' Sarah said. 'We were just about to have breakfast. Have you eaten?'

'I've had some toast,' he replied.

Sarah stepped aside. 'That's not exactly a hearty meal to start the day. You a vegetarian?' The priest shook his head. 'Good,' Sarah said. 'Why don't you join us? There's plenty to go around.'

'That sounds agreeable,' Father Janosch replied and stepped inside. As he removed his long grey coat, Sarah noticed him look nervously around the entrance lobby, particularly to the walkways above.

He doesn't like being here, Sarah said to herself. That wasn't a newsflash, as he had practically sprinted out after his last visit. In truth, she was surprised he'd come back so quickly.

Sarah then thought about her own attitude towards the house.

When she first arrived, she'd felt on edge and constantly scared. Now, however, while she was far from feeling at ease, that constant dread wasn't there anymore. Had she acclimated so quickly? That didn't seem right, especially not after seeing what happened to Chloe.

Sarah took the priest's coat and draped it over an arm.

She then led them back through to the kitchen as David continued to question their new guest.

'So have you come to study the book here at the house?' he asked.

Father Janosch was a touch slow in responding, then said, 'I have, yes, if that is okay with you, Miss Pearson?'

Sarah turned her head back over her shoulder. 'Of course. Sorry if it is less convenient, but I really don't want the book getting lost or damaged, so I would prefer it stayed here.'

'I really would have taken good care of it,' Father Janosch said.

'I'm sure,' Sarah replied. 'But accidents happen that we can't predict, so I'm afraid I need to insist.'

'Understood,' he responded, though he didn't sound happy about it.

'Well, you might be interested to know that things have been progressing quickly here,' David said. 'A lot of activity. Some we've even managed to catch on tape. I'd like you to have a quick look while you're here. It'd be interesting to hear your thoughts on what we have.'

'I'd be happy to,' Father Janosch replied.

They walked through into the kitchen and all eyes fell on them.

'Looks like we have a visitor,' David said to the others with a big smile.

The priest simply stood in the doorway and gave an awkward wave. 'Hello, everyone.'

Ralph was the first to respond. 'How do you like your eggs, Father?'

'However they come,' he replied as Sarah showed him over to the table. There weren't enough seats for everyone, but Sarah was more than happy to stand and use the kitchen counter while she ate.

Ralph soon began to plate up the food and Sarah fixed the priest a coffee—one of her hazelnut roasts. She set it down and he took a sip. The worry he had been carrying on his face seemed to melt away.

'Oh, I say, that is delicious,' he remarked.

At least he has taste.

Everyone then tucked into their food. Sarah had to hand it to Ralph—while he hadn't exactly prepared fine cuisine, as far as hearty breakfasts went this wasn't bad at all. The bacon was nice and crispy, the sausages full and juicy, and the scrambled eggs were light, fluffy, and flavourful.

There were even fried tomatoes and mushrooms as well.

Initially, the only sounds in the room were the clinking of cutlery on plates and the wet chewing noises of people devouring their food.

'Can I ask,' Sarah began, directing her question to Father Janosch, 'why are you so interested in the book?'

He took his time in answering—chewing his food and swallowing before wiping his mouth. Sarah suspected he was playing for time.

'Well, it seems extremely old, for one. And from first glance, the text within looks to deal with some dark subjects, ones that specifically go against God. So, of course, it is going to be of interest.'

'When we were upstairs,' David cut in, 'you mentioned that you had heard of the *Ianua Diaboli* before?'

Father Janosch just nodded in response, offering no further narrative. However, Sarah didn't want to let the thread go so easily.

'So come on,' she pressed. 'How come you've heard of it?'

Yet again, Father Janosch paused, this time to take a long sip from his coffee.

'Just whispers, really,' he eventually replied. 'Stories from my time back in Romania.'

Sarah waited for him to keep going, but he fell silent. She chuckled and shook her head. 'Come on, Father, you're going to have to give us more and stop your ducking and weaving. I don't know why you are being so coy, but if you don't start being completely honest, I'm not sure I want you looking at the book at all.'

His jaw tensed and the priest made strong eye contact with Sarah. Not a threatening stare, but certainly a displeased one.

'Sarah,' David started, 'I'm sure Father Janosch isn't holding back anything—'

'It's okay, David,' Father Janosch said. 'I understand where Sarah is coming from. And I apologise if I seem a little evasive. Would it be possible to speak with the two of you alone for a moment?'

Sarah frowned and turned to David, who looked just as surprised as she was.

'Something you need to keep from the rest of us?' Ralph asked.

'Not really,' Father Janosch replied. 'But it would only be right to speak with Sarah and David first.'

'That's no problem,' David said. Father Janosch got to his feet.

'We can go to the living room,' Sarah added.

'Actually,' Father Janosch replied, 'it would be better to go upstairs and see the book. Things might be easier to explain that way.'

'Fair enough,' she said, then led the way upstairs,

extremely interested in what the priest was about to tell them.

23

ONCE IN THE STUDY, David, Sarah, and Father Janosch stood around the display case. David looked to Father Janosch expectantly.

'First of all,' the priest began, 'I want to apologise. Miss Pearson was correct... I *was* being evasive with regards to the book. I am sorry for that.'

'It was pretty obvious,' Sarah replied. 'But thank you.'

David felt a little ashamed. He hadn't picked up on Father Janosch's reticence. In truth, because David trusted the man completely, he never would have thought Father Janosch would withhold anything important.

'So... what is the issue with the book?' David asked.

The priest gazed down at it, lost in a stare. Eventually, he spoke. 'The reason I haven't been forthcoming with everything is... well, first because I'm not one-hundred-percent sure this book is genuine. However, if it is, then that poses certain... difficulties... with what you are all doing here.'

'What? With us gathering evidence?' David asked.

'Yes. You see, *Ianua Diaboli* was something I first heard about back in my youth just after being accepted into the

Church. At the time, it was an off-the-cuff comment about a rumoured book which held great power. The priest who made the statement was not of sound mind, so I didn't put much stock into his words. The title always stuck with me, however.'

'And when did you next hear about the book?' Sarah asked.

'Years later, when I was in Hungary. I had an... experience there. I was assigned to assist an older priest on a case. It took a lot out of me and opened my eyes to what really exists in our world. Even beyond it.'

'Did that experience involve *Ianua Diaboli*?' Sarah asked, but Father Janosch shook his head.

'No. However, the priest leading the investigation was so overwhelmed with the activity at that Church, he wondered if the location was something he referred to as a 'Devil's Door.' Obviously, I pressed him on what that was, and he stated it was just a rumor based around a mythical manuscript.'

'*Ianua Diaboli*,' David said.

'Yes,' Father Janosch confirmed. 'But, in the end, as bad as that location ended up being, I don't think it truly was a Devil's Door. After the case, I tried to investigate the rumours regarding the book. I found out a great deal, but not much of it could be backed up with actual evidence. So I assumed it was just an urban legend.'

'So,' Sarah began, 'the obvious question to ask... what the hell is a Devil's Door?'

Father Janosch took a deep breath before beginning. 'The theory goes that a Devil's Door is a point in our world that is a direct link to Hell.'

'Are you being serious?' Sarah asked.

The priest nodded. 'Again, it was just a legend as far as I

knew, but many of the stories regarding those gateways always linked back to a certain book.' He looked down to the display case.

'So you're saying the book I've inherited could prove the existence of a Devil's Doorway?'

'Only if it is genuine,' Father Janosch stated. 'We know this thing is old, but that doesn't mean what is written inside is true, or if it even holds any power. It could just be an old book full of lies.'

'Like the Bible,' Sarah added with a smile.

David's eyes went wide in shock and his head whipped around. A look of horror drew over Sarah's face, surprised at her own outburst. Her cheeks flushed red.

'Sarah!' David snapped.

'Well,' Father Janosch said with a nervous chuckle. 'I guess some people may think that way.'

'I'm so sorry,' Sarah said in reply, holding up a hand to her chest. 'I... I don't know what came over me there.'

'It's quite alright,' Father Janosch insisted, but David felt embarrassed on the priest's behalf. He couldn't understand why Sarah had said that to a *priest* of all people. Even if she did believe it, it seemed unnecessarily mean-spirited.

'No, it isn't alright,' Sarah insisted. Her cheeks were still red. 'There was no need for me to say something like that. I'm sorry, Father. Really, I am.'

'Honestly, it's fine,' he stressed. 'Please forget it. Also, moving back to matters at hand, the validity of this book is only part of the issue. What also concerns me is the *reason* it is here in this house.'

'What do you mean?' David asked.

'Well, you probably know more than I do, but Perron Manor has quite the disturbing history, correct?'

David nodded. 'More so than any other house I've heard of.'

'And if the stories of the more... supernatural... elements are true—'

'They are,' Sarah insisted. 'I've seen them myself.'

'Well, if so, that would mean the house has a power that is unusual, even among haunted locations.'

'You're saying that Perron Manor may be a Devil's Door,' David stated, connecting the dots.

Father Janosch paused for a moment, holding eye contact, then he gave a small nod. 'Perhaps. The power of the house, and the presence of *this* book, seem to be more than just a coincidence to me. It may be that whoever found the book and brought it here was well aware of what Perron Manor *really* was. But I could be wrong about that. I could be wrong about everything I'm saying.'

'You aren't wrong,' Sarah said. Both men turned to look at her.

'What do you mean?' David asked.

Sarah didn't respond. Instead, she walked over to an old writing table in the corner of the room and picked up a ledger from it. Suddenly David remembered what she had told him the last time they were up in this study, about the ledger being able to help them learn more.

She set it down on top of the glass display cabinet so the others could see. The cover was plain brown leather except for symbols that were drawn in each corner. To David, they replicated those on the cover of *Ianua Diaboli*. In the top left was an eight-pointed star, and opposite that was a cross. The lower left was a triangle with a separate, inverted triangle within it, and the final symbol resembled the eight lines of a compass, pointing off in their respective directions.

Sarah opened the cover to the first page. There was a

handwritten note, and both David and Father Janosch leaned in to read it.

These transcriptions from Ianua Diaboli *are as accurate as I can make them, given the use of 'Old Latin' in with the more classical use of the language.*

While the original author of the book remains unknown, its purpose, and the purpose of the texts therein, are very clear. They all pertain to a very specific phenomenon that is able to exist in our world, one that is very relevant to Perron Manor.

This house is special.

It is, I believe, alive. And Ianua Diaboli *could very well be a way to harness what exists here, for those brave enough to do so.*

- A. Blackwater.

'Someone transcribed the book,' Father Janosch stated. He sounded far from happy.

'I think so,' Sarah replied.

David shook his head. 'This is unbelievable. The person who wrote the passage, this A. Blackwater, I think it's Alfred Blackwater. The grandfather of Marcus. And if he *did* translate the full book, then we have everything in this ledger that we need... right? I mean, it will tell us exactly what *Ianua Diaboli* really is.'

'Perhaps,' Father Janosch said with a frown. 'Latin isn't an easy language to translate, and there is certainly room for error.'

'But you are fluent in Latin, aren't you?'

He nodded. 'To an extent. But that note from Alfred Blackwater is worrying. It seems to imply what I feared, that Perron Manor is indeed a doorway to Hell.'

David felt both excited and terrified in equal measure. This was huge, far beyond what he'd ever hoped the investigation would yield. On the other hand, he felt woefully ill-equipped to deal with something of this magnitude.

'So what does it really mean if this place is a Devil's Door?' Sarah asked. 'Does that change anything we're doing here?'

David had no answer, so he looked to Father Janosch for support.

'There are no existing procedures in place that I am aware of,' Father Janosch said. 'No one really believed in their existence. However, I need to first determine what we are dealing with and see if it is genuine. To do that, I need to study the *Ianua Diaboli*. If Perron Manor is what I fear, then I will inform my superiors so they can escalate matters.'

'And then they will exorcise the house?' Sarah asked.

Father Janosch shrugged. 'In truth, I am not certain. You see, we don't know if that will even work.'

'What do you mean?' Sarah shot back. 'It *has* to work. The whole point of what we're doing here is to free the dead that are trapped. You know, like my sister!'

'I understand,' Father Janosch replied. 'But if we try that and it doesn't work... we could end up making things worse. For *us* as well as for those trapped here.'

David's mind was reeling. 'Why didn't you tell us this as soon as you found out?'

Father Janosch fell silent and he slowly looked down to the floor. He took a breath. 'Well, at first I had to raise the issue with my superiors and wait for their guidance.'

'Are we all in danger here?' David asked as his stomach sank.

The investigation was everything to him. He just *knew* it could be the making of him as a respected paranormal researcher. More than that, it would help someone long lost to him.

He felt like that hope was about to be pulled away from him. Was this the end of what they were doing here?

Father Janosch nodded. 'Potentially.'

'Hold on,' Sarah said, shaking her head. 'That doesn't add up. If you thought we were in danger, you would have just told us straight away. I mean, you're a *priest,* for God's sake... excuse the expression.'

'I only received my orders last night.'

'Your *orders*?' Sarah asked.

'Yes, from my superiors within the Church.'

'And those orders,' David interjected, 'are what... to investigate the book?'

'As well as the house,' Father Janosch confirmed.

'But *before* that,' Sarah said, 'when you were here two days ago, you saw the book and freaked out. You suspected the house was dangerous even then, didn't you.'

'I wasn't certain,' Father Janosch replied defensively. 'All I knew when I first arrived was David claimed the house was haunted. Then I saw a book and recognised the title. I wasn't sure about anything.'

Sarah shook her head and folded her arms across her chest. 'You're lying.'

Father Janosch's face hardened, but only for a moment. He cast his gaze once again down to the floor. 'Well, if I'm honest... I *was* scared. I've seen a lot in my years, but only once before have I ever been truly terrified to my core. I knew if this house was what I believed it to be, then I would be re-living something I dearly did not want to.'

'So you ran without warning us?' David asked. He was struggling to make sense of what he was hearing. He'd always known Father Janosch to be a good, honest man.

The priest still did not look up. 'I needed to be away from the house,' he said. His voice was small, like a child's. 'I know what happens if your soul is trapped in purgatory. It is a torment that never ends. After I was out of the house, I tried to take stock of the situation. Again, I didn't know if I was overreacting, and I was embarrassed about how I'd acted. So, I sought guidance from those above me.'

'And they led you right back here,' Sarah stated.

Father Janosch finally lifted his head to face them again. He nodded. 'They did.'

'And how do you feel about that?' Sarah asked.

'Terrified.'

David then brought the discussion back to what was weighing on his mind most, besides everyone's safety. 'So we need to stop what we are doing, don't we? We need to leave?'

'Why?' Sarah asked.

David shook his head in disbelief and turned to her. 'Because it's dangerous.'

'It was dangerous anyway, wasn't it?' Sarah shot back. 'We knew that coming in.'

'Not to this level.'

Sarah obviously didn't want things to end, and David could appreciate that. He didn't either, despite what he'd just heard. However, he couldn't put people's lives at risk.

'Well, I'm staying,' Sarah said, glaring at him.

David turned to Father Janosch for guidance. 'Father, what is your position on this. Do we have to leave?'

The priest took his time in answering. 'I cannot dictate what any of you do, I can only advise. It *might* be dangerous here, if we are actually dealing with what we think, but we still don't know for certain. So whether you stay or go... that is up to you.'

'What will you do?' Sarah asked.

'The Church wants me to investigate the house and the book, so I would ask that you grant me access.'

'And you'd be happy to stay here on your own to do that?'

David watched Father Janosch's face when asked the question. He looked horrified at the thought of it.

'I would stay on my own if I needed to,' he replied, though his tone was not convincing in the slightest. David could tell the priest didn't want them to leave him on his own here, but he had no right to ask them to stay, either.

'Tell me,' Sarah went on. 'Say you determine that the house *is* a gateway to Hell. Then what happens?'

'I inform the Church.'

'And then what?'

'That is for my superiors to decide.'

'Take a guess, Father. What do you *think* will happen?'

He thought for a moment. 'I'd assume they would try and figure out how to close the gate. I can't imagine the Church would want such a thing to exist.'

Sarah nodded. 'Okay. And how quickly would that happen? I get the feeling having an exorcism sanctioned is a slow process.'

'I think something like this would be more of a priority,' Father Janosch said.

'Yeah, I suspected as much. Last question, say the gate was closed… what would happen to the souls trapped in the house? Would they be freed… or would they be stuck?'

'I… honestly don't know,' he said.

David saw Sarah's jaw clench and she glared at the priest for a moment. Then she looked down at *Ianua Diaboli* and the ledger. 'Maybe there is a way we can find out.'

24

'AND THAT'S EVERYTHING WE KNOW,' David said to the team.

Sarah watched their faces to get a gauge on their reactions. They looked to be equal parts engrossed and worried.

David had pulled everyone into the great hall to go over what he and Sarah had learned. David stood at the head of the table with Sarah beside him, while the others were seated.

'Holy fucking shit!' Ralph stated. 'Are... are you being serious?'

David nodded. 'Afraid so.'

Silence.

Sarah could sympathise with them. She still hadn't quite gotten her head around the whole thing herself.

How the fuck am I going to help Chloe now?

'So... what does that mean for the investigation?' Jenn asked.

That was the pertinent question. Sarah was glad someone had asked it so quickly.

David turned to Father Janosch, then over to Sarah, and

finally back to the others. 'Well, that's up to us. The decision is ours to make.'

'And if we stayed,' George began, 'is the objective the same as before? I mean, would we still just be gathering evidence?'

This time Father Janosch spoke. 'Regardless of what this house is or is not, we still need evidence of any paranormal activity. The Church requires proof to act. So, in effect, nothing changes. However, the severity of activity will be a key indicator of what is truly happening.'

Ann's hand went up. 'But how will you know if the book is real?' she asked. 'I mean, you said the existence of *Ianua Dia*... whatever it's called, was little more than a rumour anyway. It's not like there's going to be a certificate of authenticity or anything. So how will you *know*?'

Ann raised a good point. It was something Sarah had been wondering herself.

'Firstly, I need to study what's written inside of it,' Father Janosch responded. 'Once I fully digest the text, I will have a better understanding of what we are dealing with.'

'And you'll know for certain?' Ann asked.

'Hopefully,' the priest responded. He didn't sound convinced.

'There is a way to know for sure,' Sarah said. All eyes fell on her.

'How?' David asked.

'The book is supposed to be full of rituals and the like, right? Well... we can try one.'

Sarah was met with silence, as well as looks of confusion and astonishment.

'You *can't* be serious,' David eventually said.

'That would not be wise,' Father Janosch added. 'Playing

with such things is not advisable. We could end up making a bad situation worse.'

Sarah shrugged. 'Fair enough. But it's one way to know for certain. And I wasn't talking about summoning a fucking demon-god or anything like that. Just trying one of the smaller rituals.'

'Like just summoning a demon-imp?' Ralph asked with a smile.

Sarah was glad of the levity he offered. 'Exactly,' she said. 'I'm sure we could all handle an imp.'

'Imp or not,' Father Janosch said, 'I don't think we mess with the rituals in the book.'

'Well, it's an option to keep in mind,' Sarah said. However, she decided not to push it any further. Instead, she changed the subject to how they would move forward. 'Anyway, we need to figure out what we do now. Everyone is obviously free to make up their own minds, but we can stay here and carry on, knowing what we do, or people can leave and call it a day. So... what does everyone think?'

The rest of the team just cast each other confused glances, each looking for someone else to take the lead. Sarah could understand their hesitation. It was a lot to drop on them and expect an instant decision.

'David, what do you think?' Jamie asked.

David took a moment. 'I'm unsure,' he replied. 'On the one hand, what we've found out definitely changes things. On the other, we've already carried out an investigation here before, and while it was tense, no one was hurt. *And* we've been here for a few days now with no real danger.'

'It's important to remember,' Sarah cut in, 'that we don't know for certain the house is actually one of these Devil Doors. It could all be bullshit.' She then turned to Father Janosch. 'Excuse the French, Father.'

He smiled. 'I've heard much worse.'

'Look,' David went on. 'I can't tell you all what to do. You have to decide for yourselves, individually.'

'But what are *you* going to do?' Jenn pressed. 'Are you staying?'

They all waited for an answer. It was slow in coming.

Eventually, David nodded his head. 'I am,' he confirmed. 'I know the risks, but I want to see this thing through. I just think the evidence we might get here would be game-changing for paranormal research as a whole. Even more so if the house turns out to be what Father Janosch suspects it is. However, I can't speak for any of you, and I don't want people staying on my account if they aren't truly comfortable with it.'

Sarah had suspected David would stay, but it was good to hear it out loud. Regardless of what anyone else chose to do, that meant things would still continue on in some fashion, and she still had a shot at helping her sister.

'Well,' Ralph began, 'I need to duck out for a few days after tomorrow regardless, since I have work commitments I can't get out of.'

That was one man down. Though not entirely unexpected, as Sarah had already been aware Ralph was going to be ducking out of the investigation due to work. The responses from the others would be a little more interesting.

'I'm staying,' Jenn firmly said. 'I haven't come this far to duck out when things get tough.'

'Not just tough,' David cut in. 'Dangerous.'

'*Potentially* dangerous,' Sarah corrected.

No, Sarah said to herself, *not* potentially *dangerous. It is dangerous and you know it.*

Chloe had been killed by the things inside Perron

Manor; Sarah had seen that herself. She'd even lied to the whole team about it in order to get them here in the first place. And now she was adding to the deception.

'I don't care,' Jenn stated. 'You say the choice is mine to make, David? Well, I've made it.'

He smiled. 'You sure?'

'I am.'

'What about everyone else?' Sarah asked.

'I'm not sure,' George cut in. 'I mean, I'm all for what we're doing here, but this sounds like stuff we shouldn't be messing with.'

'I... tend to agree,' Ann added. 'To be honest, I think this is beyond what we are capable of handling.'

'I understand,' David said. 'And I don't want anyone to feel bad about leaving. You aren't letting anyone down if you do.'

'Well, I didn't say I was *definitely* leaving,' George clarified. 'I'm just... not certain if I'm staying yet.'

'Me too,' Ann added.

David then looked over to the last remaining team member. 'What are your thoughts, Jamie?'

He shrugged. 'I'm not sure yet, this is a lot to take in. Part of me just says *'fuck it*, let's keep going.' But I need to give it some more time.'

'I get that,' David replied. 'So what do people think about taking some time away from the house until they've made up their minds? No point in staying if you are hesitant.'

The reluctant trio of Jamie, George, and Ann turned their heads to each other, yet again all waiting for someone else to speak.

'How about this,' Jamie said to the other two. 'We stay

for another night, then see how we feel in the morning when we've had time to think on it.'

Ann nodded in agreement.

'I'm okay with that,' George said. He then looked up to David. 'I guess it's decided. We're here for another night at least.'

25

THOUGH HE TRIED NOT to show it, Luca allowed himself to breathe a sigh of relief as everyone agreed to carry on with the investigation for at least a little while.

Before he'd gotten to the house earlier that day, he had been torn on whether to broach his concerns with David and Sarah, and he wasn't sure how much to tell them even if he did.

His solution had been to ease his way in by hiding the truth, just to see if he could get to the book without alerting them too much to what was going on. However, he'd quickly been called out and forced to divulge everything.

Well... *almost* everything.

He was just thankful that revealing the truth hadn't restricted access to the book. It had crossed his mind that everyone, including Sarah, could have fled, and then she may have refused to let him study the book any further. Or worse, she let him stay, but Luca would be on his own.

While he didn't feel safe in Perron Manor, Luca certainly felt better having others around him.

However, he still felt bad about keeping one last thing

from everyone. It wasn't something they needed to know necessarily, as it wouldn't impact what needed to be done. But it was important.

If Perron Manor truly was a Devil's Door, and those things actually existed in the real world, that meant other things he'd heard about the phenomenon could be real as well. And one story in particular terrified Luca.

If it was true... the Church had a lot of work to do.

26

IN ALL THE excitement of Father Janosch's visit, checking the footage of the previous night had almost slipped their minds. It wasn't until Sarah had mentioned it again to David that he'd remembered about her standing over him last night.

After the meeting, he, Sarah, and Father Janosch gathered in the makeshift headquarters to sift through the video footage, with David sitting at the computer and the other two standing over him.

Thankfully, Sarah had said she was fine with him seeing all the footage, including the video of her standing naked over David. However, David had insisted that only the three of them be present for it.

David lined up the footage so the timestamp showed three in the morning. Thanks to the night-vision capability of the camera, the image was awash with black shadows and shades of blue. David and Sarah could both be seen in their beds from the camera's high vantage point. He pressed play, and for the longest time neither of them stirred.

'You say you checked your watch at three-thirty?' Sarah asked.

'Yeah, but I don't know how long you were standing there before I woke up,' David replied. 'So I thought it best to go back a while.'

'And you don't remember it at all?' Father Janosch asked Sarah.

She shook her head. 'Not a thing.'

'And have you ever done anything like it before?'

David noticed Sarah pause for a moment. 'No, not that I know of,' she finally said.

Many minutes passed until there was movement. The three of them watched on as, on screen, Sarah slowly got out of bed completely naked. She stood for a few minutes, just swaying gently on the spot, facing in David's general direction.

David felt uncomfortable watching.

'Are you sure you're okay with this?' he asked.

She just nodded. 'I'm fine, honestly.'

'Odd that you're just standing there like that,' Father Janosch added.

'Not really,' Sarah replied, and David picked up on the defensiveness in her tone. 'It's just sleepwalking. That's hardly paranormal.'

'No,' the priest replied. 'But the *cause* of it could be.'

Eventually, Sarah on screen began to move forward, taking steady steps and looking decidedly unsteady on her feet. She reached David's bed and tilted her head down towards him. From the vantage point of the camera, it was just about clear to see that her eyes were still closed.

'There!' Father Janosch suddenly exclaimed, loud enough to make David jump. The priest thrust a finger towards the computer and pointed at the edge of the screen to a corner of the room that was drenched in shadow. 'What is that?' he asked.

Everyone leaned in. After squinting, David saw it too, and paused the playback.

Just on the edge of the darkness in the corner was a noticeable outline of a person. Nothing was exactly clear due to the pixilation and the distance of the camera. But it was definitely there.

The person looked female to David; he could make out a tall, slim build and long hair. She looked to be naked as well.

'That... that's Chloe,' Sarah said while pushing her way closer to the screen. Her eyes were wide. She then brought a hand up to the screen and touched the image with her fingertip.

'Are you sure?' David asked. He didn't know how she could be; to him, the image just wasn't clear enough.

David had met Chloe a few times, but he would never have guessed the person on the footage was her. It *could* be, he supposed, but then again it could be just about anyone.

'It's her,' Sarah stated. The conviction in her voice was absolute, but David had to wonder if that was hope rather than certainty.

He looked back to the screen, where his attention split between Sarah and the figure in the corner of the room. The shadowy stranger blended in and out of the background around her. There were times when she was clearly visible, and other times it was like she wasn't there at all as she bled into the wall behind her. Not once did the stranger move.

As the half-hour mark approached, David remembered what had awoken him the previous night.

Kill him.

An audio device had been set up in the room along with

the camera, and George had already overlaid the sound against the footage for them. David turned up the volume, raising the level of feedback and background static.

After a while, he heard it. The sound was crackly, almost like a blast of static, but the words spoken were clear.

'*Kill him.*'

'Oh my,' Father Janosch said.

David took a breath. It *hadn't* been a dream. What was worse, he'd been watching Sarah's face on screen the whole time. Her lips didn't move. It wasn't her.

In the footage, David began to stir as the words were repeated.

'*Kill him.*'

It was a horrible sound. Hoarse and almost pained.

'That didn't come from you, Sarah,' David said.

'I know,' she replied, her voice flat.

David watched himself on the video footage as he turned over in bed. 'Sarah?' he'd asked.

As he was watching, David flicked his eyes over to the edge of the screen, to the dark figure that stood watching. Yet again, she bled out of view, the pixels merging into the wall behind her. This time, however, she didn't reappear.

On the footage, David then got up and moved over to Sarah's bed, where he gathered up her duvet. He returned and draped it over her before leading her back to bed and laying her down.

After that, David spent a little time skipping forward through the footage to see if he could spot anything else, playing the video at four times its normal speed. But there was nothing of note. Of course, it would all need to be reviewed in-depth at a later date, as there could be something he had missed in their brief viewing. However, he felt like he had enough for now.

'Thoughts?' he asked the other two.

The response wasn't immediate. 'Interesting,' Father Janosch eventually said. 'Especially the person in the corner... I don't know what to make of that.'

'Pretty clear evidence of the paranormal, I'd say,' David suggested.

'I would agree,' Father Janosch replied. 'Sceptics might say the footage was doctored, but we know that not to be true. However, we do need to consider something else.' He then turned to Sarah. 'You say you have never had issues with sleepwalking before?'

She nodded. 'That's right.'

'In that case, we may need to consider that Sarah is becoming susceptible to the house.'

'Susceptible?' Sarah asked, incredulous. 'Care to explain?'

Father Janosch smiled politely and held up his hands. 'It is only a possibility. Given we saw you walk over to David, and then we heard that voice... to me, it sounded like an instruction.'

Sarah shook her head. 'Rubbish. You're implying that I'm... what? Becoming possessed? Well, I'm not.'

'Okay,' Father Janosch said, relenting, hands still up. 'I just said it for consideration. We all need to be vigilant and look out for each other.'

'Isn't it a bit quick to succumb to possession, Father?' David asked. 'We've only been here a couple of days.'

'True, but Sarah was here for a little while before that, living here with her family. Correct?'

'I was,' Sarah said. 'But I wasn't possessed.'

'And she wasn't here for very long,' David added. 'A month and a half or so. I didn't think someone could be broken down so quickly. And Sarah is pretty strong-willed.'

'I would normally agree, but we might not be dealing with a *normal* haunted location here. I don't think we can know *what* to expect.'

David thought it was certainly worthy of consideration. However, Sarah did not appear amenable to the suggestion, so David decided to move things on, though he made a mental note to follow the point up with Father Janosch privately.

'We have other evidence to look at as well,' David said to Father Janosch. 'I'd like to show it to you and get you completely up to speed.'

The priest nodded. 'Okay. But after that, I think it's important I begin studying *Ianua Diaboli*.'

'That's fair,' David replied.

'You two do what you need to,' Sarah said. 'I'm going to find the others.' She then turned and left the room, but not before glaring at Father Janosch on her way out.

David went after her, stopping her in the corridor outside.

'Sarah,' he called, grabbing her arm.

She spun around quickly.

'What!' she snapped. David noticed her hands were balled into fists, and he took a step back.

'Easy,' he said. 'Calm down a little, would you?'

'I *am* calm,' she replied, though she was clearly anything but.

'Look, I know how that must have sounded, but please just think about it logically. He's only airing a concern. One he may be wrong about, granted, but we still have to be honest with each other if we are concerned. And we can't get defensive.'

'David, he's implying that I'm fucking *possessed*. How am I supposed to react?'

'A little less angrily?' David suggested with a hesitant smile. He hoped injecting some humour would help calm Sarah down. However, she just took a step towards him.

'Do I seem possessed to you?' she asked. Her voice was low and steady.

'Not possessed, but certainly agitated,' he said. 'And come on, is it really such a leap for Father Janosch, considering what we saw on the video?'

'Yes.'

David let out a sigh. He wasn't going to get anywhere with her, though he wanted to keep trying.

'Sarah, come on. Please look at this impartially. No one is trying to offend you, here. I mean, don't you remember when we first got here two days ago? You were completely on edge, which I could understand given what you went through here. But now, the place doesn't seem to scare you anymore. Don't you think that's odd?'

Sarah paused. 'I'm just getting on with what needs to be done,' she said.

'And you feel totally safe here now?'

She looked away. 'I don't know.'

'Look,' David went on, 'I'm not saying the house has you under its control or anything, but we need to be careful. That's exactly what happens here: Perron Manor seeps into your skin and into your soul. And you likely won't even know it's happening, so we have to look out for each other. You might not be possessed right now, but it could have already begun.'

Sarah's eyes then turned to meet his. She looked calmer now, though sad. 'Can I tell you something?'

He nodded. 'Of course. Anything.'

She took a breath. 'When I was living here with Chloe,

there may have been a few times when... I don't know... I wasn't quite myself. I didn't see it then, but looking back...'

'Can you give me some examples?' David asked.

'For one, I considered running away and leaving my family when they were in danger. Purely because I was scared. That isn't me. I'm not saying I'm normally a hero or anything, but I would never do that. And I fought with Chloe *a lot*.'

'You mentioned that before,' David said.

'Yeah, but it wasn't just normal bickering. I also don't think it was brought on by stress. There were times when I really wanted to hurt her with the things I said. No matter how much we ever argued in the past, we never stooped to personal insults.'

'So... you think you *were* possessed?'

Sarah shook her head. 'No... I don't know. I didn't think so before, but after what you've just said, how would I truly know for certain, right?'

David nodded. 'Yeah, I understand. Look, to me, given what you're going through and the loss you've just suffered, I think you're acting fine. Sleepwalking aside, that is. But—'

'That's another thing,' Sarah cut in, looking embarrassed.

'What is?'

'The sleepwalking,' she said. 'I don't know why I wasn't honest in there, maybe I'm embarrassed or worried, but I *was* doing something similar when I lived here. Chloe told me she saw me walking around the house at night, though I had no memory of it.'

The confessions were a lot to take in, and David was more than a little annoyed Sarah had lied to him. It made him wonder just what else she was lying about. Still, he had to keep his annoyance in check; she had levelled with him now, and this was still her house. It wouldn't do much good to piss off the host too much.

'Okay,' he eventually said. 'I appreciate you telling me all that. But from here on out, I'm going to need you to be as honest as possible with me, okay?'

She nodded. 'Yeah.'

'Appreciate that. And don't worry, I promise to keep an eye on you and step in if I think you are acting... strangely.'

Sarah smiled. 'Thank you,' she said. 'Are *you* okay staying here after what Father Janosch told us about the house?'

'I think so,' David replied. 'It does change things a little, I suppose, but I can't just walk away from an opportunity like this. Are you okay with us staying?'

'I have to,' Sarah said. 'Chloe's still trapped.'

'I thought you might say that,' he replied. 'But I have to ask: do you really think that was Chloe on the footage we just saw? Because, if I'm honest, I couldn't see it. The girl could have been anyone.'

'I know it was Chloe. I just *know* it.'

'Fair enough,' David replied. However, if that were true, then there was a problem. 'Doesn't it concern you, though? If it *was* Chloe, and *she* was the one telling you to kill me, I mean... does that really sound like your sister?'

'No, Chloe would never say something like that.'

'Maybe the house is controlling her, like it does all the other souls in here.'

She quickly shook her head. 'I refuse to believe Chloe is a puppet. Anyway, it doesn't matter. We just need to free them all, regardless. Every last soul trapped here.'

'Yes, but we also need to be careful. Perron Manor could end up using your sister to get to you... if you let it.'

Again Sarah paused. She took in a breath. 'Fair enough.

I get what you're saying, and I won't let it affect me. I promise. Okay?'

David nodded. 'Thank you.' However, he wasn't certain if he'd truly gotten through to her or if she was just saying what he wanted to hear.

And he was troubled by what she'd just admitted.

'So what's the plan now?' Sarah asked.

'I'll show Father Janosch the rest of our evidence,' David said. 'Then, if people are up for it, we can split into two larger groups and run some experiments. But I'd like to help our priest up in the study. It isn't a good idea to have anyone working alone. You're free to join me.'

'I might come find you later,' Sarah replied. 'But for now, I'll go with the others and work with them. I think I need a break from the book and Devil Doors and all that stuff.'

'No problem. I'll walk you to the team.'

Sarah laughed. 'It'll take me less than a minute, David. Stay here, I'll be fine.' She was already turning around so as not to let him argue the point. She gave him a brief wave, and David watched her walk away.

27

LUCA WAS BACK in his study at home.

It was close to eleven at night, and he sat before his laptop with an unfinished email on the screen.

With his left hand he swirled a half-finished tumbler of whiskey. It was his third of the night.

The email was to the Bishop of Newcastle, and Luca was updating him on the progress of that day.

Luca had spent most of his time at the house studying *Ianua Diaboli*, and he'd been accompanied by David. What he'd found were pages upon pages of rituals and writings regarding the phenomena of the Devil's Door. However, there had been no indication of the author, or the date the book was written. It was therefore hard to judge the book's authenticity or true age.

Translating everything inside the book would have taken more time than Luca had available—months, he imagined—so the presence of the ledger and its transcriptions was welcome, if a little troubling. If someone had successfully translated the pages of *Ianua Diaboli*, what had stopped them carrying out one of the rituals?

Luca had found some very worrying things in the book that, if real, worried him. Particularly references to *Portae Septem*.

He'd also skimmed to the back and found the last section was titled *Claude Ianua*. Close the Door.

That ritual could prove vital. Luca remembered a sinking feeling of dread after reading it. Though it seemed surprisingly simple in its execution, the danger it also presented was worrying and required opening the door farther in order to then close it. He only read the ritual briefly, but knew it was important—a way that allowed his own world to re-establish dominance over the mirrored 'otherworld.'

That ritual needed to be carried out by a holy man, using the four elements.

No, five.

Luca shook his head and then went back to his keyboard, making mention of *Portae Septem* and *Claude Ianua* in his email to the Bishop.

Luca then took another long sip of his whiskey, which turned into a gulp as he finished what was left. He set the tumbler down and unscrewed the lid on his bottle, refilling his glass.

The buzz from the alcohol was welcome. He'd been feeling guilty ever since he'd left Perron Manor earlier that evening. David had wanted him to stay the night, but Luca had used the excuse that he wasn't prepared, and had no change of clothes. In addition, he'd said that he had duties to attend to the following day.

However, none of those reasons would have really stopped Luca from spending the night if he'd truly wanted to. After all, he'd been expressly told that Perron Manor was his priority now, and he could have easily returned home to get a change of clothing if it was that important.

Fear had kept him away.

He'd have to go back the following day, of course. All he'd bought himself was one night's reprieve.

Luca set his glass back down and started typing.

It is my suspicion that the book discovered at the house could well be the Ianua Diaboli, *previously thought to be a myth. I also suspect the house itself is therefore likely a Devil's Door. Though I cannot be sure, I feel the previous owners were aware of just what the house was. Whether they discovered this and then tracked down the book, or came into possession of the book first before making the connection, I cannot be sure. But it is too much of a coincidence.*

As you will no doubt be aware, if my assumptions are correct, we have to consider that other stories regarding the Devil's Door could also be true.

And we therefore have to consider the existence of the Seven Gates...

When he finally finished the email, Luca reread it twice. He wanted to make sure he sounded measured in his assessment and wasn't letting his fear of Perron Manor cloud his judgment. After all, they were dealing with myths and legends here.

He took another drink and then hit send. Luca eventually decided that he'd rather be accused of overreacting than not acting at all.

He then leaned back in his chair and closed his eyes.

Luca was tired, and dearly wanted to sleep. Maybe another whiskey first, though.

However, after only a couple of minutes, a chime sounded from his laptop. He checked his inbox.

It was from the Bishop.

Get the book. Bring it to us. Call me on my direct line to keep me informed.

28

SARAH'S BODY was being pulled down, sucked into the earth around her. The soil and rocks that surrounded her pressed into her skin as she dropped. An unseen force dragged her lower and lower.

The temperature rose, as did her own screams. However, those cries were overpowered by those around her.

Below her.

The earth and rock were replaced with something else. Something wet and warm.

Flesh.

It ran with blood. She heard a new voice, one that rose above other agonised wails.

'*Kill him.*'

Sarah continued to scream and struggle as she was helplessly pulled farther down. She recognised the feminine voice that was audible above all others. It was Chloe's.

'*Kill him and come home, Sarah.*'

29

DAVID ROLLED OVER, suddenly wide awake, though he wasn't sure why. He blinked and waited for his eyes to get used to the dark. The room around him was cold, more so than usual, and that alone set his mind on high alert.

As his vision adjusted, David was able to see Sarah's bed. She was sitting up and facing him with her eyes shut.

David immediately sat up himself, then cast a glance to the corner of the room, just in case a mysterious figure was again present.

This time, however, he saw nothing.

'Sarah?' he asked. He got no response.

David leaned over and grabbed his phone from the floor. When he activated the screen, he saw it was three-twenty-six in the morning.

Something had woken him. Possibly the cold, or maybe it was something else... something more instinctual.

He swung his legs out of bed, then stood with his fists clenched, readying himself.

David picked up his handheld camera and flicked open the viewfinder. When putting Sarah back to bed the previous night, he hadn't seen that mysterious figure. It was only when the footage played back that she had become apparent. With that in mind, he pointed the camera over to the corner and zoomed in.

There didn't seem to be anything out of the ordinary. He then began to slowly pan around the room and stopped on Sarah.

He could see her chest moving quickly in line with her rapid, shallow breathing. There was also a sheen of sweat over her skin, causing it to glisten. Thankfully, she was clothed this time, wearing a tank top.

Do I wake the others?

Nothing had actually happened to warrant it. Sarah was just sitting up in bed in her sleep, which was indeed odd, but not something dangerous in its own right. Although, now that David knew a little more about the house—and what it *could* be—everything was now significant. He only wished Father Janosch had stayed the night.

David suspected the priest had been scared, but he couldn't exactly force the man to stay, though Father Janosch had promised to return the following day and remain at the house for a few nights if required.

David started to turn the camera again, slowly panning around the room in an arc. He adjusted his feet and slowly swivelled so that he could capture the room behind him as well.

It was then, as he turned a full one-hundred-and-eighty degrees, he stopped and drew in a sharp breath. A female figure stood on the other side of his bed, not four feet away from him.

David didn't have time to scream before she leapt at him.

≈

Jenn felt her body shaking.

'Wake up, Jenn,' a whispering voice pleaded. It was Ann's voice, and she sounded scared.

'What's wrong?' Jenn asked, sitting up and rubbing her eyes. She felt the sting of cold air, as if a window had been left open during the night.

Ann was squatted down next to her, dressed in just a dark purple nightie. She was shivering, and her dark hair was a wild mess, sticking up in all directions. Without her makeup, heavy eyeliner, and black lipstick, Ann looked like a completely different person. She had a cold hand resting on Jenn's shoulder.

'There's someone in here with us,' she whispered, sounding terrified.

George woke suddenly. He was moving. It felt like he was being dragged. Something had an ice-cold grip on his ankle, and he was pulled across his bed.

Panic filled him as he struggled to make sense of what was happening. He then felt himself drop off the edge of the bed and hit the back of his head on the floor.

He quickly scrambled up to a sitting position and looked around in the dark. His heart raced and his skin tingled from the cold, causing it to break out in goosebumps.

Ralph sat up in his own bed and rubbed his face.

'George?' he asked. George could see Ralph's squinting, confused eyes. 'What happened? Did you just fall out of bloody bed?'

'Something pulled me,' George said.

'It *what*? Are you sure?' Ralph's voice suddenly had more

urgency to it. He quickly got out of bed and paced straight over to George to help him up.

'What's going on?' Jamie asked, now in a sitting position himself. He rubbed his shaggy blond hair and yawned. 'Something happening?'

'George was just pulled out of his bed,' Ralph replied.

'He was what?' Jamie asked as his body stiffened up. He looked quickly around the room, head swivelling from side to side. There didn't appear to be anything in the room with them.

After grabbing his phone, George shone the light from its screen onto his ankle and saw a red mark around it.

'Look,' he told the others, and they leaned in.

'Holy shit!' Ralph exclaimed. 'Wait, let me get my camera. We need to document this.' As he did, George looked up to Jamie, who had his own phone in hand as well. 'What time is it?' George asked.

Jamie checked. 'Three-twenty-six.'

'Witching hour,' Jamie added.

Ralph returned with his handheld camera and aimed it at George's ankle. 'Keep the light on it,' Ralph instructed him. Then, he addressed the camera. 'It's three-twenty-six in the morning, and our colleague George Dalton has just been pulled out of bed by something we cannot see. There is a visible mark on his ankle, which was not there before we turned in for the night.'

A slow, drawn-out creaking sound caused all three to look up. The door to the adjoining en-suite was gliding open.

Ralph lifted the camera up to capture what was happening, but George felt a creeping sensation work its way up his spine. He shivered, and it wasn't just from the cold.

'Hello?' Ralph called out. George heard the uncertainty in the big man's voice.

The door finished its swing and remained fully open. George could see nothing through the darkness inside the bathroom from his vantage point. He held up his phone, flashlight still on, and aimed it at the doorway. Now they could see a little farther into the en-suite.

Something was there.

George saw a woman, just at the edge of the beam of light. She was naked, short, and in her later years. Her greying blond hair was scraggly while her pale skin was marred with purple and yellow blotches. She wore a sinister grin and her eyes were wide with a manic, wild stare. The woman didn't move an inch.

'Fuck, fuck, fuck,' Jamie exclaimed.

They suddenly heard a scream from another room. George whipped his head around to the direction of the noise.

'That was Ann,' Jamie said.

Then, there was another cry, this one coming from a different room. 'Help me!'

David.

George quickly looked back to the en-suite, but the woman was gone. An ice-cold aura suddenly radiated from behind him.

'*Come to Patricia, dear,*' a throaty voice said. George didn't have to turn around to know the woman was now standing behind him. He felt cold, clammy hands grip his neck.

30

ANN HAD FIRST SEEN the man after she'd woken. At least... she *thought* she had. She'd looked over to the curtains and her breath had caught in her throat: a man stood there with his stomach pulled open, holding his own innards in his hands. She'd scrambled out of bed, panicked, before turning to look back.

He was gone.

Ann had then quickly snuck over to Jenn and woken her up.

No sooner had she told Jenn they weren't alone was the man there again, and he lurched forward from the shadows.

With a scream, Ann pulled Jenn away from the lumbering nightmare. Escaping to the door was out of the question—they would have to go *past* him to get to it. So, instead, Ann and Jenn huddled in the corner. Now she feared for her life, and the man with skin as pale as ash took one unsteady step after another. He lifted his hands, showing them his intestines—thick chords of meat that glistened red.

'*Please... help,*' he wheezed. The expression the man wore was one of pain and sorrow. However, that quickly darkened and a sneer crossed his lips. He raised his intestines higher. '*Let me... strangle you.*'

'We need to get out of here,' Jenn said while squeezing Ann's hand.

Ann shook her head frantically. 'No! It'll get us!' She couldn't run past him. They would die.

'We *have* to!' Jenn shouted.

Part of Ann knew her colleague was right. Surely it was better to at least try to escape than just wait to let that... *thing*... kill them. But her feet refused to move.

The man took another heavy footstep closer to them. He started to chuckle. '*You'll like it here with us.*'

'Fucking run!' Jenn screamed and shook her. That jolted Ann to life. They both dashed away, holding hands, and Ann felt fear like never before as they attempted to weave to the side of the horrific stranger.

The man raised his hands higher and attempted to drop his rope-like guts over Ann. She felt cold blood drip onto her cheek, but the pair managed to duck to the side and avoid his attempt to grab them. They then sprinted over to the door. Jenn pulled it open as Ann cast a look back.

The man was gone.

～

Ralph watched George drop to his knees as the woman behind him squeezed her grip tighter. She tittered and ran a black tongue over her lips.

George's face was twisted into a grimace. 'She's crushing my neck,' he said. His words were strained.

'Do something!' Jamie shouted, his own voice full of

panic. For half a second, Ralph was annoyed that Jamie had laid all responsibility of helping their friend at his feet. However, he didn't have time to dwell on that—George *did* need help, even though the thought of moving closer to that woman terrified Ralph.

Her eyes were milky white, with no visible pupils, and her stomach was sunken and pulled in beneath her ribcage.

'*Stay... here... forever, dear,*' the woman said. Her words were strained but had a certain sexualised lust to them. '*I'm oh... so... lonely.*'

George let out a cry of pain.

It was then Ralph acted. He lunged forward and grabbed hold of George's arms as the hag stared and grinned manically. With a heave, Ralph was able to pull George free of her grip and George fell forwards, hands on the back of his neck. Ralph then quickly pulled his friend up and dragged him to the door with Jamie leading the way. They were soon out into the corridor while the woman stood her ground, stock-still, and chuckled.

~

As Jenn and Ann barrelled down the hallway, Jenn saw a door open up ahead and braced herself for some kind of horror to reveal itself. However, she was surprised to see Jamie, George, and Ralph emerge, with George holding his neck and wincing in pain.

She ran over to them. 'What happened?'

Ralph looked up in surprise, his body tense, but Jenn saw him relax when he realised it was them. He quickly pointed back into the room. 'There's a ghost in...' but he trailed off.

With her heart pounding in her chest, Jenn looked inside. There was no one.

'There *was* someone in there,' he said. 'I swear, and George almost...'

'I believe you,' Jenn replied.

'We have to get out of here,' George said. 'It was a mistake to stay.'

Jenn could sense fear ripple through all of them, and though part of her wanted to argue, it was only a small part, overshadowed by what she and Ann had just seen.

Then, she heard another voice cry out from a nearby room. 'Help me!'

It was David. She had heard him yell for help once before already.

What the hell is happening to him?

'Let's go,' Ralph said and led the way as the others followed.

Jenn tried to push away the fear she felt as they ran to help their leader.

'I don't like this,' Ann said, her voice quaking.

Me either, Jenn thought. They reached the door and Ralph thrust it open—they all froze in shock.

David was struggling on the floor with a naked woman mounted on top of him. She had brown, matted hair, sunken, pale flesh, and twisted features that were almost demonic—as was the snarl on her face. The woman grappled with David, trying to keep his hands on the floor.

Sarah stood above them both, looking down in a trance-like state, her eyes only half open.

David turned his head to the others. He looked horrified and was clearly overpowered.

'Help me!' he yelled again. The nightmarish woman

turned to look at the others as well, locking her milky eyes on them.

Then she was gone.

Jenn wasn't sure how, but one moment she was there; the next she seemed to just bleed into the surroundings, melting away to nothing and leaving David lying alone on the ground, panting and sweating. Sarah still watched, unmoving.

'What happened?' Jenn asked as she squeezed into the room. Ralph took a few steps forward and allowed the others to enter as well.

'I'm not quite sure,' David said and got to his feet. He looked scared, which was understandable, but there was something else to his expression. Confusion, perhaps. 'I woke up and something attacked me. And Sarah was...'

They all turned to look at Sarah, who still had her glazed eyes fixed on David.

'Is she asleep?' Ann asked.

'I think so,' David replied.

'It doesn't matter,' George said. 'We need to get out of here. Now.'

'No, it's okay,' David replied, waving a dismissive hand. 'I'm honestly fine.'

'I'm not,' George stated.

David frowned in confusion.

'Look, David,' Ralph began, 'stuff happened to us as well. A woman attacked George in our room.'

'Almost killed me,' George added.

'Something attacked us too,' Ann then threw in. Ralph, Jamie, and George turned to look at her.

In the confusion of what was happening, Jenn realised neither she nor Ann had told the others about the man in their room.

'What was it?' Ralph asked.

'Something with its stomach torn open,' Ann replied. Her bottom lip quivered and she hugged herself.

It seemed like everyone had had their own experience at the same time. Jenn realised they were damn lucky no one had gotten hurt, and with reluctance accepted they should stop tempting fate.

Ralph spoke first. 'Look, David,' he said, 'I... agree with George. I don't think we should be here. I know you wanted to stay, but tonight changes things. We need to leave. And not in the morning, but right now.'

'I see,' David said. He took a deep breath then gave a solemn nod. 'You're right. We can't put our lives in danger anymore.'

'What about her?' Jamie asked, motioning to Sarah.

David turned to look at her. 'We wake her, then all get the hell out.'

'She might not come willingly,' Ralph pointed out.

'Then we'll have to make her see sense,' David responded. He then moved his hand towards Sarah's shoulder. She followed his arm as it moved, eyes still only half open with a blank expression. David gently shook her.

'Sarah?'

He got no response, so shook her a little harder. Still nothing.

'Sarah!' Ann shouted.

Jenn and everyone else jumped at the sudden noise. 'Jesus, Ann, I just about shit myself,' Ralph scolded. However, when they looked back to Sarah, they saw her eyes blink a few times, then fully open. Her pupils started to focus. Jenn watched confusion draw over her face.

'What... what's going on?' she asked.

'Long story,' Ralph said. 'But we need to get out of here.'

Sarah frowned. 'What, why?'

'We've all been attacked,' Ann said. 'We nearly *died*.'

When she thought about it, though, Jenn wasn't so sure that was correct. *Had* they nearly died? They'd all had experiences, but they'd escaped. Even David, who had been pinned down and at the mercy of that savage woman. How long had he been stuck like that before they'd all run into the room? Could he really have fought off a spirit if it didn't want him to?

Jenn glanced over to Sarah and saw that she was clearly reeling, trying to catch up with what was going on. Sarah looked back over to her bed, then to the floor, clearly confused as to why she had woken standing up like that.

'Was I sleepwalking again?' she asked.

David nodded. 'Afraid so. A woman was attacking me and you walked over, then stood there and watched it happen.'

'Jesus,' Sarah exclaimed.

'Can we not go over everything now?' Ann asked, seeming full of agitation. 'That can wait. We need to get the hell out of here quickly!'

'Okay,' David said. 'I hear you. But we can't very well run out of here in our sleeping clothes, so we should quickly get changed, pack the essentials, and then we can leave.'

'I'm *not* going back to my room,' Ann insisted.

'We'll go together,' David replied and grabbed some clothes from his suitcase. 'It'll be safer if we stay in one big group. Sarah,' he said, turning to her. 'Get dressed. Hurry.'

But Sarah didn't move.

'Sarah,' Ann snapped. 'Move it!'

'And where are we all going to go?' Sarah asked.

'Anywhere but here,' Ann shot back. 'We all have homes we can go to.'

'At this hour? I'm guessing it's late.'

'About three-thirty,' Ralph said.

'So?' Ann replied. 'Who gives a shit?'

'You all came in one van,' Sarah went on. 'By the time David drops you all off, what time would it be? Some of you live out of town.'

'That doesn't matter. I'd rather be stuck in a car for a few hours than stay here. Even if we're dog tired. I honestly don't know why you're making this an issue.'

David, who was almost finished changing, cut in. 'Look,' he said, 'we can all just go back to my house for now, to pull ourselves together. It isn't a big place, and it'll be cramped, but I have a spare bed, a sofa, and some inflatable beds as well. We can get a few hours of sleep, then decide where we go from here.'

'What's to decide?' Ann asked. 'We leave here and never come back.'

'We get it, Ann,' Jenn said. 'You're done here. Fine. You don't need to repeat yourself over and over.'

'Well clearly I *do*,' Ann snapped. 'Because we are *still* fucking standing here arguing!'

'Sarah, please get ready,' David said as he finished tying his shoes.

'I'm not going,' Sarah replied, folding her arms over her chest.

Great, Jenn thought. *Just what we need.*

'Then fucking stay!' Ann shouted and stamped her foot. She then turned to their leader. 'David, would you just *do* something!'

'Look, the rest of you go and get ready,' he said. 'Stick together and be quick. We'll meet in the corridor, then head down to the van.'

'Let's go,' Jenn said, taking the lead. She walked from the

room and the others filed out behind her. They made their way to the girls' room first, where Jenn and Ann quickly started to get dressed.

'What do you think David's saying to Sarah?' Ann asked.

Jenn shook her head. 'I have no idea.'

31

'YOU HAVE TO COME WITH US,' David said to Sarah.

'No, I don't,' she replied. Her voice was flat and cold. 'And you can't make me go. Unless, of course, you want to try and force me out of my own house.'

'I know I can't force you,' David said. 'And I would never try. But please, I'm just asking you to see sense. At least for one night, so we can process what just happened.'

'I didn't see what happened. I'm just going off what you've told me. And I still can't make sense of it all.'

'So... you think we're lying?' David asked.

Sarah's body relaxed a little and her eyes turned downward. 'I honestly don't know *what* to think.'

'I can easily fill you in. After waking a little while ago, I saw you sitting up in bed again. Given what happened last night, I was worried something was in the room with us. And I was right. There was a woman, and she leapt on me. If it wasn't for the others, I don't know what would have happened, because you weren't waking up. You just stood there, watching it all.'

Sarah was silent for a moment. She looked embarrassed.

David felt for her; none of this could have been easy for her, but she needed to stop being so stubborn.

Sarah lifted her head and her eyes widened a little.

'The woman who jumped on you,' she went on. 'Did you recognise her?'

David paused.

He was hoping she wouldn't ask that question, because he knew *exactly* who the ghostly apparition was. He'd known it as soon as he'd seen her in the viewfinder. It had become even more apparent when she was atop him. Even though her body was rotted, and her face twisted into a demonic snarl... he knew who it was.

Chloe.

She'd looked so full of hate and anger. However, he didn't want to admit that to Sarah, fearing it would only make her desire to stay even stronger. So, he shook his head and lied. 'No, I didn't recognise her.'

David hoped he sounded believable. Sarah narrowed her eyes at him, and he felt like he was being studied.

'You sure?' she asked.

He nodded. 'Of course I'm sure.'

Sarah stared at him a moment longer, then nodded. 'Okay,' she said. 'But it doesn't change the fact that I'm staying. If the rest of you want to leave, so be it, I can't stop you going any more than you can stop me staying.'

David wanted to scream at her. *Why is she being so stupid?*

He knew why, of course. Because of her sister.

David sympathised—more than she knew—but surely there was a point where self-preservation had to come first.

'Listen,' he went on. 'Just leave with us now, if only for a night, and then if you feel the need, I'll bring you back here myself tomorrow. But just get away from this house for a little while. Please.'

'Chloe can't leave, can she?' Sarah asked as if that were answer enough.

'Maybe not,' he admitted. 'But would she want you suffering like this? Or putting yourself in danger?'

'She wants my help,' Sarah said. 'And she's going to get it.'

'Not if you end up dead!' David snapped. He took a breath and ran a hand through his hair. 'Look,' he said, 'I'm sorry for yelling. But I just want you to listen to reason. Staying here on your own will do no good. And it certainly won't help Chloe if something happens to you.'

'I... don't know,' she said, looking down to the floor.

David could see the struggle within her. It was etched on her face. '*One* night,' he said. 'Just to clear your head.' He held out his hand to her. 'Please.'

She didn't move and instead looked at his waiting hand.

Please, Sarah, just listen.

Finally, she took it, and David breathed a sigh of relief.

'One night,' she said. 'Then you bring me back here tomorrow.'

'Deal,' he said.

32

'Coffee's up!'

Sarah opened her eyes at the call, though her body fought against waking. Her head pounded. She felt like she'd gone a week with only a half hour of sleep.

She was fairly sure the voice was David's, and could also faintly smell cooking meat.

The bed beneath Sarah sank as she rolled over, so much so that her hip touched the floor. It was then she remembered taking an inflatable last night, which had now lost a lot of its air. She lifted her head to see the bedroom around her. It was small and basic, with old white wallpaper, beige curtains, and a matching carpet that didn't seem to have any underlay. There was a single bed in the room as well, which Jenn and Ann had squeezed into together.

'What time is it?' Ann asked. It was more of a whining complaint than a genuine question. Sarah felt for her phone on the floor to check.

'Almost midday,' she replied.

'I'm making breakfast as well,' David shouted. 'I hope a traditional English fry-up is okay with everyone?'

It sounded good to Sarah.

'Coming,' Jenn shouted. She yawned, then added, 'I feel like crap.'

'Crazy night,' Sarah said.

Jenn turned to look at her from the bed. 'How are you feeling today?'

'I'm okay,' Sarah replied. 'My head's a little all over the place.'

'I can imagine.' Jenn swung her legs out of bed. 'I've never seen anything like last night before in my life.'

'What about back in 2014? I heard your investigation got pretty crazy.'

Jenn thought for a moment, then nodded. 'I guess. But we didn't stick around Perron Manor long after that, either.'

'So you're definitely done?' Sarah asked.

'I... don't know.'

Ann sat up as well, an angry frown on her face. 'Are you serious, Jenn? We *can't* go back.'

But Jenn just held up her hand. 'Lecture me later,' she said. 'First, I need coffee.'

Coffee sounded good to Sarah, too.

The breakfast David had served up was surprisingly good. He'd even fried up some mushrooms and poached everyone eggs.

All seven of them were crammed into an open living and dining space. The living room had a three-seat sofa as well as an old, scruffy armchair. Ann, Jenn, and Sarah had squeezed onto the couch, while Ralph took the chair, and all of them had their plates balanced on their knees.

The dining area was only around five-feet wide with a

small pine table and matching chairs, but the table only accommodated two people. George and Jamie sat there, devouring their food.

David elected to sit on the floor, just in front of an old electric fireplace with a glass front. Inside of the glass panel were fake pieces of decorative coal.

Sarah didn't think it looked too comfortable down on the floor, since the carpet underfoot didn't appear to have underlay either, just like the ones upstairs. In some places the carpet-piles had worn thin.

'I'll need to call Father Janosch,' David said. 'Tell him we aren't at the house anymore. He was planning on heading over and joining up with us today.'

There were a few nods of acknowledgement, but no-one spoke. The topic of potentially going back was clearly the elephant in the room, and it couldn't be ignored for long. Sarah had thought of nothing else since waking that morning, constantly deliberating what to do.

The house was indeed dangerous; however, Chloe was still there… suffering. Sarah's sweet, caring, pain-in-the-arse sister, whom she had loved more than anyone else in this world. Sarah pictured Chloe's smiling face and then thought about Emma, who would grow up without a mother.

How could she ever again look her niece in the eye knowing she had abandoned Chloe's soul to damnation? Sarah realised tears were building in her eyes, so she subtly wiped them with the back of her hand, hoping that no one had noticed.

She saw David looking at her as he chewed his food. He offered her a solemn smile. She averted her eyes from him.

Enough, she told herself. *You can mourn later. Keep focused. Get back to the fucking house.*

However, without the others, what could she really do to

help her sister? David and his team were the experts here... or so they said.

Sarah's mind ran back to the book up in the study, as well as the accompanying ledger. Perhaps there was something in the translations that could help.

In addition, there was Father Janosch. She had already been introduced to him now, and *he* was the one who could get the Church to help. So... did Sarah really need the others?

That's harsh, Sarah. They've given a lot to help you.

She took a breath. It was time to acknowledge the elephant.

'Have you all decided what you're doing?' she asked. 'You know, about going back to the house?'

The clinking of plates and chewing of food stopped. Silence briefly descended over them, which David eventually broke. 'Have *you* decided?' he asked.

'Yes,' Sarah said. 'I heard what you said before, and I get that the house might be dangerous. But I've lived with danger most of my life, it was kinda my job. I don't say that to be brash, but you all know why I need to go back there. You know what's at stake for me. So, I've made up my mind. I'm going back.'

More silence. Sarah went on. 'I don't expect any of you to come with me if you don't want to or don't think it's safe. You've already done enough.' She then looked up to David. 'I'd just ask that you give me Father Janosch's contact details and get him to speak to me. I'm still moving forward with the plan, because it's the only one I have. I need his help.'

She saw Ann shake her head. 'You're crazy,' Ann said.

Sarah let the comment go. *She's still freaked out about the previous night.*

Sarah saw the others cast nervous glances at each other.

It was clear not everyone had come to a firm decision yet, which was to be expected. So, it was time for them to make up their minds.

'Look,' Ralph began. 'I gotta admit, I don't know which way I fall on this. Part of me was terrified, I'll admit, but another part of me feels like we are on the cusp of something big with the house. The proof we could get there, I mean... it's why we do what we do. *But*, I also gotta work and pay the bills, and I need to take a few days away at the very least. I gotta spend some time with my girlfriend as well.'

Sarah understood that completely. Their own lives had to come first.

'Take as much time as you need,' Sarah said. 'And if you want to come back when you are able, that's great. If not, no problem.'

She then looked around the room for someone else to voice their thoughts. No one did, so Sarah forced the issue and focused on Jenn. 'What about you?'

Jenn finished her mouthful of food. 'I honestly don't know either. I got scared, but... that house is confirming everything I've ever believed in and everything I ever hoped was true. But... I dunno, I think I need more time to decide.'

Sarah nodded. 'That's fair.' She then turned her attention to Ann, who had a face like thunder.

'Don't even ask,' Ann snapped. 'I'm out. I've made that perfectly clear.'

'You have,' Sarah replied, raising her hands defensively. 'And again, that is no problem. Thank you for the time you've given me already. I really mean that.'

Jamie and George both sat at the small dining room table looking at their plates.

'Any input from you two fellas?' Sarah asked. They

looked up at each other, neither wanting to go first. It was Jamie who eventually spoke.

'I think I might be out as well,' he said and hung his head. 'Sorry.'

'Don't be sorry,' Sarah replied. 'I mean that. You've nothing to apologise for.'

'Yeah, I'm not so sure I'll be back either,' George added. 'Don't get me wrong, that house could be a game-changer. I'm just not sure we are the right people to study it.'

'How so?' David quickly asked with a frown.

George shrugged. 'I mean, come on, we all love what we do, but this is just a hobby for us. Is it really worth us putting our lives on the line?'

'*Just* a hobby?' David asked. 'I don't know about the rest of you, but I take this very seriously.'

'It's fine,' Sarah cut in. She sensed a disagreement coming, which could possibly turn into an argument she didn't have time for. 'And what about you, David?'

David held steady eye contact with Sarah for a few moments. His face was serious. 'I've given it a lot of thought,' he said, then paused and took a breath before finishing. 'I'm coming with you.'

Sarah smiled. She couldn't help it. While she was certainly prepared to go back alone, knowing David would be there was a huge relief.

He stood up and pulled out his mobile phone. 'I'm going to make the call to Father Janosch now,' he said, 'I'll update him on what happened and tell him to meet those of us who are going back later.'

As he walked from the room, Sarah caught his eye and mouthed, *thank you*.

He smiled and kept walking. She heard his footsteps ascend the stairs to the floor above.

Jenn sighed. 'Fuck it,' she said. 'I'm coming too.'

'You sure?' Sarah asked. 'You know you don't have to.'

'I know,' Jenn replied. 'But I want to see it through.'

'Appreciate it,' she said, still smiling.

Ann rolled her eyes. 'Jesus Christ... you three are fucking crazy, you know that?'

'Maybe,' Jenn said. 'But I need to do it. Same as David.'

'No,' Ann argued, '*not* the same as David. You know as well as I do the real reason he's going back.'

'Drop it, Ann,' Jenn snapped.

Ann shook her head and turned away. 'Fine,' she said and got to her feet. She walked off with her plate, taking it to the kitchen.

'What did she mean by that?' Sarah asked.

Jenn looked a little uncomfortable. 'It... doesn't matter,' she replied. 'Ask David. Not really my place to say.'

33

THE PHONE RANG AND RANG. David assumed the priest was busy and expected the call to go to voicemail. However, he was pleasantly surprised when Father Janosch picked up.

'David,' the priest said. 'Is everything alright?'

'Father, I'm glad I caught you. Everything is... okay, I guess. But there has been a development.'

'What happened?'

'Well, there were multiple occurrences last night. All of them happened at roughly the same time, about three-thirty in the morning...'

David proceeded to recount the events of the previous night, making sure to give detail about each of the three experiences.

'...to be honest,' David went on to add, 'it was quite dangerous. George could have been seriously hurt.'

'That is most upsetting to hear,' Father Janosch said. 'Where are you now? Still at the house?'

'No, most people didn't want to stay, as you can imagine. So we all left and are at my place for the moment.'

'That's sensible. The severity is troubling. Not many normal hauntings manifest in such a serious way.'

'No, but we've always known Perron Manor wasn't just a normal haunted house.'

'I suppose you are right, but I had hoped that maybe its history was false. Or at least exaggerated.'

'Well, I think we have our answers on that point,' David said.

'So I assume you are done with the investigation now?' Father Janosch asked. 'If that's the case, could I ask a favour? It would be most helpful if Miss Pearson would let me borrow *Ianua Diaboli* for study. With the house out of bounds, it may be the only way to help her sister—'

'Actually,' David said, cutting off the priest. 'Some of us have decided to go back.'

There was a pause. 'Go back? Are you serious?'

'We are,' he replied.

'But David, if the house is so dangerous, then why?'

'I want to help my client,' David said. 'And I want proof that everything I've devoted my life to is not just make-believe.'

That wasn't the whole truth, but it was as much as he was prepared to give.

'Well, maybe there is another way. The book. David, if Sarah lets me have it to study and report on, I think the Church would act. So, really, there isn't a reason to go back to the house.'

'I thought you said the Church still needed substantial evidence to act?'

'I would count what happened last night substantial, wouldn't you?'

'Of course,' David said. 'But the trouble is, we didn't

capture any of it. It would just be our testimony. Not really irrefutable proof to an impartial adjudicator.'

'I'll vouch for you,' the priest said. David picked up a hint of desperation. He knew Father Janosch was scared of the house—they all were, to an extent, but he wondered if the priest was letting his fear cloud his better judgment. Or, on the other hand, was David letting his need to get back there cloud his own?

After all, even though he'd persuaded Sarah to leave temporarily, David knew he was just as guilty of wanting to return. He wanted the exact same thing. The difference was, his desire to help a loved one in need had been stretched out over thirty-five years.

'I will speak to Sarah,' David said, 'but I already know the answer. She's single-minded in what she wants to do, and won't let the book leave Perron Manor if she thinks it could delay things.'

'How would it possibly—'

David cut in. 'Because if the book is gone for you to study at your own leisure, then the urgency is gone, Father. Sarah will have no guarantee on how long things will drag out, or how quickly the Church will act—if they even choose to at all. If you need *Ianua Diaboli,* I think you will need to come to the house.'

'I assure you,' Father Janosch replied, 'I would work as fast as I possibly could. And it would be quicker that way, too, as I could work late into the night from home.'

'Well, like I say, I'll speak to her for you.'

'No need,' Sarah's voice said from the open doorway of the bedroom. She walked over to David and held out her hand, requesting the phone. He gave it to her.

'Father Janosch?' she said. 'This is Sarah Pearson. Forgive

me, but I overheard a little of the conversation you were having. And I can tell you that David is correct. I'm sorry, but I won't be letting that book out of my sight. It's not like I think you're going to take off with it or anything, but I just don't have time to fuck around. You are welcome to come over and help us; in fact, I'd like it if you could. But that's final.'

David listened intently as he heard the mumbles of a reply come from the priest, but he couldn't make out the exact words.

Sarah shrugged. 'It might well be irresponsible and dangerous, Father, but that's where I'm at with the whole thing. If you want to make sure we don't accidentally summon the Devil or something, I suggest you get your arse over to the house and help us.'

David's eyes widened in surprise. Sarah then smiled and nodded a few more times as Father Janosch replied.

'Okay,' she eventually said. The phone was handed back to David. 'He wants to talk to you.'

David held the phone up to his ear. 'Yes?'

'Fine,' Father Janosch said. 'I'll come.'

David looked up to Sarah and she flashed him a smile and a wink. 'Just gotta play hardball,' she whispered.

David said his goodbyes and finished the call with Father Janosch. 'Well played,' he said with a chuckle to Sarah.

'Thank you. I figured we could use his help, but he's been entirely too evasive for me.'

'Yeah. I think he's terrified of Perron Manor, to be honest.'

'Understandable. But he needed to make a decision, just like the rest of us. I just hope he follows through with it.'

'Were you serious?' David asked.

'About what?'

'Accidentally summoning the Devil. I mean, I know it was kind of a joke, but would you really be willing to attempt some of the rituals in the book? I remember you suggested something like that a little while ago.'

'I don't know. Maybe, I guess. I mean, if there is something in there that could help us, wouldn't you?'

'It's awfully dangerous,' David said. 'We might not summon the Devil, but we could very easily get something wrong and cause a great deal of harm. We really need to be careful.'

'Fair enough,' Sarah said. 'We'll be careful.'

David didn't know what to make of the answer. It was decidedly... ambiguous.

'I wanted to ask you something,' she went on.

'Shoot,' he said.

Sarah paused for a moment. Her eyes flicked to the side, as if she were considering her words carefully.

'What's the deal with you and Perron Manor?' she asked.

David cocked his head to the side. 'What do you mean?'

'Like... why are you so interested in it?'

He wasn't sure where the questioning was coming from. 'Because of what it is,' he replied. 'It's like the holy grail to people like me.'

'Paranormal investigators?'

'Right. It's what I live for. I've always believed that if I could carry out a prolonged investigation in the house, I'd get indisputable proof that death isn't the end.'

'And that's the only reason?'

He frowned. 'Should there be another one?'

Sarah was obviously pressing for something. *What exactly does she know?*

'Well,' she went on, 'Ann made a comment downstairs, about why you are so obsessed with the house.'

'*Obsessed*?'

'Okay, maybe she didn't use that word, but you know what I mean. She made it clear there was something beyond just your interest in the paranormal. Jenn wouldn't tell me anything, though, and said it was best to talk to you about it. So...' she held her arms out to her side, 'here I am, talking to you about it.'

David looked down to the floor and tucked his hands into his pockets. He let out a breath.

Shit.

He was annoyed Ann had let that slip after specifically telling his team not to do so. David wanted to appear professional—hell, he *was* professional—and not like someone who had lied just to get inside the house to further his own agenda.

Still, if anyone could understand his true motivations, surely it would be Sarah. At least he hoped so.

'You read my book on Perron Manor, right?' he asked.

Sarah nodded. 'Of course.'

'Well, do you remember the part in Chapter 17, where I mention a girl named Katie Evans?'

He saw Sarah squint as she thought about the question. However, she shook her head.

'Sorry, not really. Should I?'

'Probably not,' David said. 'It was only one line, about a girl that went missing in 1985. She was last seen at the house.'

'Okay, so what's so significant about that?'

'Well, I kept the details vague on purpose. Thing is, I know more about that incident than any other in the book. Katie Evans was my stepsister.'

Sarah's mouth hung open. 'Wait... are you serious?'

David nodded. 'Yeah. My mother got together with

Katie's father when I was young, and Katie and I grew up together.'

'Jesus,' Sarah uttered. 'I... had no idea.'

'There's no reason you should have. She was a little older than me, but we did everything together. We used to stay up late at night telling ghost stories, usually ones involving the creepy house in town. We'd hike up to the grounds sometimes, always in the daytime, and dare each other to run up to the gates and touch them.

'One evening, she was going out with friends, and I'd overheard them talking. They were heading up to the house. I could tell Katie was excited and a little nervous. I wanted to go as well, but she wouldn't let me. And when she left that night, it was the last time I ever saw her... kind of.'

'What do you mean?' Sarah asked, tilting her head to the side. '*Kind* of?'

'Well, this story will probably sound familiar, but a year or so later when the investigation died down and she was never found, I wandered up to the house myself one day. I just *knew* Katie was inside. I hopped the boundary wall and walked up to the house. I was terrified. But, in one of the windows upstairs, I saw someone staring back at me.'

'Katie,' Sarah said.

'Yup. She looked horrible. Almost like a corpse. And she appeared to be in pain, too. I was so scared I just ran. But ever since, I've been trying to get back here to learn as much as I can in the hopes that I can help her one day.'

Sarah looked astonished. She shook her head, trying to find the words. 'I... um... don't know what to say. If it was in 1985, wouldn't my uncle have been living there?'

David nodded. 'Yeah, but he always said no one entered the property that night. Said there were a bunch of girls hanging around out front, but he went out and told them to scram, which he says they did. Katie's friends said the same thing, but they also swore that Katie turned back and was adamant she wanted to at least get over the wall. Apparently,' his voice cracked a little, 'she said to one of them that it would really impress her little brother. But the police searched the house and didn't find a thing. After a few years, they gave up looking. Just another missing person in this town. But that's not all.'

'Go on,' Sarah said.

'In 2014, when we carried out our investigation, we unleashed something in the basement...'

'I remember that part.'

'Right. Well, whatever was down there had a message for me. Not the group, just me. 'Return here. Help another in need.' I'll never forget that. I've always assumed it was about getting back to help Katie.'

'David... how come you didn't tell me any of this before?'

'I don't really know,' he said. 'I wanted you to think we were serious about what we were doing, not that I had an ulterior motive for helping. I didn't want to piss you off.'

'But your motive is the same as mine,' she said. 'Why the hell would it piss me off?'

He shrugged. 'Again, I don't know. I guess I'm just not used to sharing that story.'

'But the team all know about it?' Sarah asked.

He nodded. 'Jenn pieced it together a while ago, before our investigation in 2014, so I told everyone what had happened. But, to be honest, every person in the team has their own story of why we do what we do. That just happens to be mine.'

Sarah shook her head but smiled. 'You should have just told me, you know. Although I... do have another question.'

'Again, shoot,' David said, feeling relieved.

'Given what's on the line for you at that house, how come you were so quick to convince me to leave last night? I mean, I get you were scared, I think everyone was, but didn't you want to stay? You know, for Katie.'

'Of course I did!' he replied. 'But I also know how dangerous things can be if you push yourself too much. Running away last night didn't have to be the end, but if something happened to us in that house... well, who would help Katie then?'

'Fair point,' Sarah said. 'I just get a little impatient with the whole thing. Knowing Chloe is stuck there, suffering...'

'Yeah, I get it. So let's make sure we don't mess up and that we both set our sisters free. Agreed?'

He held out his hand. She laughed, then shook it. 'Agreed.'

'Okay, then. I suppose we need to get the others home, and then we can head back to the house.'

'Sounds good,' Sarah said. 'Jenn is still in as well, by the way. She's coming with us.'

'Really?' he asked. 'That isn't too surprising, I guess. I've never seen her shy away from anything.'

'She's a trooper,' Sarah agreed. 'Now come on, I'd like to be back at the house while it's still daylight. I want to find out more about that bloody book, because I'm willing to bet it has some answers.'

34

THE VAN AMBLED down the long gravel driveway, causing Sarah to bounce in her seat. When she peered out through the front window, she could again see those distinct three peaks of Perron Manor.

While she had been desperate to return, Sarah couldn't deny it had felt good to be away from the oppressive house, if only for a little while.

David drove, and Jenn sat up front with him. Sarah was in one of the seats behind, looking over their shoulders. She saw her car parked outside in the carport where she'd left it. It had occurred to her to take it last night when everyone was fleeing, if only to turn around when the others were out of sight and come back on her own.

Now, she was glad that David had convinced her to get in his van with the others.

Gazing out at the house again, Sarah was reminded of the first time she'd laid eyes on it, only a couple of months ago. And yet, it seemed like a lifetime. Perron Manor had become such a big part of her life recently. All dominating. All consuming.

Hopefully, she would soon be free of it. As would Chloe.

They pulled to a stop in the carport, and David killed the engine. No one moved. The tension in the van was palpable, and Sarah was sure they were all thinking the same thing.

Are we crazy coming back here?

But she knew they couldn't just sit out in the van all day. There was work to do—namely, looking more closely at *Ianua Diaboli* and the ledger. Previously, Sarah had been happy to let other people worry about the book, but now it was time to take more of an interest herself.

As they waited, the sound of another car engine from behind alerted them.

David checked his side mirror and let out a laugh. 'He showed up quick.'

Just before they had set off, David had called Father Janosch to tell him they were on their way. The priest had said he'd join them as soon as he was finished with what he needed to do. Yet here he was, arriving only five minutes after them.

The three of them exited the van and Sarah turned to see Father Janosch's small, light-blue hatchback approach. It was a basic, unassuming car, which suited his role. She could hardly see a priest racing around in a sports car or a Bentley. They waited for him to pull up next to them before getting out.

'Hello, everyone,' he said with a bright smile, though it looked rather forced. Still, Sarah appreciated the effort. He *was* here helping them, after all, and she had to be thankful for that. He had a leather case with him that dangled from one hand, and a rucksack over his shoulder. He wore a long black coat, jeans, and white trainers.

Sarah held out her hand to him and gave a big smile of her own.

'Thanks for coming, Father,' she said. 'I know I put the pressure on you a little, but I'm grateful you're here.'

He shook her hand. 'Just remind me never to haggle with you in the future,' he joked. Father Janosch turned to David and Jenn. 'Just the four of us, I assume?'

'Yes,' David replied. 'The others decided against it for now.'

'Very well.' Father Janosch then looked to the house, and his happy expression faltered.

'Do you have a plan of attack?' David asked.

The priest shrugged, not taking his eyes off Perron Manor. 'Spend as much time as I can with the book and the ledger, and keep the Church updated.'

'Just tell them it's real,' Sarah said. 'The book, the house, the fact that it's a Devil's Door. We know that's true anyway. Tell them what you need to so they can send in the cavalry.'

'I wish I could,' Father Janosch said with a hint of sadness. 'And believe me when I tell you they *are* taking this seriously, but they need to know for certain before they act.'

'Does it matter?' Sarah asked. 'If they turn up here and Perron Manor just turns out to be a regular old haunted house, they can still help us, can't they? They can still sanction an exorcism and all that. But if it *is* what we think, then we'll have saved them time. So again, does it matter?'

'It matters,' Father Janosch confirmed. 'Because if we are correct, then we have more to worry about than just…'

'Than just what?' Sarah asked.

Father Janosch shook his head. 'Forget about it. It doesn't change what we need to do here. So, I suggest we start as soon as possible.'

He then walked off towards the house. Sarah cast David and Jenn a confused look, which they returned.

More to worry about?

Sarah wanted to push Father Janosch on that point, but there would be time for that later. For now, they needed to get started. The priest was right about that.

Sarah unlocked the main door, and they all entered and stood quietly in the entrance lobby. The house was silent. She looked to the floor at the foot of the stairs and remembered the sight of Chloe's body as it lay there in a crumpled heap—her head twisted and neck broken after that... monster... had killed her like she was nothing.

But Chloe *was* something. To Sarah, she had been everything. And now she was gone.

No, not gone. She's still here... suffering.

'I don't like how quiet it is,' Jenn said. 'Last time we were here, we were running for our lives.'

Sarah remembered the panic of their escape as well, even if she hadn't seen what the others had.

She felt on edge just being here, and she was sure David and Jenn were as well. It was like they were just waiting for something to happen.

Father Janosch spoke up. 'Should we go upstairs and get started?'

'As good a plan as any, I guess' Sarah replied. 'It's what we're here for. But why don't we bring the book and ledger down here, to somewhere more comfortable?'

'That would be appreciated,' Father Janosch said.

'And don't forget the rule,' David added. 'No one goes off alone. That was true before but *especially* after last night.'

The group took off their coats and Sarah noticed that Father Janosch wore a blue denim shirt underneath, one that was tucked into his jeans. However, despite his casual look, he still had his white clerical collar on show, as well as a small, silver crucifix that hung around his neck on a thin chain.

The four of them made their way up to the top floor and over to the study. Sarah approached *Ianua Diaboli* and looked down through the display glass to its leather cover.

Could it be true? Could this book hold power over the house? She noted again the strange symbols at each corner. Those were replicated—if a bit more crudely—on the ledger.

'Father Janosch?' she asked. He walked over beside her.

'Yes?'

She pointed down. 'Those markings on the book... what are they?'

'Protective seals, I believe. Markings that prevent anything from happening to the book.'

Sarah turned to him and frowned. 'Seriously? Are you saying I couldn't destroy it, even if I wanted to? Like, some spell would stop me?'

'They'd only stop you if you were possessed,' Father Janosch said. 'If not, you could destroy it without any problem. You see, the protection doesn't extend to the living.'

'So what does it protect from?'

'Well, to put it bluntly, the supernatural.'

She looked back to him. 'What, so ghosts don't rip it up?'

Father Janosch laughed. 'Kind of. You see, that book—if legitimate—could contain great power. The power could work against certain insidious forces here at this house. And they may want to destroy it. These markers prevent the dead, or undead, from doing so.'

'Undead?'

Father Janosch nodded. 'Just my term for things that have never truly lived. At least, not in the sense we know it. Demons and things like that.'

Sarah shook her head. 'That's crazy. Not that I don't believe you, of course, I've seen too much to be blind anymore. But I always took that kind of thing... spells, occult, demonic symbols... as horseshit.'

Father Janosch laughed again and patted her on the shoulder. 'I do love your way with words, Miss Pearson.'

'Just call me Sarah, Father. Please.'

'Okay, then I insist you call me Luca.' He then turned to David and Jenn. 'That goes for both of you as well, if you would. No need for formalities.'

David nodded as he and Jenn moved beside them.

Sarah's mind started to turn over as she looked back at *Ianua Diaboli*. An idea came to her.

'What if we *did* destroy the book?' she asked.

Father Janosch's head whipped round to her. 'Destroy it... why?'

'Well, if the book is linked to the house, and the Devil's Door, would destroying it close the door?'

Father Janosch shook his head vigorously. 'No, certainly not. At least, I don't think so. The thing is, if Perron Manor is a gateway to Hell, then it has been that way long before the book was brought here. So if we destroyed *Ianua Diaboli,* the door would simply remain open, but we would have lost a truly valuable weapon.'

'Understood,' Sarah said. 'We keep the book safe. But do we even know if the house has always been a gateway? I mean, has the land just been that way since the dawn of time, or was the door opened at some point?'

Father Janosch scratched at the back of his neck. 'Hard to say. You have to understand, what I do know of these phenomena are all based on rumours and stories. Until I saw *Ianua Diaboli*, I didn't believe there were such things as physical gateways to Hell in the first place. I *believe* the door-ways have to be opened, but I can't be certain of it.'

'So how was *this* one opened?' Sarah asked, but then

shook her head. 'Never mind,' she said. 'I appreciate you are as much in the dark as we are here.'

'Not quite,' David said and turned to the priest. 'Your knowledge of the occult and paranormal is going to be invaluable.'

'So he knows even more than *you*?' Sarah teased with a smile.

David laughed. 'Yeah. Consider him the Yoda to my Luke.'

'And what does that make me?' Sarah asked. 'And don't say the princess, or I'll smack you!'

David held up his hands. 'But Leia is awesome! Fine, you can be Han.'

'I'm okay with that,' Sarah said.

David then turned to Jenn and narrowed his eyes while he chewed his lip.

'I swear to God, David,' Jenn said, 'if you make me the big hairy thing I'm going to be furious.'

Father Janosch just looked confused and completely out of his depth. He leaned in toward Sarah. 'Who on earth is Yoda?'

35

AFTER THEIR CONVERSATION UP in the top-floor study, the group retired to the dining room with the books.

The ground-floor dining room was David's idea, as the room was smaller and more intimate than the great hall at the back of the house, but had a large enough table for them all to fit around.

A single chandelier hung above them, lighting the room, and the only other piece of furniture of note was a chest of drawers set against the far wall.

Father Janosch sat at the head of the table, with David on one side of him and Sarah and Jenn on the other.

'So then,' Father Janosch said. 'Let's begin.'

'How are we going to do this?' David asked. 'Is there anything we can do to help?'

Father Janosch slid *Ianua Diaboli* over, so it was directly before him, and traced a finger down the cover. 'I think the best course of action is for me to read a section, then cross-reference it with the ledger here.' He tapped at the book next to *Ianua Diaboli*. 'I can then determine if I think the translations are accurate. Having a copy of *Ianua Diaboli* already in English would be a great help. However, I think the process will be slow and laborious, unfortunately.'

'Did you learn much from the time you had with the book yesterday?' Sarah asked.

'Some,' he replied. 'But I tried to take in as much as I could, flicking back and forth through its pages. Now is the time for completeness. But as you can see,'—he held up *Ianua Diaboli* with a groan, and pointed to its thick spine—'it will take a while.'

The process Father Janosch suggested made sense to David. The priest was by far the most fluent in Latin, and so was the best-placed person for the work. Of course, that would make David and the others little more than bystanders.

'We could read from the ledger,' Sarah suggested, as if reading David's mind. 'That would at least give us something to do.'

'Sounds like a plan,' Father Janosch said.

'Wait,' Jenn interrupted. 'I'm still not clear on something. I get why we're doing this, reading through the book and all. But at the end of the process... how best to word this... *so what?* I mean, even if you study all the book's contents, would that prove one way or another if it was legitimate? Or if Perron Manor really was one of these doorways to Hell? It's just words on a page. Not proof.'

The question gave David pause. It was a valid point. All they would know for sure was if the translations were correct or not.

He briefly thought of Sarah's earlier idea of testing out one of the rituals themselves, then quickly chastised himself for even considering such a thing. It would be stupid and dangerous to try.

Still, at least they would *know*.

'Well, that is why we need to keep gathering evidence,' Father Janosch said. 'From what I have seen, we have a good amount already. If we get more, and present it all along with the *Ianua Diaboli* and the translations, I think the Church will act.' He then leaned over to Sarah. 'However, I do want to reiterate that if you allow me to take the book home to study, and then show them in person, it will move things on much quicker.'

David looked to Sarah as well and waited.

She shook her head firmly. 'Sorry, Luca, no can do. I've made my position clear on that. But, since we are covering old ground, I want to again ask, would you bend the truth for us? Just tell them what they need to hear so they act. We all pretty much know what we are dealing with anyway, right?'

'But we are not *certain*,' Father Janosch said. 'And lying isn't something I'm in the habit of doing, being a priest.'

Sarah crinkled her nose. 'Really? You've been a little loose with the truth with us, wouldn't you agree? What with saying you couldn't stay here last night as you had duties to attend to, yet you magically showed up straight away after David's call?'

Father Janosch's face turned a deep shade of red. David wasn't certain if it was from anger or embarrassment. The priest then looked down to the table in front of him.

'Sarah,' David said, 'we don't need to go over that again.'

Sarah held up her hands. 'Fair enough,' she said. 'I don't want to fight. I just don't like the insinuation that I'm the one being difficult by insisting my own book stays in my possession.'

David addressed Father Janosch. 'Look, Fath—sorry, Luca... I'm sure Sarah didn't mean—'

But Father Janosch just raised a hand and cut David off.

'She's right,' he said with a sigh. 'I haven't been completely honest with you. And given the sacrifices you are all making by being here, I think I owe you that much. But please understand, what I am about to tell you is sacred knowledge. It is something I was expressly *forbidden* from sharing with you.'

David's heart began to quicken. Father Janosch, someone David had known for years, looked like a broken man. What knowledge was he about to impart?

'You don't have to tell us if it will get you in trouble,' David said, drawing a scowl from Sarah, which he ignored.

However, Father Janosch just shook his head and raised his eyes back up to them. 'I *have* been bending the truth. Or at least, I've been hiding some of it, which is just as bad. However, one thing I cannot do is lie to my superiors about this. If I get it wrong and we aren't dealing with what I suspected, then I would be finished. The idea that Devil's Door could really exist is a serious concern—'

'We get that, Luca,' Sarah said. 'That's why we're here.'

He shook his head. 'I mean beyond just Perron Manor. You see, if this one exists, there could be more.'

'Okay,' David chipped in. 'I understand that could be bad...'

'No,' Father Janosch replied. 'I don't think you *do* understand. Not really. One of the stories told along with the Devil's Door, was about the Seven Gates, or the Seven Doors. I've heard it called different things, but the idea is always the same.'

'Which is?' Sarah asked as she leaned forward.

'That if seven of these doorways are open at any one time, then... well, then it is all over.'

'What's all over?' David asked.

Father Janosch took a breath. 'Everything.'

David looked over to Sarah, and then to Jenn. They both seemed to be just as confused as he was.

'You're going to have to explain that more,' Sarah said. 'What do you mean everything is over?'

Father Janosch took a deep breath. 'It is said that if seven of the gates are open, then the connection to Hell is complete and at its strongest. Hell and our own world would merge.'

'Armageddon,' David added as his body slumped back onto his seat. He felt as though the wind had been knocked out of him. 'But surely that is just a story,' he went on. 'All religions and societies have their own tales about the end of the world, and that doesn't make any of them true.'

'No,' Father Janosch conceded. 'I know of many such stories, and to be honest, none keep me up at night. Indeed, the Seven Gates was never something I was concerned about, either. Like you said, just another myth and legend. Until this...' He tapped on *Ianua Diaboli*.

'But it could still all be bullshit,' Sarah said.

'And I hope it is,' Father Janosch replied. 'But you can see now why I need to be certain that, firstly, the book is genuine, and second, Perron Manor is actually a gateway. Because the resources the Church will then need to put into place would be... well, I can scarcely comprehend it.'

There were a few moments of silence between them all. It was Sarah who eventually spoke up, evidently trying to be the voice of reason. 'Well, even if this *is* all true, surely we know there can't be seven of those doors already open. Because, you know, we're all still here. It isn't raining fire or brimstone outside. So nothing has changed from what it was before we learned about the book. And nothing likely will change—the world has survived for this long without being sucked into Hell, so it's hardly something to be concerned about... right?'

No one answered. How could they? Each and every one of them was fumbling in the dark here. The gravity of the situation was overwhelming, and David had no idea what to say next. Part of him wished the priest had kept that information to himself.

Only a few days ago David had been excited at the prospect of getting back inside Perron Manor, to find indisputable proof of the afterlife, and also help his long-lost stepsister.

But things had moved on. Gateways to Hell had never been on David's agenda when he'd agreed to help Sarah, and now they were even talking about the end of the world. It was just too much for him to get his head around.

He realised that no one else had answered Sarah's question, and she shook her head in annoyance. 'Look,' she began, 'we need to just continue as we are. If the Seven Gates thing is real, then fuck it, we deal with *this* gate for now. That's the mission.' She looked over to David. 'Chloe and Katie still need our help.' Then, she pointed to the book. 'And that is still our best shot at finding out what the hell is going on. So, I think we should get started.'

She folded her arms over her chest, sitting with her back straight and head slightly tilted up. Her little speech was an attempt at a rallying cry, and she was absolutely right in what she was saying.

David still felt overwhelmed, but he nodded in agreement. 'You're right.' He turned to Father Janosch. 'Luca, I think we get to work.'

36

JENN'S HEAD swam as Father Janosch began reading aloud from *Ianua Diaboli*. The Latin he was speaking sounded beautiful and exotic, despite her knowing the actual words likely had sinister connotations to them.

End of the world. Armageddon. Seven Gates.

What the hell had she gotten herself involved in?

Sarah had insisted on pushing on, but Jenn had remained silent, fading into the background as she fell deep into thought.

Jenn had believed in ghosts for as long as she had lived, and often thought about Heaven and Hell. As contradictory as it seemed, she'd always had trouble believing in those two things, though she couldn't explain why.

Others had suggested that surely the paranormal and things like Hell were one and the same. To Jenn, however, they had always seemed like separate ideas. She believed ghosts were a mere function of the universe—that our souls continued on in some form after the human body failed.

But that didn't mean heading off to eternal bliss and

sitting on fluffy clouds while playing harps. Or being thrown into pits of fire to be immolated for eternity.

Jenn now hoped the book and the idea of portals to Hell were, to quote Sarah, horseshit. She could then go back to EVP sessions, Ouija boards, and ghost hunting: the things she signed up for.

They were clearly all ill-prepared to handle apocalyptic prophecies.

Father Janosch finished his reading and sat back. No one had followed along with the ledger, so Jenn had no idea what the first passage he'd read meant.

'Well?' David asked. Father Janosch looked ashen. He then sat forward and pulled the ledger closer.

'Please give me a moment,' he said, raising a finger. 'That was a lot to process, and I want to check the translation.'

Jenn braced herself. She wasn't sure she wanted to know what he'd read.

After a few minutes, Father Janosch sat back again. 'Okay,' he said after letting out a long sigh. 'The first section answers a question we all had about the gates: whether they have always existed, or if they have to be opened. Turns out, it is the latter.'

'What does it say?' David asked.

'It goes into detail about how the doors are opened,' Father Janosch responded. 'It is very... graphic, and against God. Human sacrifice. The spilling of innocent blood, and things that are...' he made a face like he was going to vomit, 'not something I want to repeat. But, according to this, gates *can* be opened, as long as a number of steps are met. So if that is true, then it means someone opened the door here. Either when the house was built, or before.'

'I would think before,' David added. 'During the research for my book, I discovered that the people who first built the house had to disperse a group of nomads from the area. The only descriptions were that those people didn't speak the King's tongue and, apparently, worshipped ungodly things. The document I found also claims those people were 'strange to look at,' though there was no other information on them to be found. I'd wager the land Perron Manor was built on was sacred to these people. And sacred for a good reason.'

'You think they opened the door?' Sarah asked. 'That's a bit of a leap, isn't it?'

Jenn had to agree.

'Depends how you look at it,' David replied. 'It's not like the tragic events that have happened at this house took a while to get going. They started pretty much straight away after the building was opened as a monastery. One of the monks went mad and killed his brethren. The horrific events just escalated from there. It makes sense to me that the land was already tainted.'

'But how could a group of nomads open a gate to Hell?' Sarah asked. 'They wouldn't have had *Ianua Diaboli* or anything like that.'

'Well,' Father Janosch began, 'I don't think this book here is the precursor to the existence of these doorways. The book is written in such a way as to impart a previously learned knowledge. The author, I think, is somebody who studied these gateways in great detail. So it is likely that the doors existed before *Ianua Diaboli* was written.'

'Okay,' Jenn started, finally finding her voice. 'So how did people back then figure out how to open these gates?'

Father Janosch slowly shook his head. 'As yet, I don't know. And that is something we may never know.'

'But,' Sarah began, 'if these nomads were able to do it, then *something* must have shown them how. I'm guessing the steps in that passage aren't just something you could stumble upon?' she asked Father Janosch.

'Correct,' he replied. 'But that mystery is probably irrelevant for the time being. There is a lot to get through here, and we have just scratched the surface.'

37

SARAH YAWNED and rubbed her eyes. It felt like granules of sand were trapped beneath the lids. Her body ached from sitting down for too long.

Empty bowls sat at the far end of the table, having been pushed back out of the way. Tinned food was just about all Sarah had left in the cupboards since her time living there with Chloe, and no one had stopped to think about going out for more supplies.

Sarah drained the last of her lukewarm coffee, hoping the caffeine would help keep her energised. It had been a long afternoon.

After setting her mug back down to the table, she looked at the open book in front of Father Janosch. Despite working for hours, the pages they'd completed were dwarfed by the ones still to come.

This is going to take forever.

The information gleaned from the book so far had been interesting, and mainly covered rites and rituals that could summon different entities. Apparently, there was a demonic presence known as Pazuzu that often travelled through these doorways, and was described as an evil and detestable being that hated the living. He was considered vile and uncontrollable, even in the realms of Hell.

However, Sarah didn't know how much more she could listen to. If Father Janosch had the translations covered, shouldn't the rest of them be trying to gather more evidence?

'We should be doing more,' Sarah said to David.

He frowned. 'In what way?'

'Well, Luca seems to have this in hand, so shouldn't we be carrying out some investigations?'

'Too dangerous to leave Luca here alone,' David replied while firmly shaking his head. 'And I don't like the idea of splitting into two groups. There aren't enough of us here.'

'And when do you think we're actually going to get the evidence we need, then? Because Luca himself said the book on its own isn't enough.'

'She's right,' the priest agreed. 'We still need more to present to the Church.'

David took a moment, and Sarah could see his mind working behind his narrowed eyes. 'Okay, how about we take a break from the book and go check the footage from last night, see what we caught there. I'd rather not try and draw anything out tonight, at least until we know a little more.'

'But we have a priest,' Sarah said. 'Fix him up with some holy water and surely we have a ghost-hunting Rambo.' She smiled as she said it, hoping to add some levity. Thankfully, she got a laugh from Father Janosch.

'I wish I were so brave,' he said. 'Or so useful. Though I do have my Bible.'

'See,' Sarah said to David. 'A Bible is practically an assault rifle in situations like these.'

'How about this,' Father Janosch offered. 'I finish up the section I'm working on, then we spend a little time trying to gather evidence?'

David sighed. 'I guess that makes sense. But everyone needs to be careful. No unnecessary risks.'

They waited a little while longer for Father Janosch to reach a natural break, then cleaned up the bowls from the table and carried them through to the kitchen. It seemed ridiculous that such a simple task needed all of them, but David had insisted they all had to stick together. Sarah had to wonder how that would work at night when they needed to sleep. She didn't know if there was a room big enough to squeeze four beds in, so Sarah guessed she would be sharing with Jenn, while David and Father Janosch would probably bunk together.

Sarah took a moment to look around the kitchen. The room had been the heart of the house when she had lived there with Chloe, Emma, and Andrew. She could almost see Emma sat at the table in her highchair, while the rest of them sat around chatting, with Andrew panicking about the next job that needed doing at the house.

'First, we'll check the cameras,' David said, pulling Sarah from her thoughts. 'We need to make sure they're still running. And we can have a quick look over last night's footage.'

'Isn't there anything else we can be doing?' Sarah asked. 'Something a bit more proactive?'

'After we check, yes,' David said, much to her annoyance. 'But to be honest, our best successes have come in the dead of night anyway, between three and four o'clock. That seems to be the time when the house is most alive. I think we need to be ready for that.'

'Plus,' Jenn said to Sarah, 'checking the cameras from

last night is important. If we caught that woman attacking David, then that would be huge.'

She was right. They could have something just waiting for them that could be sent on to the Church straight away.

However, something was off. David's face was clouded with worry as he made eye contact with Sarah.

'There's... something I need to tell you first,' he said to her.

Sarah frowned and cocked her head to the side. 'Okay. Anything I need to worry about? Because you look like you've seen a... well, wrong choice of words.'

'It's about last night,' he said. 'When I was attacked. Remember when you asked me if I recognised the woman in our room?'

Sarah slowly nodded, and a feeling of dread came over her. She had an idea where this was going.

David lied to me.

'Who was it?' Sarah demanded through gritted teeth, though she suspected she already knew. Even so, she wanted to hear him say it.

He took a breath, then let out a long exhale. He looked like a schoolboy about to be chastised by his teacher. 'It was Chloe,' he eventually said, and his head hung low.

Sarah began to shake. Her hands balled into fists. 'Chloe?' she asked, teeth still clenched. 'So when I asked who it was before... you just lied to my face?' He nodded. 'Why?' she asked.

'Because I didn't know how it would affect you. You're here *for* her, and if you knew that she'd attacked me, I...' He shrugged. 'I honestly don't know. I guess I just didn't want you worrying about what she's become.'

'She hasn't *become* anything,' Sarah shot back. 'Chloe

wouldn't attack you. That was something else. It must have been.'

David didn't reply, and just stood in silence with his head still hung low. Everyone else was quiet, trapped in awkward silence.

Sarah wanted to step forward and tear David's head off.

How could he keep something like that from me?

Regardless, he had to be mistaken.

'That couldn't have been Chloe,' she went on. Tears welled up in her eyes. 'She would never hurt anyone. It had to be the house playing tricks: another spirit made to look like my sister or something.'

Father Janosch slowly walked over to Sarah and laid a gentle hand on her shoulder.

She turned to him, trying to keep from breaking down completely. The thought of Chloe turning into one of those monsters was starting to dawn on her.

'He's wrong,' Sarah said to Father Janosch. 'That wasn't her. He's *wrong!*'

Father Janosch smiled. 'He is,' the priest said. 'And... he isn't.'

'I... I don't understand.'

'Places like this are evil, Sarah. And the souls of the dead who are trapped must obey the will of the house. I know this isn't going to be easy to hear, but I feel you must. The spirits are puppets, used as needed. *But* that isn't who they really are. The good person your sister was still exists. So, if David is correct and it *is* your sister we see on the footage, then you have to remember that the house is using her. Chloe's actions are not her own.'

That image of her strong sister, so utterly helpless and without agency being used against her will, broke Sarah.

What had Father Janosch called her... a puppet?

Sarah couldn't hold back the flood of tears anymore. What had been a steady flow suddenly erupted and she broke down sobbing, bending double as pain and anguish suddenly overwhelmed her.

Whether Sarah had fully admitted it to herself or not, she had always known deep down the kind of purgatory Chloe was in. Their last night at the house, when Chloe had died, they had both seen scores of spirits meaning to do them harm. In life, those people could not *all* have been evil or murderous. They were just being used—manipulated on strings by a master behind the curtain.

Helpless.

However, Sarah had not allowed herself to think of Chloe being used the same way. It was too painful.

She felt a hand on her back and realised the others had gathered around her. Someone pulled her upright and hugged her tightly. It was Jenn. Sarah continued to cry, the dam now completely broken.

'Why didn't I believe her?' Sarah asked between sobs. 'She told me about the house and I... I just wouldn't listen.'

Chloe had tried *so* hard to make Sarah see the truth, but Sarah didn't want to hear it. She'd thought she knew better—knew that Chloe was just stressed or worrying over nothing. She knew that it all had to be in Chloe's head.

And then Chloe had been killed. She had been right, and it was Sarah's fault she was dead.

The house had wanted Chloe all along, ever since she'd escaped it as a child. Now it had her.

Another death. More blood on Sarah's hands.

Just like Tania—Sarah's best friend who had died while they served together in the army. Sarah had been supposed to take point, but an overwhelming feeling came over her, gripping her with a fear she wasn't used to. Tania had filled in... then stepped on a landmine.

It should have been Sarah.

Two people she should have protected; two people she had failed.

'It's okay,' Jenn whispered. 'Just let it out.'

But Sarah didn't want to let it out. She didn't want to feel weak and helpless. She wanted to help Chloe. She wanted to put right, in some small way, one of the many wrongs in her life.

The biggest one.

Sarah pulled away and wiped her face with the sleeve of her jumper. 'I'm fine.' She shook her head, trying to clear away the hurt.

Then something drew her attention. A scent... one that was very familiar to her.

Lavender.

Sarah turned in the direction the smell was coming from, but there was nothing there—the scent evaporating just as it had become noticeable.

Chloe?

The last time Sarah had smelled lavender like that, she had been cradling Chloe's lifeless body, nuzzling her cheek to Chloe's head and taking in Chloe's familiar shampoo.

Was it just in her head? Thoughts of her sister triggering a phantom olfactory sensation?

Or was it something more?

'What is it?' David asked.

'Nothing,' she said, then once again wiped her face. 'Let's go. I want to see that footage.'

'You don't have to,' David began. 'We can review it for you and—'

'David,' she said sternly. 'I *want* to see it.'

38

THEY WERE BACK in the makeshift headquarters, once again gathered around one of the laptops. David sat before it and lined up the video.

Sarah, Father Janosch, and Jenn all stood behind him, looking over his shoulder.

David felt terrible.

He was pretty sure Sarah hated him because of him hiding the truth.

Hiding the truth is still a lie, David.

He couldn't blame Sarah for being angry. It wasn't his place to keep something like that from her in the first place, even if he thought he was doing the right thing.

In his mind, Sarah had displayed certain tendencies during their time here, which were understandable but worrying: being overzealous, careless, and sometimes antagonistic with people. She was suffering loss, so her attitude was understandable, but David had tried to handle the situation and guard Sarah from... well, from herself.

But that wasn't his place.

He played the footage from 3am. On it, he and Sarah were in the room alone. Both were asleep.

David sped up the video while nothing was happening, then set it back to normal speed when Sarah sat up in bed. The timestamp showed three-twenty-two.

Sarah simply stayed in a sitting position, watching David.

'Can you remember this?' Father Janosch asked.

'No,' Sarah replied. 'Not at all.'

It wasn't long before David started to move on the video, rolling over and looking towards Sarah. He then sat up and moved his head to look around the room.

There didn't appear to be anyone else in the frame.

On the recording, David got out of bed and grabbed his handheld camera, panning around the room with it.

'This is where it happens,' he said to the others. 'Keep your eyes peeled. It wasn't until I'd turned to look behind me that I saw...'

He trailed off as he heard Jenn draw in a gasp.

Something had bled into the image. A figure, standing behind David on the other side of the bed. He felt goose-bumps form on his arms as he watched. From the vantage point of the camera, it was hard to make out any definite details, other than the long, scraggly hair on the naked form of the woman.

There was no way to tell from this angle that it was Chloe.

On screen, he slowly turned around. As expected, the figure dove atop him.

'Jesus,' he heard Jenn utter from behind.

There was a struggle, and the woman forced David to the ground. She mounted him, lashing out with her arms, which he managed to grab in an effort to push her off. But she was a wild animal. The struggling continued as, on screen, Sarah got out of bed and walked over. She stood above David and his attacker and looked down—not moving or making an attempt to intervene.

'You still don't remember any of this?' Father Janosch asked.

'I don't,' Sarah replied.

'I remember your eyes were half-open,' David added, 'but you didn't seem awake. It was like you were in a trance.'

They continued to watch for a few minutes before the door to the room on camera opened. That was when the others filtered in. Just before they did, the savage woman looked up to the doorway... then disappeared, fading out into her surroundings as David lay alone on the floor.

The rest of the footage played out as David remembered, with him being helped to his feet and Sarah coming to from her sleepwalking state. But the footage offered up nothing that David wasn't already aware of. He paused the playback.

'Did that look like your sister to you?' Father Janosch asked Sarah.

'I... don't know,' she replied. 'It's hard to make out.'

'There is a way we might know for sure,' David offered, then pointed to the paused image, specifically to the hand-held camera on the floor. 'I saw Chloe on that as I turned around. It scared the hell out of me. But... the footage on it might be a little more clear. It was certainly closer.'

David spun around in the swivel chair to face the others.

'Is the camera still in the bedroom?' Jenn asked.

'Should be,' David replied. He then looked to Sarah. 'Are you sure you want to see it?'

After a moment's pause, she nodded. 'Yeah. I'm sure.'

They all walked upstairs to the bedroom. As David opened the door, they were met with darkness. All the natural daylight was blocked out due to the thick curtains still being drawn. David reached in and flicked on the light. There, on the floor, was the camera.

Sarah strode into the room first and retrieved it. She flipped the viewfinder open, and the others crowded around.

'You will need to rewind it,' David said. 'When I dropped the camera, it would have just kept recording until the tape stopped.'

Sarah did, and they saw nothing but the dark bedroom from the camera's vantage point on the floor. Eventually, in reverse, the camera moved quickly up from the floor, and there was a flash of a person in view. By the time Sarah had hit the pause button, the footage had skipped farther back and was now focused on her own image as she sat up in bed.

'Play it again and try to pause the image as soon as you see the person behind me,' David told her.

She hit play, and the camera panned. The woman came into view and dove forward just as Sarah hit pause.

The image was a little blurry, given the lunge of the woman on camera, but there could be no denying who it was. Her skin looked decayed and her face was twisted up into a hateful snarl, but it was Chloe.

Sarah quickly snapped the camera closed and let it drop to the floor.

'I'm sorry,' David said.

'It's fine,' Sarah replied, though her voice made it sound anything but.

'Remember what I told you,' Father Janosch said. 'She is being controlled. Don't let that image be the way you remember her.'

'Hard to think of anything else now,' Sarah said. She then turned around and looked at David. 'I suppose there's something I need to tell you, too,' she said. 'Something I should have been honest about from the beginning.'

David frowned. 'Okay... what is it?'

'It's about how Chloe died. I told the police she fell down the stairs when we were running and broke her neck. I told you the same thing.'

David nodded. 'Right. But that's not what happened?'

Sarah shook her head. 'No. *Something* caught her. I don't know what it was, exactly, but it wasn't like the other spirits we saw that night.'

'A demon?' Farther Janosch asked.

'Possibly,' Sarah said. 'It broke her neck right in front of me. Just snuffed out her life like she was nothing.'

David was silent for a moment. They all were. By rights, he should have been mad at the deception, the same way Sarah had been at him. However, David had always suspected there was more to Chloe's death than Sarah had shared. He'd never pressed her on the issue because it suited his needs to think there was less of a danger in the house.

'That is worrying,' Father Janosch said. '*Very* worrying. In fact, it changes quite a lot.'

'I'm sorry,' Sarah said. 'I was just nervous that if I told the truth, David and his team wouldn't help, and I'd be helpless to save Chloe.'

'So we've been in more danger than we thought the whole time?' Jenn asked, obviously annoyed. Sarah turned to her with a genuine look of regret.

'I'm sorry,' she repeated.

'If the house was able to physically hurt someone and kill them after only a month and a half,' Father Janosch started, 'then that is beyond anything I've ever heard of as far as demonic activity goes. It's just too quick.'

David knew what he was driving at. 'Proof that the house is indeed a doorway to Hell?'

The priest took a deep breath. 'I think so. That knowledge would have been *very* useful upfront.'

'Seems like we've all been holding back the truth,' David said.

Sarah had lied to him; he'd lied to her; Father Janosch had been keeping his own secrets...

The whole thing was a mess.

No one spoke for a long while. Eventually, David broke the silence. 'We keep going then,' he said. 'As far as I see it, we still have a job to do.'

'Unless you have enough evidence now?' Sarah asked Father Janosch. 'What happened last night, plus how Chloe died, as well as everything else... is that enough to take to the Church?'

'Possibly,' Father Janosch replied. 'I'm going to call the Bishop to update him, see what he says. If it is enough, can I please take the book and the ledger away from the house?'

'I guess so,' Sarah said, finally relenting. Her face was still tear-streaked. The poor girl looked broken.

It had been a difficult day for all of them, made worse by the recent revelations. David felt punch-drunk.

'Come on,' Jenn said to Sarah. 'Let's get you cleaned up.' She took Sarah's hand and started to lead her off to the en-suite.

Sarah stopped her. 'I really am sorry,' she said yet again.

'I know,' Jenn replied, but didn't say anything else. The two disappeared into the bathroom, and David felt Father Janosch touch his elbow.

'We need to talk,' the priest said in a whisper. 'Privately.'

David shook his head. 'I don't think it is the time for any more secrets.'

'This one is needed. Trust me.' He then ushered David from the room, closing the door behind them.

39

LUCA STOOD close to David out in the hallway. He didn't want to risk the others overhearing if they came back in from the bathroom.

'I'll be brief,' Luca said. 'I think we have something else to be concerned about.'

'Something *else*?' David asked with wide eyes. 'How much more can there be?'

'It's Sarah,' Father Janosch went on. 'I'm worried about her.'

'Why?'

'What we saw on last night's video. And the previous one. It's the sleepwalking.'

'Okay,' David said. 'Are you thinking it's a sign that the house is trying to take hold of her?'

'I do,' Luca replied.

'I've been thinking the same thing, but it's something I've been keeping an eye on. I really don't think we are at the stage of possession yet. Not even close.'

Luca shook his head, trying to hide his frustration. David was too naïve. Though, perhaps he himself had been as well. 'I think things may be further progressed than you think,' he said. 'That's twice now I've seen her in a trance-like state. And she admitted that kind of thing happened back when she lived here with her sister, correct?'

David nodded. 'Correct.'

'Well, given what we know now about how Chloe died, that is proof of how quickly things can escalate in this house. I'm just concerned Perron Manor may have more of a hold on Sarah than even she is aware of.'

'You think it's possible to become fully possessed in such a short space of time?'

'Normally no, not at all. It would take a few months at least. But we are not in a normal situation. Either the forces behind Perron Manor are able to take hold of people quicker than I've ever seen, or there is another factor at play. Regardless, I'm worried the situation could get out of hand.'

'Then we'll keep a close eye on her,' David said. 'Unless you have another idea?'

Luca did not. He still needed to complete his work with the book, as ordered.

He let out a sigh. 'Fine. But make sure you don't let her out of your sight.'

David gave a firm nod. 'No problem.'

'You best go back inside,' Luca continued and retrieved his mobile phone from his pocket. 'I'm going to call the Bishop and update him. With any luck, he might agree that we don't need to be here any longer.'

'You're going to stay in the corridor on your own?' David asked with a look of concern.

'I'll be fine, David,' Luca replied. 'I'm right outside the door and will be straight back in after I've finished the call.'

David hesitated, but soon relented and went back into the bedroom, closing the door behind him. Luca unlocked his phone, scrolled down to the Bishop's private number, and hit dial.

It rang a few times then clicked to voicemail.

'It's Luca,' he said into the phone. 'There have been some developments. Activity in the house is... severe, and though I'm not certain yet, I am confident the book in Miss Pearson's possession is the real *Ianua Diaboli*. I also believe the house is indeed what we feared it to be. Again, I can't yet be one-hundred-percent certain, but I can see no other explanation for the level of activity we've seen here. Not only that, it has become apparent that the sister of Miss Pearson—Chloe Shaw—was killed by a demonic presence after only a month and a half inside the house. Please call back and advise. Until then, I will continue as ordered.'

He then ended the call and stared at his phone, hoping the Bishop would quickly get back to him and end the investigation. Then Luca could be free of this accursed house forever.

Bishop Turnbull strode down the hallway of the Cathedral Church of St Nicholas on his way to his meeting. The marble floor echoed his footsteps as he walked, the ceremonial purple robes he wore billowing around his legs. He had a file gripped in one hand, and his mobile phone was wedged between the document and his thumb. The phone lit up, showing he had received a voicemail. He stopped with a frown.

Strange it didn't ring first.

Bishop Turnbull placed the phone to his ear and listened to the message. However, he heard nothing but a few seconds of static. The Bishop then checked his call log.

The only call he'd received had been that morning, but there had been nothing recent.

So he listened to the voicemail again, hearing the same static, and at the end he selected the option to ring back the caller. As soon as he did, it clicked to a voicemail of its own, and he heard Father Janosch's voice:

'You have reached Father Janosch. I am unable to come to the phone right now, but if you would please leave a message, I will get back to you as soon as I am able.'

'Luca, it's me,' Bishop Turnbull said. 'I think you tried to leave me a message, but I couldn't make anything out. Get back to me if you need anything. Also, I am keen to get an update. We *all* are, Father. So please carry on and get what we need. There can be no mistakes.'

He ended the call and carried on to his meeting. It would have been good to speak to Father Janosch before going in, as there were some important people waiting to hear what Luca had found out.

40

JENN WAS EXHAUSTED.

They all were. She could see it on the faces of everyone as they again congregated in the dining room and watched Father Janosch work.

Thoughts of running any sessions to gain further evidence had gone out of the window. After David and Sarah's confessions, the mood was grim. Everyone was wiped, and setting up another activity seemed like too much work. At least for tonight.

Instead, Father Janosch had insisted they keep going with the book, so the others had joined him.

However, as well as being tired, Jenn was angry. She kept it to herself for the good of the group, but the fact Sarah had lied to them about what happened to her sister enraged Jenn.

She was also angry that David hadn't told anyone else that it was Chloe who had leapt on him the previous night. Jenn had seen the face of that crazed woman; however, she had never met Chloe in life, so she hadn't made the connection. But it seemed like important information they all should have been privy to.

Apparently everyone had been harbouring their little secrets. Everyone except Jenn.

In truth, she just wanted to go home now. She needed sleep.

Evidently, she wasn't alone in that respect. A light snoring beside her drew her attention. David's head had dropped forward and his eyes were closed. Everyone turned to look at him.

'Is he asleep?' Sarah asked.

Jenn chuckled. 'It's been a long day.'

'Quite,' Father Janosch agreed. 'Perhaps we should all call it a night.'

He checked his phone again, something he'd been doing a lot in the past few hours, always followed by a look of disappointment.

Expecting a call, Father? Jenn wondered.

'That sounds like a good idea,' Sarah said. She pushed her chair back and rose to her feet, stretching her arms up above her head and letting out a groan.

'Where are we all sleeping?' Jenn asked. Her gear was in the room she had been sharing with Ann the previous night, but she'd be damned if she was staying in a room on her own tonight.

'I'm not sure,' Sarah replied. 'Do you think we'll all fit into one bedroom?'

Jenn thought about that, and she doubted it.

Father Janosch stood up as well and laid a hand on David's shoulder, giving him a gentle shake. David's eyes snapped open and he straightened up in shock. He looked up at the others in obvious confusion.

'I fell asleep, didn't I?' he asked.

Father Janosch laughed. 'You did. Come on, it's time for bed.'

David ran a hand through his hair, shook his head, then got up. 'Yeah, I think that's wise.'

'Jenn has raised a good point,' Sarah said. 'I'm not sure if four of us will fit into one room. Unless we clear out all beds and just use mattresses. But that's gonna be a lot of work.'

'I don't want us splitting into two rooms,' David stated.

'Okay,' Sarah went on. 'The biggest room is the one Jenn and Ann were using. I'll share a bed with Jenn'—she looked over to Jenn—'if you're okay with it? And then we can pull in some mattresses for you two,' she then pointed at David and Father Janosch.

'Makes sense,' David said. 'Yeah, let's do it.'

Jenn wasn't sure how happy she was with that, especially given Sarah's penchant for sleepwalking. The idea of waking up to see Sarah standing above her made Jenn shiver. Was it too late to just back out of the whole thing entirely? Jenn subtly checked her watch and saw it was close to midnight.

Come on, she said to herself, *you're here for a reason. Get on with it.*

While that was true, how far did her desire to find out the truth really go? After all, she probably had all the evidence she really needed now. Of course, there was still the issue of Chloe and the whole fucking Devil's Doorway business.

And also David's sister...

He was her oldest friend. Could she really abandon him when he needed her most?

After brief consideration, she decided she could not, and that realisation gave Jenn extra resolve to continue.

The group got to work rearranging the room as needed and pulling in the extra mattresses. In the end, the room looked like it was hosting a kid's sleepover. Everyone brought in their clothes and bags, and when finished, it was a tight fit.

'There aren't any cameras in here,' Jenn said.

Father Janosch, who was sitting on one of the mattresses on the floor, frowned. 'What do you mean?'

'We set up cameras in the other room to film Sarah and me during the night,' David clarified. 'But we don't have one mounted in here.'

'Do we need to get one ready?' Jenn asked. It was David's turn to check his watch now.

'It's going on twelve-thirty,' he said. 'That might take close to another hour.' He chewed his lip for a few seconds. 'We'll leave it for tonight,' he finally said. 'With four of us in here, we should be okay. If Sarah does try to sleepwalk, she'll probably trip over someone before she gets very far anyway.'

With that decided, everyone got themselves ready for bed, each using the adjoining bathroom to change into their sleeping clothes, though they kept the door open as they did. Finally, everyone settled down, but Jenn couldn't shake how uncomfortable she felt lying next to Sarah.

Stay in fucking bed, she silently pleaded. *Just for tonight.*

41

SARAH WAS SINKING into the earth again, getting dragged lower and lower through the soil and rock.

Kill him.

Farther down.

Kill him and come home.

Farther.

I'm waiting for you... Sis.

The earth around her changed the lower Sarah got. It eventually became flesh. Warm and wet. She saw faces grafted into the meat.

Some of them were strangers. One she knew.

Tania.

Tania's face was fixed into a scream.

The flesh around Sarah contracted, pressing into her.

Tania spoke. '*Release me. Kill him and release me.*'

Lower and lower.

Come home, Sis.

Sarah's eyes slowly opened. She felt cold and exposed, and it was dark all around her.

Her eyes slowly started to adjust, and through the thick shadows she was just able to make out her surroundings. Sarah quickly drew in a panicked breath.

She was down in the basement. Alone. Instinctively hugging herself in a vain effort to ward off the cold, she turned around, taking in as much of the area around her as she could. Everything was quiet, with only her own jagged breathing breaking the silence.

How the fuck did I get down here?

She knew the answer almost as soon as she'd asked the question. Her sleepwalking had taken her farther than usual. And, evidently, she hadn't woken the others when leaving the bedroom. They were likely still asleep. Unless, of course, something had happened to them.

Get a grip and stay calm, she ordered herself. *You've been in worse situations.*

Sarah closed her eyes and slowly brought her breathing under control, taking long inhales and letting out slow exhales.

Calm. Keep focused.

She opened her eyes again. There didn't seem to be any immediate danger, despite the strangeness of the situation, so all she had to do was get to the steps and head back upstairs. Simple.

A hoarse, gravelly, feminine... and familiar... voice cut through the silence.

'Hi, Sis.'

Sarah gasped and turned her head towards the furnace, which she could barely see due to the lack of light. The archaic heating device was almost completely covered in shadow.

Almost.

Sarah could, however, just make out its front, where the grills were open. There was no one inside.

It turned out Chloe was not inside of it, but on top of it. Her decayed face came forwards, swimming out from the darkness, as she crouched on the metal structure.

Her eyes were a dull white with no pupils, her skin was mottled grey, and her brown hair was thin and greasy.

My beautiful sister, reduced to this.

Chloe opened her mouth into a grin, revealing cracked and yellowed teeth, as well as blackened gums. A purple tongue slithered from her mouth and ran across her dry lower lip.

Sarah couldn't move, rooted to the spot in fear. Her sister then pulled back and once again disappeared into the darkness.

'*We've been waiting for you,*' Chloe said from the shadows. '*But you're home now.*'

A giggle. Chloe's voice was not her own, not quite like Sarah remembered it. It had a strained and almost distorted quality to it. Sarah then heard a noise from behind her, a sound that was something between a growl and a laugh. Not human. Sarah turned to the old cells that lined one of the far walls. The growl had come from one of them, though whatever had made it was hidden away.

'*Don't worry about him,*' Chloe said. '*You'll meet him soon enough.*'

Sarah snapped her head back towards the furnace.

'What do you want?' Sarah asked.

Another giggle from Chloe. '*Stop fighting, Sarah. Give yourself to us.*'

There was a skittering sound of something crawling over metal. Then Chloe emerged from the shadows again, this time standing next to the furnace. Sarah was now able to take in all her horrible, naked form: her sagging breasts, concave stomach with overhanging ribs, peeling and dry skin, and black fingers.

Chloe took a step forward.

'Stay back,' Sarah said, though her voice was a whimper.

This can't be Chloe. It can't be.

'*Our mother was alone in this basement once as well, just like you. The house took her.*'

'Leave me alone,' Sarah said, taking a step back.

'*And then the house* made *you, Sarah. Can't you feel the connection to it? To Mother. And to your dear Papa... Marcus?*'

Chloe stepped forward again. Another growl sounded from behind Sarah.

It occurred to her that she could break for the steps and take her chances, but the overwhelming fear that held her would just not let go.

'*You're special, Sis. And we're going to take you now. You've been resisting, but no more. We need you to do something for us.*'

'Get away from me!' Sarah bellowed.

'*Kill him, Sarah. Kill him and come home to me.*'

Chloe then dropped to all fours and let out another horrible giggle. Sarah screamed as the twisted version of her sister quickly scuttled forward with her belly pressed low to the ground. She moved like a spider, and cackled while wearing a manic grin.

Sarah turned, managing to overcome her fear enough to finally move. However, she screamed again as she turned straight into the thing that was looming behind her; it was tall and black, with a hideous mouth full of nightmarish teeth as well as melted facial features. A sickening smell of sulphur overpowered Sarah.

Despite the terror she felt when the monster grabbed

her, Sarah recognised what it was—the demon that had killed her sister.

And now it had her too.

It lifted her easily from the ground, talon-like hands gripping her upper arms, and brought her closer.

Sarah kicked and flailed as the demon's mouth opened, then closed it over her own.

42

JENN OPENED HER EYES, disturbed by movement in the room.

It was still dark. She could hear something shuffle about at the end of her bed and lifted her head, peering through the darkness.

'Sarah?' she asked.

Sarah seemed to be bending down, but quickly straightened back up and looked at Jenn.

'Yeah?'

'What are you doing?' Jenn asked.

'I needed the toilet,' Sarah whispered in response. 'It's a bit tricky climbing over everyone to get back to bed.'

'Okay,' Jenn said. 'What time is it?'

'Not sure. About four, I think.'

Jenn watched as Sarah stepped over David, moved back around to her side of the bed, and got in. As she did, Jenn felt a coldness radiate from the woman, enough to make Jenn tense up and shiver.

'Jesus,' she said. 'Have you been sitting in a fridge?'

Sarah gave a light laugh. 'No, but it's fucking cold in

here.' Sarah then lay down and pulled the covers over her body.

Jenn wrapped her side of the duvet tightly around herself as well, hoping to ward off some of the cold Sarah was generating.

Despite the chill, Jenn was just glad Sarah hadn't been sleepwalking again.

~

Sarah had almost had her hands around David's neck when that bitch Jenn had woken up and ruined everything.

Still, it was a lesson. With the four of them together, could she really have gotten the job done without anyone else intervening?

She would need to get him alone.

Then, Sarah would be allowed to come home. For now, however, she had to be patient.

43

LUCA TOOK another sip of his coffee.

They'd had a full day at it and evening was drawing in again, darkening the skies outside. They were in the dining room with *Ianua Diaboli* and the ledger. A constant *tap, tap, tap* of rain hitting the window could be heard.

Yet again, Luca was at the head of the table, with David and Jenn on one side of him and Sarah on the other.

It had been another long day and they had not left each other's sides. They had continued researching the book for a while, and Luca had noted references to the Seven Gates. That troubled him greatly. They also ran some sessions to try and draw out the spirits of the house. However, the results had been... disappointing. Luca had still not seen anything in the house with his own eyes.

The only thing of note was the phone call from Ralph, where he'd told David that he and the others were coming back to the house to get the rest of their stuff. They wouldn't be staying, however.

Sarah was certainly eager to get things moving. Though

she physically looked exhausted, she moved with enthusiasm and energy, like a madwoman. She had been like that all day.

'We should split up into two groups,' she said at the table. 'It'll be fine. Jenn can stay here with Father Janosch to work on the book; David, you can come with me and we can run a vigil or EMP experiment or something.'

Luca could tell by David's expression that he wasn't about to go along with her idea.

'No,' he replied. 'We should stick together as much as possible.'

'But we need to be doing *two* jobs,' Sarah argued. 'Luca needs to do his thing with the book, but we also still need to be cataloguing any evidence we can. Last night was a bust, so we need to be proactive.'

'Then we'll just keep alternating,' David argued.

'We were going to do that last night,' Sarah said. 'But then we just ended up back in here, twiddling our thumbs while Luca carried on with the book. The rest of us are nothing more than third wheels.'

'Sorry, Sarah, but that's final.' David folded his arms over his chest. 'We need to be cautious here. You heard what Luca told us yesterday about what this place *could* be. I'm not going to put people at any more risk than we absolutely have to.'

Sarah shook her head in disgust. Luca could feel the anger radiate from her. Thankfully, she stayed silent and sat back in her chair, folding her arms as well.

David looked over to Luca. 'Please carry on.'

Luca started to read from the ledger.

He had picked up an unclear voicemail earlier from Bishop Turnbull. It seemed the message had been left the previous day, though Luca had been unaware of it until now.

The message was mostly just static but cleared up at the end, where Luca heard the Bishop state: *'So please, carry on and get what we need. There can be no mistakes.'*

Though the rest of the message was lost to a bad line, the intent of it had been clear: keep going.

That made sense. While he acknowledged the evidence David had shown him was compelling, as was *Ianua Diaboli*, Luca had seen nothing for himself as yet. It was all second-hand accounts, along with the footage. It was certainly enough to convince *him*, but could he claim with absolute certainty that what he'd been shown wasn't doctored or manufactured somehow? There was a chance the others were all in on it together in an attempt to gain some kind of plaudits.

He didn't believe that, of course. Not one bit. But other people might. And he knew the Church would be reluctant to involve itself in something that could damage its reputation—especially since that reputation had already eroded immensely over the last few decades. Attendance at sermons across most European countries was at an all-time low, and people were turning away from God in droves. So now the Church was nothing if not careful.

Luca had spent the previous day cross-checking the ledger against *Ianua Diaboli* to ensure the translations were accurate. Everything he'd seen indicated they were. So, feeling a desperate need to speed things up, he decided to focus purely on the ledger itself, which he could get through much quicker, only checking *Ianua Diaboli* to reference some of the hand-drawn sketches within its pages.

Whoever had written that book seemed to have a deep knowledge of what a Devil's Door was, and also how to leverage its power. If it was all genuine, Luca had to wonder about the book's author. How could he—or she—know so much? Where had that understanding come from? And what was the purpose of writing it all down? Who was the author looking to share his knowledge with? So many unanswered questions.

There was another mystery as well. Because the ledger and *Ianua Diaboli* had been at the house for such a long time, at least before Marcus Blackwater took ownership, Luca wondered if the book was somehow related to the horrible events back in 1982. The massacre had long been unexplained.

The others sat in silence as Luca worked. It was a little uncomfortable, having all eyes on him, and he could indeed sympathise with Sarah. It *did* seem like a waste of resources to have everyone sit and watch him read from the ledger when they could be doing something more productive. However, David was ultimately right—splitting the teams into smaller groups was just asking for trouble.

As he continued to read, Luca found himself skimming the pages, satisfied once he got the gist of each particular section, whether it be a ritual, a curse, even a rite. One part even detailed how it was possible to reanimate a dead body using a soul or demon via a Devil's Door. That was something Luca didn't want to think about for too long.

He moved quicker, only scanning the titles of each section in order to get an idea of what was ahead. After another hour of reading, he hit on something interesting.

Luca quickly crossed-referenced what he saw against *Ianua Diaboli*, just to satisfy himself. The title of that chapter in the old book read *Impius Sanguis*.

Accursed Blood.

As Luca read through the pages of the ledger, a growing sense of unease worked its way up from his gut. The point of the ritual was to impregnate a host, one that was possessed by the forces that flowed through the door. The reward for the man giving his seed was free will after death, along with great power. The only requirement was the man himself was not under the control of any supernatural forces.

One phrase stood out: *Enim sanguis clavis est*. The blood is the key.

The ledger stated that the newborn child would be *clavis* —the key—and would unlock *Portae Septem*, the Seven Gates.

Luca's stomach tightened up. To complete *Impius Sanguis*, it said the doorway needed to be opened wider to draw power, and it needed souls to do that.

His mind immediately ran back to 1982 and the massacre on Halloween. How many people had gone missing that night? Luca couldn't remember exactly, but possibly enough to further open the door.

Could *Impius Sanguis* have been carried out that night by someone at the hotel? And if so, was an unholy child created?

He kept reading as the passages went on to detail the role of the Accursed Blood. After reaching adulthood, they needed to return back to a Devil's Doorway so their minds could be 'soured.' Then, when under possession, they had to offer up the soul of an innocent—killing someone by their own hand.

Their transformation would then be complete. If all Seven Gates were open during or after the Accursed Blood's transformation, the merging of Hell and Earth would begin.

Luca sat back in his chair, feeling all energy drain out of him.

'Are you okay, Father?' David asked.

However, Luca was not really paying attention, instead

staring at Sarah. He knew her age, so could work out her birth year from there.

1983. *Could it be?*

'Sarah?' he asked.

She looked up. 'Yeah?'

'This might sound like a strange question, but could you tell me what month you were born?'

She paused, then her face fell. Her jaw tensed up and her eyes narrowed.

'Why is that important?' she asked.

Luca felt a knot in the pit of his stomach.

'Didn't you say you were a July baby?' Jenn cut in.

Nine months prior to July would put the conception at around October 1982.

'Why is that important?' David asked.

'Do you realise you may have been conceived at this house, Sarah?' Luca asked, keeping his eyes firmly on her. He saw her jaw tense again.

She slowly nodded. 'Yes, of course. I've always realised that was a possibility. I *can* count, for God's sake.'

Sarah made his question sound like a ridiculous one, but Luca could tell from her hate-filled glare that she knew he knew.

'And your father,' Luca went on to ask. 'Did he ever take in interest in *Ianua Diaboli,* or the ledger, when he lived here?'

Sarah shrugged and slid her empty coffee mug over towards herself. She cupped it in her hands and started to slowly rotate it on the table. 'How could I possibly know that for sure?' she said. 'But I doubt it. Dad was never one for that kind of thing. He was a simple man.'

Luca wasn't sure whether to believe her. If Sarah was the

key, either her dad *had* to have used the book... or her father wasn't who she thought.

Luca's mind raced. *What do I do?* The book said that the key needed to be possessed again before taking a life. So... was Sarah possessed at that moment, or was the house still working on her?

He brought up a hand and took hold of the crucifix he wore, rubbing it between his fingers. He always did it absent-mindedly when nervous. And he was *definitely* nervous.

Jenn spoke up. 'I'm confused here, are you two angry at each other over something? You could cut the tension with a knife. What's going on?'

'Not angry,' Luca said. 'Just curious. How are you feeling, Sarah? Like yourself?'

She smiled. It wasn't a pleasant one. 'I'm fine, Father. Just eager to move things along. So how about we put those books away and go and gather some evidence? You can come with me if you want? Then we can talk more.'

'We don't split up,' David said. 'You *know* that, Sarah.' He turned from Sarah to Luca, then back again. 'Seriously, what the hell's going on here? It's like you two are having a stand-off.'

'Care to tell them, Sarah?' Luca asked.

'I have no idea what you're talking about... *priest,*' she said, the final word spoken with pure hatred. Her face suddenly twisted into a hideous snarl and, in the same instant, she raised her coffee cup and drove it down onto the surface of the table. The ceramic mug shattered. Luca instinctively pushed himself back from the table, as did David and Jenn.

'What the...' was all David managed to get out before Sarah snatched up a long, jagged shard. With frightening speed, she hopped up onto the table and lunged at Luca, who held his hands up to stop her. He managed to wrap his fingers around the wrist of her leading arm.

Luca fell backwards to the floor and Sarah on top of him. She screamed like an animal and tried to force the point of the shard down into his throat. Luca cried out, pushing up against her with everything he had. However, she was too strong, and the makeshift ceramic weapon lowered slowly until the point found his neck.

He felt the skin puncture.

No! Not like this!

Luca sensed movement around them both. Sarah was then yanked off him and thrown back. David and Jenn stood above Luca, looking horrified. Luca quickly brought his hand to his throat and felt a sting. He looked at his fingers and saw spots of blood, but knew the wound wasn't deep or serious.

He had been lucky.

'Sarah, what the fuck are you doing?!' David screamed.

Luca pulled himself to a sitting position, where he was just able to see Sarah over the top of the dining room table. The horrible snarl was still etched on her face. She looked at him, then at the other two. Luca saw that the shard was no longer in her hand, but now on the floor close to him.

Would she attack again without a weapon?

'Stay back from her,' Luca said as he climbed to his feet. 'She's possessed.'

David and Jenn both looked shocked. 'What... when?' David asked.

Sarah began to laugh. 'You're all fucking pathetic, you know that? You'll die tonight. Every last one of you. By *my* hand.'

She then turned and ran from the room.

'What the fuck is going on?' David asked with urgency.

'It's true,' Luca replied, trying to take deep, slow breaths. 'There can be no doubt any more. The book, the house, everything is as we'd feared. Sarah is at the centre of it all.'

'I still don't understand,' David said.

So Luca explained as quickly as he could. About *Impius Sanguis, Portae Septem,* and about Sarah being the key. He also told them how she needed to take a life while under the control of the house.

'If she kills one of us, then the results could be… unimaginable,' Luca finished.

Jenn slumped down to a chair. 'I… I don't fucking believe this.'

'I understand,' Luca said. 'But you need to come to terms with it quickly. There may still be hope, but we need to be very careful.' He lifted *Ianua Diaboli* from the table. 'The first time I looked at this, I skimmed the very end of the book, just out of interest. There is a ritual there, *Claude Ianua*. It could help us.'

'Phone the Church,' David stated. 'This is too much for us. You have to get someone else here quickly.'

'I can try,' Luca said, 'but time is of the essence. If Sarah manages to kill one of us—'

'Then we run!' Jenn snapped. 'We get the hell out of here and leave Sarah alone until someone better equipped can get here.'

'And what if she got to someone else in that time?' Luca asked. 'Dragged them back here after we ran?'

Luca didn't want to disagree with Jenn. He wanted to run every bit as much as she did. To stay could mean not just the end of their lives but also eternal damnation for their souls. It would be pain and unimaginable torture… forever.

But what were their own lives compared to the lives of everyone on Earth? They had to try.

'Shit,' David said and ran a hand through his hair. He looked ashen. Jenn did as well. And Luca couldn't blame them. The situation was madness.

But they had to get through it.

'I'm scared,' Jenn said.

'I am too,' Luca admitted. 'But if we stick together, then the three of us should be able to hold her off if we need to.'

'But what about the house?' Jenn said. 'We wouldn't just be fighting against Sarah. We'd be fighting everything else inside this place.'

'Then we need to be quick,' David said. Luca saw that his hands were trembling. 'The ritual you mentioned, *Claude*... whatever it was. How does it work?'

'I'll explain later,' Luca said and set the book down, flicking through the pages to the back. He then opened the ledger up to the same place and started to read. The other two had their eyes fixed on the open door to the room.

He was thankful that *Claude Ianua* was not a complicated ritual to carry out. It brought with it great danger, but if everything went well it would be relatively easy to set up and follow. It surprised him that closing the doorways could be so straightforward, but then again, it could well have been a safeguard—a way to quickly cut off the book's power if needed.

A sound drew their attention. The low rumble came from a distance, but was getting close.

It was an engine.

'Shit,' David said. 'It's Ralph and the others. We have to warn them. If Sarah gets to them first... They don't know what's happening here.'

Luca gathered up both books, and the three of them

sprinted towards the front of the house. As they broke through to the entrance lobby, Luca saw the front door was already open.

He heard Ralph's voice outside. 'Hey, Sarah, how have things been? Any other... Sarah! What the hell are you doing?!'

Ralph screamed.

44

JENN'S MIND was in overdrive trying to catch up with what was happening. She had heard Ralph scream, followed by the panicked voices of the rest of the group outside. David got through the front door first, with Jenn, then Father Janosch following close behind. Jenn heard a thud on the marble floor beside her while still in the entrance lobby, and turned to see that Father Janosch had dropped the books. She didn't need to ask why. The rain outside was heavy, and could damage or ruin *Ianua Diaboli.*

Jenn ran out onto the front porch and into the driving downpour. The scene before her was one of chaos. Sarah was being dragged off Ralph, and he lay on the ground writhing in agony as the rain hammered down on him. George and Jamie wrestled with Sarah as she fought like an animal. The two men were clearly struggling but managed to push her to the ground. Jamie had an obvious gash across his forearm, and it was then Jenn saw that Sarah was holding a long kitchen knife which glistened with blood. Her hair was matted to her head.

Jenn's eyes snapped back over to Ralph as they ran towards him. He was clutching his stomach with his teeth clenched together in a pained expression. Though he was wearing a dark blue hoodie, Jenn could see an even darker wet patch pool out from beneath his hands.

'What the fuck are you doing?' George screamed to Sarah as Jamie cradled his arm.

Sarah took a step towards them with the knife raised. Her teeth were clenched and her eyes were filled with fury and hatred.

'Sarah!' David screamed. She turned to see David, Jenn, and Father Janosch advance. At first, she stepped forward towards them, seeming ready to take them all on. That terrified Jenn. However, a look of hesitation flashed over Sarah's face. She then turned and ran, sprinting over to the van the others had arrived in. Sarah thrust the knife into the front tire. Once, twice, three times.

'What the fuck are you doing?' Jamie screamed at her. However, neither he nor George dared to get to close. Sarah moved on to the other front tire and slashed at it wildly before running off again.

'Leave her,' David ordered to Jenn and Father Janosch. 'Get to Ralph.'

The three continued over to their fallen friend, the wet gravel crunching underfoot. Ann knelt next to Ralph and had his head on her lap.

'Help,' Ralph wheezed. He looked terrified, clutching his stomach. The rain hammered down on him.

'What do we do?' Ann asked, close to tears.

George was suddenly next to them, and he already had his mobile phone out. 'We need to call an ambulance.' He typed the emergency number into his keypad and put the phone to his ear. Jenn surveyed the area around them, but was unable to spot Sarah.

'She ran,' Jamie said to them with a hand clutched around his bleeding forearm. 'Over there.' He pointed over to one side of the house where the carport stood, covering the vehicles inside in shadow.

'She's going to slash the tires!' Jenn yelled.

David lifted up Ralph's hoodie to see a gash, the width of a knife blade, in his lower left side. Blood ran freely.

'Shit!' George yelled. 'I can't get any reception. What the hell! Anyone else?'

Jenn tried her phone but got a similar result to George. 'How can that be? Reception isn't great here, but we've never had this happen before.'

'It's the house,' Father Janosch said. Jenn heard a bang over in the carport.

Sarah was getting to work.

'We need to get Ralph inside,' David said, 'and out of the rain. I have a first aid-kit in there. Come on, help me.'

Jenn didn't want to go back in the house, but they were out of options. They couldn't use any of the vehicles to get away, Sarah had seen to that, and it had proven impossible to get through to the police or an ambulance.

She again looked over to the cars and saw Sarah standing watching them, smiling. The woman then slowly turned and ran into the shadows, towards the back of the grounds.

'Help us!' David yelled at Jenn. The others had crouched around Ralph, ready to lift his bulky frame. Jenn squatted down as well.

'On three,' David stated. 'One... two... three!'

They all strained. Ralph was even heavier than Jenn had been expecting, but they managed to lift him.

'What the hell is going on here, David?' George asked, panicked.

Jenn felt her fingers straining under Ralph's weight.

'I'll explain inside,' David replied. 'But we have to be quick.' They then shuffled their way back over to the door, accompanied by Ralph's screams of pain.

45

'TAKE HIM TO THE DINING ROOM,' David said as they re-entered the entrance lobby. He was drenched to the bone and struggling with Ralph, his arms aching as the large man's weight became difficult to handle. 'We'll put him on the table.'

It was the best place he could think of. Already David's mind was racing through what to do next. If they couldn't get Ralph to a hospital, or get an ambulance out to the house, David would need to do his best to keep his friend alive.

However, his first-aid training probably wouldn't be enough.

Ralph's weight grew heavier as Father Janosch broke away from them.

'Father!' George snapped.

But the priest simply ran over to the corner of the room and picked up *Ianua Diaboli* and the ledger, which had been discarded on the floor.

'We need these!' he insisted and led the way over to the

dining room. His head was on a constant swivel as if expecting something to leap out.

When David and the others were finally able to lower Ralph down to the dining room table, David felt relief in his arms. He lifted Ralph's hoodie again and saw the blood still running from the wound. David moved his hands over the gash and pressed down, applying as much pressure as he could, and drawing out another yowl of pain from Ralph.

Shit. This is beyond me.

'I need some blankets and my first-aid kit,' David ordered the others, while still trying to keep his focus. Blood pooled on the table below Ralph, and it seeped out quickly along the polished surface. David just hoped that no major arteries had been cut. 'The kit is in my room,' he said. 'Just grab the brown leather bag up there.'

Father Janosch had moved to the far end of the table and set both books down, opening them towards the back. He scanned the pages, mainly looking at the ledger.

What the hell is he doing?

'I'll go,' Jenn said to David. She looked pale and terrified, but David was glad she was brave enough to offer. There was zero chance of her going alone, however.

'George, Jamie, you two go with her.'

Neither looked enthused, though Jamie appeared to be the more hesitant of the pair. He had his own injury, still holding his bleeding forearm. The long cut was across the top, however, and away from the veins beneath the wrist.

'Wait!' Father Janosch said. 'We need some other things as well.'

'What are you talking about, Father?' David asked, still pressing down on Ralph.

'We need to stop what is happening here. If Ralph dies, you know what that means.'

George threw his hands up in the air. 'Can someone please explain what is going on?!'

Father Janosch ignored the frantic question and again addressed David. 'I need my Bible. And I also need some salt, candles, water, and some soil. A mirror, too.'

'For what?' David asked.

'Something I'm ill-prepared for... but we have no other choice. There is a ritual in *Ianua Diaboli* that I think closes the door. But it is dangerous.'

'Ralph is in trouble,' Jenn said. 'We need to—'

'I know how this is going to sound,' Father Janosch cut in. 'But if Ralph dies before we close the door... the consequences could be dire.'

'What the fuck is going on?!' Ann screamed in utter frustration. Her voice bellowed so loudly it momentarily drowned out the sound of rain outside.

'David can explain it to you,' Father Janosch said. 'I'll go with the others to get what we need, and I'll update them as best I can as well. But we all need to hurry.'

'Go,' David said to him.

'And everyone remember,' the priest added. 'If you see Sarah, avoid her. Run. Do *not* let her harm you.' He took a breath. 'Kill her if you must.'

'You can't be serious,' Jamie said in disbelief.

David felt for Jamie. For all of them. They had walked into a nightmare that he himself could scarcely wrap his head around.

'There is a mirror in the bag with my first-aid kit,' David said.

Katie's mirror. His good-luck charm.

'My Bible is up there, too,' Father Janosch said. 'And I have a flask we can use to collect the water. But we also need soil, candles, and salt.'

'You can get soil from the gardens,' David said. 'But candles... I don't know.'

'The kitchen,' Jenn said. 'There are some in the kitchen.'

'Be careful,' David added. 'All of you.'

Father Janosch nodded. 'Protect the books,' he said and motioned towards *Ianua Diaboli* and the ledger.

Father Janosch, Jenn, Jamie, and George then all walked from the room, leaving David with Ann and Ralph.

'I need something to cover the wound,' he said. Ann looked terrified but slipped off her coat. She then ripped at the arm of her net top that covered a purple blouse beneath. The material tore easily, and she handed it to David. He clamped it down onto the seeping cut in Ralph's stomach.

'What... did he mean, David?' Ralph said, struggling with his words. 'About closing the door before I die?'

David let out a sigh, and began to tell them everything.

46

Luca strode through the hallways of Perron Manor, keeping his hands clenched into fists, if only to stop them from trembling. He was on edge, and as alert as he'd ever been in his life; his eyes darted about and checked all corners as they moved. Sarah was in the house somewhere, lurking and waiting.

I can't do this. I'm going to fail.

En-route to the stairs, the group quickly ducked into the ground-floor study to try the landline there. It was dead.

Unless they ran off into the night, they were trapped at Perron Manor. However, there was no way they would be able to take Ralph if they did run, not without exacerbating his injury. And if he died before they got off the grounds...

As much as Luca hated the idea, he knew that closing the door was the only option.

I can't do this!

He was terrified, and the task ahead overwhelmed him.

They had been careless and hadn't taken the danger the house posed seriously enough.

He should have just followed Sarah's advice and told the

Church that Perron Manor was indeed what they feared, even if he hadn't been certain. Consequences be damned.

If he had, then someone far more capable could have come to handle things. The rest of them could have gotten Sarah out of the house before she was turned. But no, Luca had hesitated and second-guessed himself. His handling of the whole situation had been terrible.

Now they could all lose their lives because of it. No, not just their lives. They would be prisoners of Perron Manor for eternity, stumbling among the dead in pain and agony—forever suffering the rot of their decaying souls.

Undead puppets to an unknowable master.

'Spill it, Father,' Jamie said as they started up the stairs. 'You owe us an explanation. Why was Ralph attacked? What the hell happened to Sarah?'

'She's possessed,' Luca replied. 'The house has her now. However, there is more...'

He managed to briefly explain their situation—at least, as best as he could in such a short space of time: Perron Manor *was* a Devil's Door, Sarah was under its possession, and she was also born of the house—her bloodline tinged with evil.

'Impossible,' George said after the explanation. 'That can't be true.'

'It is, George,' Jenn said.

But George shook his head. 'I'm sorry, but there is no way this whole thing has devolved into the possibility of the world ending.'

'Not ending,' Luca replied. 'Merging with Hell.'

'Same difference.'

True enough.

They entered the bedroom, where everyone had earlier dumped all their belongings, George ran over to grab

David's bag as Luca retrieved his flask and Bible from his satchel. Luca then ran a hand over the front of the holy book. It had a burgundy leather cover with gold writing and a black embossed cross in the centre. The flask was glass and fit comfortably in the palm of his hand, with a plastic screw cap at the top.

'We need to get the first-aid kit to David before we get the rest of the stuff,' Jamie said.

'I really think we need to gather the other items we need first,' Luca insisted.

'And why the hell do we need all that? Candles and earth and whatever?'

Luca strode from the room first as the others kept pace.

'*Claude Ianua,*' Luca replied as they moved back towards the stairs. 'The ritual to close the door.'

'It needs candles and water?' Jenn asked.

'Fire, water, earth, and air,' Luca confirmed. 'The four elements. They need to be blessed by a holy man, and used as part of the ritual. The elements come together to join our own world to the other, to Hell, so we can then close the door.'

'Sounds insane,' Jamie said.

It was. The whole thing was insane.

Once they reached the bottom of the stairs, Jenn spoke up. 'There are candles and salt in the kitchen,' she said. 'But we need earth from outside. Do we split into groups?'

'It's dangerous,' Luca said.

'I know,' Jenn replied. 'But we don't have a lot of time. If we do split up and we're quick, we can all meet back up in the dining room in no time at all.'

Luca was torn. David would no doubt insist they stick together, given the group was already split, but Jenn was right: speed was of the essence.

He couldn't risk it.

Luca shook his head. 'You might be right, but if we thin our numbers any more and Sarah is hiding, there's a higher chance someone could lose their life. Come on, let's get to the kitchen.'

They ran as one and cut through the house. Luca hated the waiting. Their passage had been easy so far, which meant Sarah wasn't likely close, but that in itself unnerved him. He would prefer to know for sure where she was hiding. In addition, Perron Manor itself hadn't tried to hinder their progress at all. Was it just leaving them to Sarah, or biding its time?

In the kitchen, Jenn dug through a set of drawers. 'The candles are in here,' she said. 'Matches too. How many candles you need?'

'Grab as many as you can carry,' Luca said, and Jenn tucked a bundle of them under her arm. The packet of matches was thrust into her pocket. The candles were short and wide, but would do for what Luca needed.

Luca himself rifled through the cupboards and found some table salt, and he also grabbed a Tupperware container, knowing he would need something to carry the soil in. Lastly, he filled his flask with water from the tap.

He hadn't yet told the others that the ritual couldn't be done in the dining room. They would need to get as deep in the ground as possible.

That meant getting everyone down to the basement.

Hold out, Ralph. Just a little longer.

When they had everything they could get from the kitchen, that left only one element: earth.

'Out the back,' Luca ordered.

They ran through to the great hall and continued over to the rear door. Luca stepped outside first, and a security light flicked on, pushing away the darkness. The rain hammered down onto the uneven paving, leaving stretches of puddles.

No one was out there.

Where are you, Sarah?

The others stepped outside as well. They all slowly made their way through the courtyard to the gardens beyond, getting drenched by the rain once again. Luca still expected *something* to happen.

But there was no attack and no spirits blocking their way.

'Quickly,' Luca ordered the group. They ran over to a flower bed and he filled the Tupperware container with black mud, then pressed the lid down.

That was everything they needed. He stood up and turned around.

Sarah was there, standing on the patio, knife in hand.

'Hello, Father,' she shouted over the sound of the falling rain. 'Care to come over here? I have something I want to show you.'

She had discarded her jumper, now wearing only a tank top and jeans. The wet and cold didn't seem to bother her at all.

'Let us pass, Sarah,' Luca shouted back. 'This isn't you. You're being controlled. Surely you know that?'

Sarah shook her head and gave a humourless laugh. 'No, priest, I am finally free. No more worry, no more doubt, no more pain... and no more guilt. It's a beautiful thing, Father. True freedom.'

'You're a puppet, Sarah,' Luca shouted back. 'A puppet to the house.'

'Better a puppet to something real than a servant to a false god. You're ruled by fear, little wretch. That's all you have in your life.'

She took a step forward.

Luca tensed up. With Jenn, George, and Jamie beside him, they had numbers on their side. But Sarah was an army girl, and she held that glistening knife. She didn't have to beat them in a fight—she just had to bury that blade into one of their throats.

And Luca was the oldest and slowest.

'If only your sister could see you now,' Luca yelled. 'How do you think she'd feel?'

'She *can* see me,' Sarah shouted. 'And I can see *her*. She's proud of me. If I plunge this blade into your flesh, then I can come home to her and be with her forever. She's waiting for me.'

'No,' Luca stated, shaking his head. 'The *real* Chloe exists here somewhere, yes, but *beneath* the evil. And she's horrified at what you're about to do. Don't you see? She wants you to fight this, Sarah. She *needs* you to. We all do.'

Sarah laughed, then tilted her head back to let the rain fall on her face. She lifted the knife and traced the blade down her throat, over her chest, and towards her crotch.

'There's nothing to fight, priest,' she said, dropping her head back down. 'Chloe tried to get away from this place, but it wanted her. *Needed* her. It called her back. She couldn't get away from it. Perron Manor always gets what it wants. So why resist?'

Something clicked into place for Luca.

'No, Sarah. It was never about Chloe. The house wanted *you* back. It almost had you, too, but Chloe managed to convince you to leave. So it took her, and showed her to you to lure you in. Don't you see? Perron Manor needed to keep you here just a little longer in order to finish what it started with you. If you give in to it, the house wins.'

It was all so obvious to him now. Chloe was never the

focus of the house. It had always been about Sarah. Both sisters had been called back when needed, and it had gotten to work on Sarah, even killing Chloe to keep Sarah there longer.

Luca had always been confused at how quickly she was showing signs of succumbing to the forces here after only a few days during their investigation, and after only a month and a half when she'd lived here with Chloe. But she was the key. She was born of the house. She was one with it.

It was troubling to think how far into the future the tendrils of Perron Manor could reach in order to manipulate things. Did that mean events were already set in stone?

No, he couldn't accept that.

Sarah had stopped advancing, and he saw a flash of something on her face. Resistance. The real Sarah *was* in there. Perhaps he'd gotten through to her.

'Fight it, Sarah! For your sister!'

She gritted her teeth together and brought a hand up to her head. She winced. Luca could see the conflict and fight going on inside her.

'Sarah, please,' Jenn yelled over to her. 'Just stop this. Ralph could die. Let us help him.'

Sarah's eyes then opened wide. Her hand fell back down to her side and a hideous smile crossed her lips.

Sarah shook her head. 'No, you're planning something. You want to close the doorway. I can't allow that.'

Another step forward.

'What do we do?' Jamie asked Luca. Luca had no clue.

47

WHERE THE HELL ARE THEY?

The others were taking their time and it was worrying David.

Ralph was struggling. He was still conscious but in tremendous pain. He looked pale. So very pale.

Ann had raided the chest of drawers at the far end of the room and found some tablecloths that they had used to press onto Ralph's wound in an attempt to stem the flow of blood. David still pushed down with as much pressure as he could safely exert.

But he needed his first-aid kit.

Quick footsteps outside of the room drew his attention —a pitter-patter of someone running past the open doorway. A shadow had passed as well, but it moved too quickly for him to see anything clearly.

Ann's head swivelled around. 'What was that?' she asked.

'Hello?' David called, hoping it was one of the others coming back. Deep down, he knew it wasn't.

He heard a feminine giggle from the hallway outside.

Ann quickly moved over to stand next to David. The table, with Ralph atop it, was between them and the door.

'I don't fucking need this right now,' Ralph said.

David took Ann's hand and put it on the blood-soaked rags over Ralph's stomach.

'Keep pressing down,' he ordered. He then walked around the table to the other side. As scared as he was being closest to the door and whatever was out there, David didn't like the idea of Ralph being the one nearest to the danger.

'Show yourself,' he demanded.

Another giggle.

'*Are you sure... you want that... Brother?*' a voice said. It was crackly and gravelly... like the voice of the dead.

David's heart froze. While the voice was horribly twisted, it did trigger a pang of recognition within him, like a long-lost memory suddenly pulled to the fore through the mists of time.

It was Katie's voice.

He heard the slap of a bare foot outside. Then another. A shadow was cast on the floor of the hallway, and it moved closer with each step.

He trembled in fear and anticipation, and David was quickly reminded of his time back in 2014, when a disembodied voice had delivered a message to him: *Return here. Help another in need.*

David had always assumed that the 'other in need' was Katie, as he knew she was trapped at the house. Now he'd found her.

However, David was ill-prepared for the horror that stepped out from behind the door frame. He'd seen ghosts in the house before. Even a demon back during their first investigation, so David thought he was ready for anything...

He let out a scream and backed up into the table, banging into it and causing Ralph to cry out.

The thing that stood in the doorway was little more than a walking corpse: decay, rot, and death given form. The flesh on the woman's spindly frame was dry, wrinkled, and a mix of browns and greys. Some areas of skin were missing, showing bone beneath; ribs poked through the paper-thin flesh, shins had no covering, and the jawbone was also stripped bare, giving the woman a skeletal grin.

One eye was missing, just a dark pit boring into her cranium, and the remaining eye was cloudy and milky with no pupil. The only hair she had was a few wispy strands. On top of that, the horrific girl was completely naked, with sagging, punctured breasts drooping low.

Yet despite the disfigurement, the rot, and the ruin, David knew it was Katie.

'*Hi, Brother.*'

Though her jaw moved, the voice didn't seem completely in-sync, as if it were coming from another space behind the walking nightmare.

A black tongue rolled out from Katie's mouth and licked her dry upper lip. It then moved over the bottom teeth of the exposed jaw. Her hand came up to one ruined breast and squeezed.

'*Am I still beautiful?*'

She was mocking him. No, it wasn't her. This wasn't Katie. It was the house. *Perron Manor* was mocking him, trying to make him feel as much horror and revulsion as was humanly possible. And it was succeeding. However, David hoped Katie—the *real* Katie—was somewhere beneath it all and that she could hear him.

'I've come back for you, Sister,' he said. 'I never gave up.

And I'm going to help you. The message: 'Return here, help another.' That was about you, wasn't it?'

The hideous woman just threw her head back and let out a humourless cackle.

'*Idiot*,' she said with hatred in her voice. '*That message was* never *about your dear sister.*'

David shook his head. 'Lies,' he replied. 'I won't let you fool me.'

Katie took a step forward, her motions jerky, like her body was on fire and she was walking on hot coals. '*I don't need to fool you. Perron Manor delivered the message, but the person you were supposed to help? That was never me.*'

David frowned, unsure of what to believe. If the message was never about Katie, then could it have been about...

'Chloe!' he exclaimed, as something suddenly made sense to him. 'Is that who I'm here to help?'

Katie slowly shook her head.

'Sarah?'

A nod.

He tried to make sense of it all. Was that the truth, the message was about Sarah? If so, it kind of made sense, given the circumstances of how he'd returned to Perron Manor. He *was* here helping Sarah in what she needed to do.

'It was Sarah that needed me,' he stated in realisation.

Katie laughed again. '*You still don't understand. The message was just the bait. A worm on a hook, and you bit into it. We kept you dangling on the line until we needed you. Sarah was always going to return home. But we knew her sister would convince her to leave before we had taken her completely. So... we took her sister and gave Sarah a reason to come back, though she was never going to come back alone. She needed help. An 'expert.' Someone we had dangling on a line, just ready to reel in.*'

Katie laughed again. David's head swam. That couldn't

be true. 'Bullshit!' he snapped, feeling his anger rise. 'That's impossible.'

Katie then started to fondle her other breast, and David heard the crunch and crackle of dried skin. Dust fell to the floor from beneath her squeezing hand.

It's trying to sicken you, David said to himself. *To get under your skin. Don't let it.*

'*Afraid not, little brother. That's why it first took me, you see. The pieces for this night were put into place a long time ago. This house... it knows things. Sees time differently. We all do now. And it is... horrifying.*' She cackled and squeezed harder. '*Not something your simple brain would be able to comprehend. But know this: you're a pawn, David. You and all your friends. Now you're where we want you. There's nothing you can do about it. You'll join me soon enough, Brother.*' She then pulled her hand away from her now-crushed breast and waved her fingers at him. Katie backed up, one step after the other.

She wasn't quite finished. Her hand quickly found its way between her legs and she let out a moan. '*Then we can do what I know you always fantasised about. Isn't that right, Davey-boy?*'

David clenched up. His hands squeezed into fists and his teeth ground together. 'That isn't true!' he snapped, eyes wild in anger. 'I was too young. Not once did I ever—'

'*Sure, sure,*' Katie said, her tone one of pure conde-scension.

She then disappeared from the room.

David was motionless, trying to make sense of it all. He had been horrified at her final words.

He hadn't. Ever. Not once!

Not... once.

David quickly ran out of the room to again confront the horror, but found only an empty hallway.

48

WE HAVE TO CHARGE HER, Jenn thought to herself. *We're just standing and waiting.*

Sarah slowly advanced on them. All it would take was one swing or stab from that knife. Even if they all tried to flee and scatter in different directions, the likelihood was that only three out of the four would get past her.

And it only took one.

Sarah kept moving forward at a slow and steady pace.

'We need to tackle her,' Jenn said, hopefully only loud enough for the others to hear over the rain.

'We need to *what?!*' Jamie asked.

'You heard me,' she replied. 'We rush her. Better than waiting for her to come over and swing at us with that knife.'

'That's insane,' Jamie shot back.

But it wasn't. It was dangerous, certainly. Jenn knew it would take all of them to subdue her, but it was still four against one.

'She's right,' George added.

That was a relief—at least she wasn't alone. And Jenn

had an idea of how to make it work. She pointed to the house behind Sarah, up to the top floor.

'Chloe! she yelled. 'She's there, in the window!'

Father Janosch, George, and Jamie all looked up there to see nothing. Thankfully, Sarah turned her back on them to look up as well.

'Now!' Jenn cried and charged forward. It took the other three longer than she would have liked to figure out her plan. However, they soon ran as well, with Jamie and Father Janosch bringing up the rear. George kept pace with Jenn, and the two of them bore down on their target, who then started to turn back around.

Jenn leapt. She and George barrelled into Sarah, knocking her to the ground. The knife slipped from her grasp and skittered along the paved ground. Jenn grabbed one of Sarah's arms, and George seized the other. Both dropped their weight down onto her to keep Sarah pinned.

Jamie and Father Janosch soon reached the melee, but Jamie looked terrified. Sarah kicked and bucked wildly, exhibiting more strength than Jenn had expected, making holding her down difficult.

'Your belt!' she shouted up to Jamie. 'Tie her ankles together!'

Jamie looked confused for a second as Sarah continued to fight. She snarled and swore.

'Fuck you all! I'll bite your fucking throats out and watch you die!'

Eventually, Jamie snapped into action and removed his belt. Father Janosch, his hands still full of everything they needed for the ritual, dropped his weight down onto Sarah as well to keep her hips and legs from writhing.

After struggling for a few minutes, his hands slipping in

the rain, Jamie managed to wrap the belt around Sarah's legs, tighten it up, and then tie it into a knot.

'We need to restrain her arms,' Jenn said.

'Jamie,' George shouted while straining. 'Get my belt, too. Quickly!'

Jamie once again sprang into action and pulled George's belt free.

'We need to get her onto her front, then tie her arms behind her back,' George said.

'I'll kill you all!' Sarah said. Her face was twisted into a furious and hateful glare. 'I'll tear your fucking guts out with my bare hands.'

Jenn tried to ignore the threats. 'On three we roll her,' she said, then began the count. The rain continued to hammer down, soaking Jenn to her core. 'One, two... three!'

She and George worked as one and flipped Sarah over, driving her face-first into the paving slabs of the courtyard. The hand George had been holding managed to get free, however, and Sarah managed to quickly grab him by the balls.

George let out a pain-filled shriek, but Father Janosch and Jamie were quick to force Sarah's arm behind her back, where it met the one Jenn was fighting with. George, with tears in his eyes and wincing in pain, then wrapped his belt around Sarah's wrists and tied a strong knot in it.

The four then backed away from Sarah, who lay on the ground, still writhing and swearing, but stuck.

'I'll fucking kill you all!' she bellowed.

'We need to move quickly,' Father Janosch instructed. 'Back to David. Now.'

49

BACK IN THE DINING ROOM, Jenn handed off the first-aid kit to David while Luca set down everything they had gathered.

The salt, for drawing out the protective symbol.

The Bible, for reciting the words of God.

Candles, earth, and water, which combined with the air around them to make up the four elements.

And the mirror, as well, to reveal the otherworld. It would be the anchor that held everything together. It would need to be broken in order to end the ritual.

While Ann removed Ralph's hoodie, David opened the first-aid kit and pulled out an alcoholic wipe—it wasn't much, but it was all he had. He used it to clean Ralph's cut as the big man screamed in pain. Ralph moaned as he bled onto the dining room table, his blood staining the wooden surface beneath him.

However, Luca concentrated on the ledger, reading through the ritual again and again to make sure he could commit it to memory. It was relatively straightforward, which was good, but unbelievably dangerous.

He added some of the salt to his flask of water, then

recited a prayer over it in order to bless it and create holy water. He repeated the same prayer over the mud in the container.

Air and fire would need to be blessed downstairs when inside the seal.

David applied a thick layer of gauze over Ralph's wound and took out a roll of tape from the first-aid kit. He stretched a length over the gauze, crudely sealing it down.

Ralph looked pale, and in a great deal of pain. However, he was very much conscious. Luca wasn't a medical expert, but he was sure that was a good sign.

Luca noticed David looked odd as well. He almost seemed distracted somehow. Ann too. Luca had to wonder if something had happened while the rest of them were away gathering supplies.

'We ran into Sarah outside,' Jamie said to David and Ann.

'What happened?' Ann asked.

'She tried to attack us, but we managed to subdue her,' George answered. 'We tied her up, but I don't think it will keep her down for long.'

'We had our own run-in,' Ann replied.

'Don't,' David quickly snapped. 'We don't have time.'

Ann looked surprised at being shut down so abruptly, and more than a little annoyed, but she didn't press the point.

Luca was keen to hear their experience but didn't have time to probe it either. They needed to work quickly.

'Okay,' he said to the rest of the team. 'We need to get down to the basement.'

All of them, even Ralph, turned to look at him.

'Are you serious?' Jamie asked. 'Why?'

'We need to get to the lowest point that we can. It will help speed up *Claude Ianua*.'

'Why does that make any difference?' George questioned. 'Why can't we do it here?'

'The farther down we are, the stronger the connection with the doorway. That's what it says in *Ianua Diaboli*, and we need all the help we can get. So we need to move.'

'What about Ralph?' Jenn said. 'We can't risk moving him.'

'We have to,' Luca replied. He hated pressing the matter, as Ralph was clearly struggling, but the result of them failing in their task didn't bear thinking about. Their own lives, though he didn't say it outright to them, had to be expendable.

The realisation caused Luca to pause. It was hard not to be overwhelmed by how quickly the stakes had risen.

'I'll need you all to help carry me down there,' Ralph said. 'But if that's what we need to do, let's go.'

Luca was worried about the big man. His pallor was not a healthy one, and a film of sweat covered his face. However, Ralph seemed to be aware of the urgency of the situation, and Luca was thankful for the support.

Of course, Luca sincerely hoped Ralph *didn't* die. But more critically, he really hoped Ralph didn't die before they closed the door. That was all that was important.

Perhaps that made Luca a terrible priest. However, it was a guilt he would have to wrestle with another day. They needed to move, but the others also needed to know their roles going forward as time would be of the essence when downstairs.

'When we get to the basement we need to keep together so that I can mark out a protective seal with the salt. Then I'll put the mirror at the centre of the seal. Lastly, I'll need to spill my blood on both. Once that is done, we should be safe inside the seal. Step one will be complete, and the spirits here will not be able to reach us.'

'Could Sarah get to us, though?' David asked.

Luca didn't have the answer. 'I... don't know. Because of that, we need to be alert. Regardless, we then light the candles and place them around the perimeter. I will sprinkle the earth and the water there as well. These are the elements we use to re-establish the dominance of our reality: fire, earth, and water, and even the air we are breathing. Then I will recite a passage from *Ianua Diaboli* to start the ritual. Doing so will create a temporary merging.'

'A fucking *what?*' Jamie asked. 'Are you serious, you're going to join our world to... Hell?'

'I will only be merging Perron Manor, but yes, that is correct,' Luca confirmed. 'Doing that will give the house much more power, so it will be a very dangerous time. That is why we need the seal. Once the door is fully open, we smash the mirror, the anchor, and it closes the door permanently.

'Is that it?' David asked. 'Seems simple.'

'It is,' Luca replied. 'Opening the doors is more difficult. They require sacrifice, but closing them is only about re-establishing the Earth's dominance. At the moment, Perron Manor exists with a foot in each reality. Closing the door changes that. But remember that the house will be fighting us. As will Sarah, if she gets free.'

'Then we need to get moving,' Ralph said, pushing himself up to a sitting position.

David and the rest of the group quickly moved over to Ralph and helped him from the table, while Luca gathered up what they needed for the ritual, including the books and his Bible.

He just hoped his faith was strong enough.

Claude Ianua had to be initiated by a holy person. The specific faith did not matter, as long as the person had turned their back on darkness and dedicated their life to the light.

Once the merger was in full flow, Luca would need to keep reciting words from a holy text—in this case, the Bible —to fight the power coming through the Devil's Door. However, if his belief was not absolute... they were in trouble.

'Okay everyone,' he said. 'Let's go.'

50

I can't fail.

Sarah continued to roll and slither over the wet pavement, feeling the rain soak through her clothes. She was cold and angry, and had to resort to wriggling across the ground like a worm.

She had been stupid—tricked far too easily. Now the others were inside and had locked the door behind them.

But they had also been stupid. Very stupid. Sarah's knife, which had fallen from her hand after Jenn and George had tackled her, had been forgotten.

All she had to do was reach it, and then use it to cut herself free. Doing so while tied up with her arms behind her back would be difficult but doable. She would just have to be careful not to accidentally slice her wrists in the process.

Fight it!

Sarah shook her head to try and exorcise that dissenting voice. She had to ignore it and listen to the will of the house.

Her skin tingled, feeling alive and almost on fire. It had felt that way since the previous night. On top of that constant sensation, she could now also feel an anger radiate from the house. It was aimed directly at her.

'*Get up!*'

Sarah quickly rolled over to her back and squinted through the cold rain that cascaded down onto her face.

'Chloe?'

Sarah's sister stood above her, naked and rotted. Her milky eyes burned with anger.

'*You need to kill to come home to me,*' she said in a hoarse, pained voice. '*If they succeed and close the door, you'll lose me forever. Get up and kill!*'

'I will,' Sarah promised. Before her very eyes, the form of her sister started to dissipate, then blew away like dust in the wind.

Just before Chloe did, however, Sarah noticed something; the hateful expression faltered, if only for a second, and was replaced by something entirely more mournful.

Sarah shook her head and rolled back over, again making her way towards the knife. She planned to get free of her bonds and gut every single person inside the house.

Then she would be home. Back with Chloe forever.

51

DAVID WAS STRAINING under Ralph's weight. He had one of the man's arms draped over his shoulder while George held the other.

Ralph had insisted he could walk, but needed aid. That helped, as there was no way they could have carried his full weight down the narrow stone steps without dropping him.

The big man was in a great deal of pain still, made worse by being moved around, but he was still conscious and alert. It gave David hope that the stab wound might not be fatal... as long as they could get him medical attention soon.

Father Janosch and Ann led the way through the corridors towards the great hall, with Jamie and Jenn bringing up the rear.

'Jesus, Ralph,' George exclaimed as they neared the hall. 'How much do you weigh?'

Ralph managed a laugh as he winced. 'That's a bit of a personal question, George.'

As they moved, David kept his eyes peeled. It was hard not to expect something to leap from one of the doorways they passed, but they managed to get to the great hall unhindered.

Once inside, however, all of the lights blinked off and plunged them into darkness.

'Shit!' Ann said.

David was scared but not surprised. Did he really expect the route down to the basement to be a simple one?

'*Ring-o-ring-o-roses*,' a throaty, distorted voice called out from the far side of the hall.

Through the darkness, David could make out the form of a tall, pale man standing against the far wall. He was dressed in a dirty suit, and his eyes were little more than black pits.

'Shit!' Ann said again. 'Shit, shit, shit! What do we do?'

'We keep going,' Luca said and held out his flask of holy water before him, the top unscrewed.

The door to the steps was on the same side of the hall as they were, so the ghostly watcher was not blocking their path, though it was certainly a worrying presence.

David cast a glance out through the rear glazed door. He knew the others had tied Sarah up out there. However, he could see no sign of her. The security light was off, limiting how far he was able to see, which in itself was strange. If Sarah was in the courtyard and moving—even wriggling— she should have activated the light's sensors.

Ralph's weight was starting to cause David's neck to cramp up, but he kept on going. Soon they were at the door, with the pale man doing nothing but watching. Father Janosch pulled it open.

Ann screamed first.

George quickly stepped backwards, pulling Ralph and David with him as David nearly lost his footing. Father

Janosch instinctively raised his hand again, holding the holy water out before him like a weapon.

Chloe stood on the other side of the door.

She was naked, her body resembling a decomposed corpse —just as Katie's had—and her face was twisted into something demonic. Her mouth was wider than it should be, and her teeth were sharper and blacker than they had been in life.

'Back!' Father Janosch commanded, but even David could sense the older man's fear.

Chloe giggled. *'You're all going to die here.'*

Luca quickly flicked his arm forward and sprayed Chloe with a mist of water from his flask. It coated her face. Her milky eyes went wide, and she dropped her head back then screamed.

It wasn't a human noise, too high-pitched and animalistic, and David could have sworn he picked up the sound of a bleating goat mixed in with the cries.

The spirit of Sarah's sister then backed up, bringing her hands up to her face as she continued to shriek. Father Janosch doused her again and again.

Chloe then looked up. David was startled to see she now looked different. Though her body was still ruined, her face was more reminiscent of when she was alive. The skin was smoother and pale, with red cheeks, and her eyes once again had their brown irises.

Most importantly, she no longer looked hateful. She looked... terrified.

'Help me,' she said before quickly vanishing right before their eyes. Her voice still echoed even after her form had disappeared.

'What the hell was that?' Jamie asked.

However, there was no time to deliberate. A light had

drawn David's attention, and he turned again to the rear door. Sarah stood outside, soaked to the bone, with wild eyes and a knife in hand.

He hoped to God the others had locked that door after coming inside.

'We need to go,' Father Janosch instructed. It was then the tall, pale man finally moved, drifting over to the door. David couldn't help but watch the slow, silent glide.

A long, spindly hand rose up and touched the glass of the door. It shattered in an instant, exploding outward and coating Sarah, who didn't take her eyes off David the whole time.

'We need to go *now!*' Jenn then yelled. She grabbed hold of David and George, pulling them all forward towards the steps. Jamie slammed the door shut behind them, but there was no lock to hold Sarah back.

As a group, they all thundered down the narrow stone stairwell but were moving too quickly, and supporting Ralph proved impossible. He fell from their grasp, pitching forward into Father Janosch and Ann. David tried to grab at Ralph again but succeeded only in being dragged forward as well.

David tumbled down with the others, with the slapping of bodies on the hard stone steps ringing out along with the groans of pain from his team.

52

JENN RAN down the steps with Jamie and Ann beside her, looking on in horror as the others lay in an intertwined heap.

'Are you okay?' she shouted.

The replies were groans of pain. Ralph held a hand to his stomach, where Jenn could see fresh blood wet his t-shirt again.

'Everybody up!' she quickly demanded. Sarah wouldn't be far behind, so they needed to move. Jenn carefully stepped over David and entered into the dark basement, helping Father Janosch up, who looked unsteady on his feet.

The items he needed had fallen to the floor and were strewn about the area.

'Quickly!' Jenn ordered. She helped up David and George, before finally assisting with Ralph.

Father Janosch began gathering his things. Then, the door above them opened with a long, slow squeak.

'Move!' Ann yelled.

As one, they all shuffled farther into the basement and

were swallowed up by the dark. It was bad enough upstairs in the great hall, but at least there had been moonlight seeping in through the windows. Down here, they were underground, with no natural light to help them.

'I... I'm missing something,' Father Janosch said, panicked. Jenn felt the toe of her shoe strike something, and she bent down to retrieve a container she had kicked. It was the salt.

Jenn could hear slow and steady footsteps make their way down the steps. Suddenly, a burst of fire erupted from the furnace at the far side of the basement, powerful enough that it sounded like an explosion, blowing open the doors on the front. The flames continued—a roaring inferno with a figure caught inside.

A man with blackened, melted features leaned out from the metal structure, glaring at them with his one good eye.

The flames from the furnace cast a flickering glow over the whole basement, and Jenn could see that other spirits of the dead were also there with them. They stood around the perimeter of the area, watching: a man holding his own insides; a short, stocky blonde woman of advanced years; and the man with brushed-back hair and an open throat, whom they had earlier identified as Marcus Blackwater.

There was also a corpse-like woman with a crushed breast, and half a man who writhed around on the floor in a pool of his own blood, his bottom half completely missing. In fact, the more Jenn looked around, the more other spirits seemed to appear.

But it was not just spirits. There were tall, spindly forms in amongst the dead, with elongated arms, twisted faces, and obsidian bodies.

Demons.

One in particular was taller than the others, with a large mouth full of nightmarish teeth and facial features that had melted like wax. She had seen this thing before, back in 2014.

Pazuzu.

Jenn thrust the container of salt into Father Janosch's hands. 'The seal!' she shouted. 'Hurry!'

'I need the book!' Father Janosch shouted back, looking around frantically.

The spirits around the edges of the room started to slowly advance.

'Here,' George said and passed *Ianua Diaboli* to the priest.

Father Janosch set the book down on the ground, turning the pages to the back to study the illustrations shown in *Claude Ianua*.

'Get the other things,' Father Janosch demanded. 'Quickly.' He started to pour the salt out into a crude circle wide enough to fit everyone in it.

The ghosts continued to move closer, and Sarah emerged out into the basement from the steps. She walked at a leisurely pace.

With Ralph lying on the floor within the salt circle, the others quickly stepped inside as well, now with all the elements they needed. Jenn double-checked to make sure they had everything.

Father Janosch then started to work around them, drawing out additional lines inside the circle.

'Is that... a pentagram?' Jenn asked.

'It is,' Father Janosch replied. 'The tip needs to point north. Then it is a symbol of protection. If it is inverted, that's when it invokes the demonic.'

He worked quickly. However, Jenn was concerned. Sarah didn't seem to be in any rush, and neither did any of the horrific entities that slowly closed in as well.

Why?

'It's done,' Father Janosch said. He positioned the mirror in the centre, shuffling Ralph aside, then grabbed at the thin, silver crucifix he wore around his neck, yanking and snapping the chain.

Jenn winced when she saw the priest drive the edge down into the flesh of the back of his hand, piercing the skin. With gritted teeth, he sliced the bottom of the crucifix down over his hand, cutting through the prominent veins and drawing blood.

Father Janosch was clearly in pain, but he pinched the skin together along the cut to force out more blood, then let it drip down onto the mirror and the salt outlines of the seal.

He let out a visible sigh of relief.

'It's done,' he said. The closest spirits to them slowly moved to the outer edges of the symbol and stopped. There, they just watched. More and more gathered around, and Jenn felt panicked as they became trapped and surrounded. But just as Father Janosch had said, it seemed that they could not gain entry. Pazuzu and the other demons all stalked their way to the front of the crowd, bearing down on the team and glaring with eyes that burned yellow.

'Leave us alone!' Ann yelled as she cowered in fear. David looked horrified... but also defeated.

Father Janosch was still working, setting up the candles around the inside edges of the seal. Jenn pulled out the box of matches she had earlier jammed into her pocket and began to light the candles.

She saw movement through the crowd. Sarah was

pushing her way through to them, wearing a condescending smile.

'Ignore her,' Father Janosch said. 'She can't hurt us now. We are safe.'

Regardless, Jenn still stepped back away from the edges as Father Janosch sprinkled dirt from the container on the ground, followed by holy water from his flask.

With everything set, he grabbed his Bible and began to recite words from its pages.

'I will bless the Lord at all times; praise shall be always in my mouth.'

Sarah laughed.

Something's wrong, Jenn thought to herself. *She's too confident.*

'Are you sure you are so safe, *priest?*' Sarah asked. Her voice dripped with malice.

Father Janosch kept going for a little while longer, reciting more from his Bible. When finished, he turned to Sarah.

'I am quite sure,' he said, staring her down. 'The elements are blessed. Fire, water, the earth, even the air around us. And the fifth element, too: the souls within the circle. We are protected, and *Claude Ianua* has begun.'

He then bent down and retrieved *Ianua Diaboli,* and he started to read from the open pages, loudly uttering Latin verses from the ritual.

'Oh Father,' Sarah said, waving her hand to get his attention. 'Your little seal will only hold me back if the faith of those inside is strong enough. I wonder... are you confident of that?'

'We all believe!' Jenn snapped and stepped forward. 'How can we not? Look at all the souls trapped here—

damned and in purgatory. If Hell is truly real, then Heaven and the Lord *have* to be.'

Sarah shook her head. 'Not necessarily. And besides, David over there knows you are all fucked, don't you, David?'

David said nothing; he just scowled at Sarah. Father Janosch continued with his rites.

'And,' Sarah went on, 'your priest has about as much true faith as I do. He's a liar, a coward... a wretched excuse for a so-called 'holy man.''

Father Janosch continued unabated, repeating the same phrases over and over.

'Aperi ostium conjungere mundos. Infera et terra inter se illigantur. Vera forma revelatur ut ancora auferatur.'

'Keep going,' Sarah said. 'Open the door wider. Give me more strength.'

A rumbling sound from all around them drew shrieks of fear from the team. The thundering increased to an intense booming sound, as if something massive were striking the very reality of their surroundings.

'What the hell is that?' George asked as he moved his hands over his ears. Father Janosch kept going.

Jenn knew what was happening. The door was opening.

She happened to cast her eyes down to the mirror and drew in a breath at what she saw.

Instead of the concrete beams of the ceiling above, the reflection in the mirror showed something else. No longer concrete, the surface was made up of... flesh—red, glistening meat. And worse, it writhed and moved as human bodies emerged from within it, all of them trapped and screaming.

The souls of the dead.

It occurred to Jenn that *this* was how they existed in Hell. Fused to the form of the house.

The booms continued, getting louder and louder.

'Look!' Ann screamed, pointing to the walls.

What the fuck... Jenn could scarcely believe what she was seeing. The walls, floor, and ceiling of the basement were all changing, matching what she had seen in the reflection.

The walls bled as they turned to meat. Withered, human forms partially broke free, arms and legs flailing. Some were only faces, trapped within the fleshy surface around them and screaming manically. The noise around Jenn and the others rose dramatically, with the cries of agony becoming deafening.

'David!' Father Janosch yelled. 'Grab the mirror.' David was slow in moving, but eventually picked up the mirror from the ground.

Father Janosch turned to Sarah and gave a forced smile. 'It worked,' he shouted at her.

Though what was happening might have been part of the plan, he still looked as terrified as Jenn felt.

'It has indeed,' Sarah replied, just audible over the chaotic cacophony. 'As I said, your seal may keep out my brothers and sisters,' she motioned to the watching dead and demons that surrounded the circle, 'but now that you have opened the door and infused me with power, you can only keep me out if your faith is absolute.'

'My faith *is* absolute,' Father Janosch shouted back.

Sarah shook her head. She then picked up a foot and dropped it onto the salt line of the circle. With a swipe of her leg, the seal was quickly and easily broken.

Jenn was shocked.

What the fuck?

Sarah quickly stepped forward, lunging towards Jenn, who was unable to react in time.

She felt the knife penetrate her gut and bury itself right up to the hilt.

'No!' Father Janosch yelled.

Sarah yanked the knife sideways across Jenn's stomach. Jenn screamed, feeling her insides bubble free.

53

DAVID WAS IN SHOCK.

Jenn dropped to the ground, holding her stomach as blood poured free through the slash in her t-shirt. She looked utterly surprised, eyes wide, not really comprehending what had just happened.

Fleshy red intestines pushed their way out through her split skin.

Sarah stood above her and raised the knife again. At the same moment, with the seal broken, the masses of the dead, along with their demon brothers, advanced onto the helpless team.

They were dead. All of them. They had failed.

Something inside of David snapped, and he bellowed out a roar born of both fear and fury. He threw himself forward and crashed into Sarah, forcing her down to her back and landing on top of her. The mirror he held fell from his hand down beside them. He saw her knife drop as well, clattering down close to the mirror.

David was vaguely aware of Father Janosch screaming

something at him, but he was so focused on hurting Sarah that he didn't take the words in.

However, just as he positioned himself atop her, Sarah's hands reached up and grabbed his throat. A leg then snaked its way up in front of him, and she drove the sole of her foot up, connecting with the bridge of his nose.

David felt cartilage break and crunch beneath her driving heel. The world spun and pain erupted in his face.

Before he knew it, Sarah had reversed their positions, and he was easily forced to the ground. She quickly rolled on top of David, straddling him.

As chaos erupted around him, and he saw his team dragged away by the hordes of the dead in the basement, he heard Jenn spluttering and wheezing from somewhere close, gasping for breath.

Sarah stared down at him with a look of wild glee on her face.

54

I'VE DONE IT!

Jenn was going to die; she wouldn't last long with her stomach cut open like that. Sarah's role was complete.

She could then forever be with the one person she had failed most of all—Chloe. They could be together forever at Perron Manor. Sarah's skin still tingled, and it made her feel alive. A constant, buzzing sensation seemed to emanate from her very molecules.

What are you doing? Stop this! Fight it!

She shook her head. That dissenting voice needed to be quashed. It had been lingering in the back of her mind since the previous night, when she had been fully turned. That was when her eyes had been opened.

Killing David would finally snuff out the annoying remnant of her former self.

Sarah reached down towards the knife beside her, using her fingers to push the mirror out of the way.

'*Don't!*'

It was a voice she recognised, and Sarah gazed up to see

her sister standing before her. However, Chloe looked different than she had out in the courtyard.

While much of her body still exhibited the exquisite rot and ruin bestowed by Perron Manor, her face now seemed almost... human.

And she appeared to be in great pain. Chloe was clearly fighting against something, as her body was locked and shaking. Straining.

'*Don't do it. Fight it.*'

'I'm coming home to you, Sis,' Sarah said. 'There's no need to be scared.'

Chloe was crying. '*This isn't you. Fight it. You're a warrior. Fight it!*'

Sarah paused. What the hell was Chloe saying? She couldn't go against the house.

Screams from the others drew Sarah's attention as her fingers felt around for the knife. She turned her head and saw that Jenn lay on her back, holding her stomach, taking short sharp breaths. Her eyes were wide and staring at the ceiling.

Death was coming for her.

Father Janosch was being pulled to the ground, helpless as the spirts of the damned clawed for a part of him.

Jamie screeched in pain when Pazuzu, the stubborn and rebellious one, the opener of gates, took hold of his jaw in one long, talon-like claw. The jaw was ripped clean off. Then long fingers of the other hand bored through his eyes.

You're doing this. Jamie is dead because of you. Jenn will be soon. And Ralph. Listen to Chloe. Fight it.

Sarah looked down to David, who looked utterly defeated. He was crying.

But this was good. It was what the house wanted. All was right.

'*Fight it!*' Chloe yelled.

Fight.

Sarah clenched her teeth together. Her body tensed up and her mind swam with confusion, like it was about to split in two.

She just had to kill David. Grab the knife that was close to her hand and drive it down into his throat. Then all would be well.

Fight it.

Obey.

Fight!

Sarah let out a scream as her body shook. Her fingers found what she was looking for.

She brought the object up high above her head, gripping it in both hands. David turned away and closed his eyes.

Sarah thrust her arms down as she continued her scream.

The mirror in her grasp crunched and broke on the hard ground next to David's head. The lid snapped off and the glass shattered into small pieces.

Everything stopped.

The chaos that had previously surrounded Sarah drew to an immediate halt. All eyes turned to her.

The pale faces of the dead stared in confusion, as did the demonic entities. Pazuzu, with a blood-stained hand, dropped Jamie's lifeless body and stepped closer to her. It tilted its head. Even the previously writhing bodies trapped within the walls stopped moving and crying in pain.

Pazuzu let its head drop back and bellowed out a horrible, deafening screech.

Sarah's mind, previously so clouded and confused, suddenly became clear, like a terrible and painful fog had suddenly dissipated. Her skin still tingled, like pins and needles across her entire body.

She looked again to Jamie, then to Jenn.

What have I done?

Sarah quickly backed off David and pulled her knees up to her chest.

Oh God, oh God, oh God. No, no, no.

Jenn's breathing was growing slower, becoming more laboured. Still none of the dead moved. David quickly scrambled over to his fallen friend.

'Jenn!' He took her hand and cupped her face. 'Jenn!'

No, no, no.

The walls around them began to change yet again. The wet flesh melted away, running down to the floor and disappearing to reveal once again the stone structure behind. The bodies within the walls fell free. Their appearance softened and became more human.

So too did the appearance of the gathered dead who stood in watch. All their deformities and disfigurements were stripped away. The rotted bodies changed, soon looking much more healthy and normal.

Then, the dead slowly started to disappear. The sensation Sarah felt on her skin, that tingling, started to fade away with them.

Pazuzu let out another roar before it melted into the darkness that swallowed up the room once again when the furnace dampened out to nothing. Sarah felt something approach her.

She turned her head up to see Chloe. However, her sister didn't seem pained anymore. She looked beautiful, without pain or worry.

Chloe was flanked by Jamie... and Jenn.

Sarah quickly turned to see David crying over Jenn's

motionless body—blood still spilling out to the floor below her.

No!

Sarah looked up to her sister, Jenn, and Jamie. They were smiling. Jenn just gave Sarah a sad wave, took Jamie's hand, and then moved away into the darkness.

'I'm sorry,' Sarah said. 'I'm so, so sorry.' Tears fell from her eyes. Her heart was broken.

I caused this.

She had lied in order to bring the team here in the first place, and then she had killed Jenn with her own hands.

Chloe knelt down in front of her, and Sarah picked up on the familiar scent of lavender. A warm hand touched her shoulder.

'I'm sorry for everything, Chloe,' Sarah said. 'It's all my fault. Chloe... I'm so sorry.'

'Sarah?' a soft voice asked. It was Father Janosch, who was sitting up, his clothes in tatters and his hair a mess. However, he looked unharmed. 'Who are you talking to?'

She looked back to Chloe. 'Don't you see her?' Sarah asked.

He shook his head.

Ann was sobbing on the floor, and George had moved close to Jamie, his face a picture of revulsion and shock. David continued to cry over Jenn's body.

Chloe leaned forward, and Sarah felt a flood of warmth radiate out from the lips that touched her forehead.

'Thank you,' Chloe said. Her voice was little more than a whisper.

Chloe then stood up and turned around.

'Don't go!' Sarah cried. 'Please, don't go! I can't cope without you!'

Chloe's eyes were sad, but she stepped away into the darkness, disappearing from Sarah forever.

55

LUCA STOOD TO HIS FEET. Everything was a mess. Jamie and Jenn were clearly dead. Ralph's breathing was growing more laboured.

It had been close to twenty minutes since Sarah had broken the mirror, and everything had ceased in an instant.

The house around him felt different. He knew without question they had done it: completed the ritual of *Claude Ianua*.

The Devil's Door had been closed permanently.

But at what cost?

Everyone sat numb. Ann still cried loudly. Sarah's sobs were soft. Ralph stared up to the ceiling; if they didn't get him help soon, he would die as well.

Luca walked over to David, his legs shaking beneath him as he did. He knelt down. Jenn's terrified expression was frozen on her face, eyes wide open, hands on her stomach. Luca moved a hand over to her eyes and closed them.

'David,' he whispered. 'Ralph still needs help. We need to call an ambulance if we can. Or get him to a hospital somehow.'

David didn't look away from Jenn.

'What the hell happened here, Father?' he asked. His voice was so full of pain that Luca's heart broke for him. It broke for them all.

'I don't know,' Luca replied. 'It's hard to comprehend. But we did it. We stopped what was happening. That's something.'

'Two of my friends are dead,' David said angrily. There was a silence between them for a few moments. Eventually, David turned to Luca. 'I saw someone I knew here, you know,' he said. 'Just before we came down to the basement. It was my stepsister, Katie. A long time ago she went missing in this house. That's... that's what has always drawn me to it. Katie—or the thing pretending to be her—told me that the house had a plan. Something it had been orchestrating for a long time. Apparently that's why my sister was taken in the first place. And why Chloe was killed, too. All to get Sarah here to... to do what she almost did.'

'I know,' Luca said. He hadn't known about Katie, that was a surprise to him, but he was aware the house had been manipulating events for many years prior, even if he could scarcely comprehend *how* that was possible.

'What I don't get,' David went on, 'is if the house was able to line things up like that... how were we able to stop it? How could we stand in the way of a force like that?'

It was a good question. 'Perhaps,' Luca replied, 'because there was a force working with *us* as well.' The words made sense as soon as he said them. In fact, he got an over-whelming and unexplainable feeling that he was absolutely correct, despite making it up on the fly to help make his friend feel better. After all, what were the chances of a priest with a prior knowledge of the Devil Door's and *Ianua Diaboli* being called to Perron Manor to give aid? 'Maybe that other force helped the house align everything and make sure we were where we needed to be. Just not in the way the house wanted.'

'All so that Jenn and Jamie could die?'

Luca paused. How could he answer a question like that?

The truth was that, unfortunately, the sacrifice *was* worth it, given the stakes. But as a survivor, did he have any right to feel that way?

'David,' Luca went on, 'if we don't act quickly, Ralph could be next. And we don't want that to happen, do we?'

David, still looking at Jenn, shook his head.

Luca held out a hand to him. 'Come on, let's go.'

56

THE RAIN HAD EASED. Everyone except Ralph and Ann was outside. Sarah stood on her own as Father Janosch, David, and George all huddled together away from her, speaking in hushed whispers. Ralph lay just inside the entrance door with a coat over him. Ann knelt by his side.

Sarah hugged herself, pulling tighter the coat Father Janosch had handed her on the way out.

As numb as Sarah felt, she was aware of the disgusted glances she was getting from David and George. And every time she turned around to look at Ann, she was met with a furious death stare.

Sarah couldn't blame any of them.

She had killed Jenn. She was the reason Jamie was dead.

More blood on her hands.

Luca had insisted they all come outside to try and call an ambulance. This time, the call connected straight away. He had told the operator there had been a terrible accident, but when he divulged the nature of the injury—a stab wound— the operator said the police would be sent as well.

Luca then told the operator that there were also two

dead bodies. After all, how could he hide something like that?

Sarah could only imagine how many police would now show up.

More death at Perron Manor, the creepy old place in the middle of nowhere. More souls to add to its legend.

'Devil's House has struck again,' the locals would say.

However, Sarah knew the truth. This would be the last tale about Perron Manor. Its story was finished.

She saw Father Janosch turn from the others and make his way over to her.

'How are you holding up?' he asked.

It was a ridiculous question considering what they had all been through, as she was holding up the same as the others: in a total state of shock.

Though she had more weighing on her than the others, as *she* was the one who had taken a life. Possessed or not.

However, Father Janosch had asked the question from a place of concern, and Sarah was appreciative of it.

'I honestly don't know,' she whispered.

Father Janosch nodded in understanding, then waited for a little while before he went on. 'Sarah, down there in the basement, when everything ended... you were talking to someone. Chloe, I think you said.'

Sarah nodded. 'She was down there, but she looked normal again. Like she did in life.'

'We didn't see her,' he said. 'After you broke the mirror, it was like a snap, and then all the madness around us was gone in an instant.'

'I saw things a little differently,' Sarah said. 'The world slowly changed back to normal. All the spirits shifted as well, turning into something more peaceful. I think they're finally free. All of them. In fact, I'm sure of it.'

'And did your sister speak to you?'

'A little. She said 'thank you.' I know how this is going to sound, but I saw Jenn and Jamie as well. They were next to Chloe.'

Father Janosch drew in a deep breath. 'Okay.'

'Do you think I should tell the others?'

He looked over to them, then back to Sarah. 'I'm not sure. Maybe not at the moment... it would be a lot to take in. What happened to Chloe and the others when she finished passing on her message?'

'They turned and all walked away into the darkness. They left. I don't know exactly where they all went, but they're gone now. I know that for certain, because I can't feel them anymore.'

Father Janosch cocked his head to the side. 'Feel them?'

Sarah bit her lip, thinking how best to put her experience into words. 'Ever since I woke up under the control of the house, my skin... it almost felt like it was on fire. A tingle, or an itch, over every inch of me. It's not something I've ever felt before. But when the door was closing down there in the basement, and the spirits were leaving, the sensation dulled. And when Chloe left, it stopped completely. That's when I knew the door was fully closed... I just *felt* it. And now I know there are no more souls trapped in the house.'

'Because you can't feel them anymore,' Father Janosch said.

'I suppose that sounds stupid.'

The priest smiled. 'Not at all. Considering what we've been through, nothing sounds stupid.' He then narrowed his eyes and rubbed his chin. 'I wonder if being under the possession of the house has left its mark on you.'

'How do you mean?'

'Well, you saw things the rest of us did not. And you sensed when the door had been closed. Perhaps you are left with a gift: seeing and sensing things others can't.'

Sarah shook her head, dismissively. 'I don't think that's true...' But she paused. It wasn't the first time in her life that notion had entered her mind.

'What is it?' he asked.

'Back in the army,' she replied, 'when I lost my best friend. I was supposed to be on point that day, but an inexplicable fear took over me. I just couldn't do it. I've never been able to explain why that happened. My friend took over the duties that day and died for it. I lived. I could never understand why.'

'The house,' Father Janosch said. 'It kept you safe, so that it could call you back. Perhaps you've always had the gift, because of who you are and how you were born. And now it is... I don't know, amplified?'

'So I'm a freak,' Sarah said angrily.

He shook his head. 'No, not a freak at all. None of us can help how we are born; all we can do is control our own decisions in life.'

'I couldn't even do that,' Sarah said. 'I was a puppet.'

'But not anymore,' Father Janosch stated firmly.

They both heard the police sirens in the distance. 'Actually, Father,' Sarah said, 'I don't think I'll be making any of my own decisions for a long time.'

'What do you mean?'

She was surprised at how naïve the priest was being. Hadn't he thought it through?

Sarah again looked over to David and George. 'They're never going to forgive me, are they?' she asked. 'Any of them.'

'Well, they're a little bit shellshocked at the moment. We

all are. But they'll come around. You weren't acting under your own power, Sarah. It was the house, not you. In fact, you even managed to beat it. Don't forget it was *you* who broke the mirror and completed the ritual. *You* closed that door and *you* released all the souls inside Perron Manor... including David's sister.'

'It was *me* that brought everyone here because of a lie. *I* got Jenn and Jamie killed.'

'And if you didn't bring them, how many more lives would this house have taken in the future? It would have brought you back here eventually. Who knows, it might have succeeded and turned you completely. Perhaps everything that happened here played out as it was supposed to.'

'If that's the case, it's only going to finish one way now.'

'The police,' Father Janosch said with a slow nod. So he *had* thought about it.

'Yes. Jenn's stomach has been cut open. Ralph's been stabbed. My fingerprints will be all over the knife, because I was the one wielding it. Jamie's injuries are not going to be easily explained, but the police will want answers.'

'We'll tell them the truth,' Father Janosch said.

'The truth is insane. They won't believe us.'

'I will seek assistance from the Church, then. They can help us and—'

'It was *me*,' Sarah said as the siren drew nearer. She saw vehicles heading down the drive.

'What was?'

'When the police ask who did it, you tell them *I* did. All of it. I stabbed Ralph. Killed Jenn. Did... *that* to Jamie. Tell them I was driven mad at the loss of my sister or something. No sense in any of the others ruining their lives over this.'

Father Janosch shook his head. 'I can't lie about that, Sarah. I won't.'

'Then they'll think you're nuts too. Just tell the others to go along with it. They won't speak to me and I know they'll never forgive me. I don't blame them. But I can do this much for them. They shouldn't be hard to convince.'

'Sarah, I—'

'Tell them!' Sarah yelled.

Father Janosch jumped in shock and took a step back. An ambulance and two police cars pulled up.

'Please,' she begged with tears in her eyes. She then turned and walked over to the police, though not before turning her head to give Perron Manor one last glance. She looked at the window where she had seen Chloe only a few weeks before, begging for help.

The house was clear.

TWO WEEKS LATER...

Luca sat in one of the back offices at Newcastle Cathe-dral—officially called the Cathedral Church of St. Nicholas.

With the room's polished hardwood floors, dark wooden panelling to the walls, and high ceilings with ornate coving, for a moment Luca thought he was back in Perron Manor. It was unnerving that a house so evil could have so much in common with the house of God. Thankfully, Luca just had to look out of one of the high windows at the city of Newcastle outside—and not the landscape of rolling hills and countryside—to know he was back in civilisation.

Perron Manor was behind him now. But the effects and fall-out were not.

Bishop Turnbull sat opposite him, on the other side of a large, mahogany meeting table. The Bishop was flanked by older men, four on one side and three on the other. Luca had no idea who the other people were, but they carried an air of authority about them. Each was dressed in a cassock, as was Bishop Turnbull, and they looked at Luca intently.

He felt like he was sitting down for a job interview.

'Thank you for coming in,' Bishop Turnbull began. He was a thin man in his late fifties, and his bald head had some liver spots showing. He wore rimless glasses which were perched on a long, thin nose, with dark-brown eyes behind them. 'I passed on your report and debriefing to my superiors.' He gestured to the men that flanked him. 'We owe you a great deal of thanks.'

'Not just me,' Luca was quick to point out. 'Miss Pearson, David Ritter, and also David's team did just as much as I. Probably more. Some even gave their lives.'

Bishop Turnbull nodded. 'Yes, we appreciate that. Truly. And we will make sure those who are still here with us are thanked as well. I take it Mr. Cobin is recovering well?'

'Ralph? I believe he will be okay, yes.'

'We need to talk about the others, actually,' Bishop Turnbull said.

'Is that so?'

'Yes. We need to discuss what they experienced. I understand they captured a great deal of footage and evidence as part of their investigation.'

'That's right,' Luca confirmed. 'I'm sure some will still decry it all as fake, but it is there nonetheless.'

Bishop Turnbull looked uncomfortably to the three men sitting to his left. One of them nodded to him, and Turnbull turned back to Luca.

'That evidence can never come out,' he said.

Luca frowned in confusion. 'What do you mean?'

'Exactly what I said. They can't make what they've found public.'

Luca didn't know what to say to that. 'I... don't follow. It's *their* evidence, how are we supposed to stop them doing what they want with it? And more importantly, *why* should we stop them?'

'Because of what the house was. There can be little doubt anymore, given your testimony.'

'And?'

Bishop Turnbull shook his head. 'If word spread of the existence of these doorways—and worse, they were backed up by actual evidence—what do you think the reaction of the public would be?'

Luca thought about it. His answer probably wasn't what they expected. 'Scepticism,' he replied. 'I honestly don't think many people would believe it anyway.'

'No, maybe not everyone. But enough people would. And what if the wrong kind of people or organisations found out about these doors, and tried to use them for their own gains?'

Organisations?

'So you want to keep the truth hidden,' Luca stated.

'We *have* to,' Bishop Turnbull replied. 'Because we still don't know enough. For example, with regards to the Seven Gates—were all open prior to you closing the door at Perron Manor? And who opened the gates in the first place? Can more be opened? Surely you can see our concern and what's at stake.'

Luca could.

Not *everyone* needed to believe what David and his team might announce to the world for it to be a problem, only a few of the wrong sort. Especially if word of *Ianua Diaboli* got out as well. For the Church, it was easier to hide something that no-one knew existed in the first place.

He realised what they were going to ask in regards to the book as well.

'You need *Ianua Diaboli,* don't you.'

'Of course,' Bishop Turnbull said like it was the most

obvious thing in the world. Perhaps it was. 'The book is still at the house, I presume?'

'Yes,' Luca replied. 'And the owner is still locked up awaiting trial, as I'm sure you are also aware. So, if you want it, you would need to speak to her and ask her to give it up. Miss Pearson can be... difficult... to deal with at times.' He smiled fondly as he said it.

'Luca,' Bishop Turnbull went on, 'we want you to ask her to donate the book to the Church. You know her already, so we hope you can convince her.' His voice then took on a grave tone. 'If not, we will have to get the book by other means. But we *will* get it.'

Luca sat back in his chair. 'Wait... you're admitting you would *steal* someone's possession? The Church would stoop that low?'

The man to Bishop Turnbull's right leaned forward, lacing his fingers and setting them on the desk before him. He had a full head of grey hair, a square face, broad shoulders, and grey eyes that showed no emotion. 'You think the Church is above that, Father?' he asked with a gravelly, Eastern European accent. 'Do you not know how our history was built?'

Luca was dumbfounded. 'Of course, but I would have thought we'd moved on from mistakes of the past.'

'Then convince this woman to give us the book,' he stated, and slowly sat back.

Luca looked to Bishop Turnbull for support.

What they were threatening was ludicrous. Had they forgotten just who they were and who they served? Stealing was not something that should be permissible.

And despite Luca asking the Church for assistance in helping Sarah, they had ignored him. It looked like she was going to rot in prison while everything else just moved on.

Bishop Turnbull just looked down, embarrassed. He wasn't calling the shots here, Luca realised. Whoever these men were, they had Turnbull dancing on their strings like a puppet. Turnbull was only the mouthpiece for the meeting, and nothing more.

'We also need to discuss Miss Pearson,' Bishop Turnbull went on.

Luca had no idea what to expect anymore, so he just shrugged. 'Go on.'

'You say that she is now *clavis*—The Key?'

Luca shook his head in exasperation. 'Yes, but she is no longer controlled by anything other than her own free will. The door at Perron Manor is closed now. It has no hold over her. In fact, she beat it. She fought against the possession and defied it long enough to save us all. So she isn't a danger.'

'But she is still the Accursed Blood,' Bishop Turnbull said. 'Whether at Perron Manor or another of these gates, she could still be used as The Key.'

That much was true, but Luca still had no idea what they were implying. 'And...?'

'You say you believe she is now 'sensitive,' after her ordeal?' the Bishop asked, sounding like he was changing tack.

'Well, I believe she always has been sensitive to a degree, given who she is and her bloodline. However, I think the recent possession, where she touched the other side, has heightened those... abilities.'

Bishop Turnbull looked to the man at his side with an uncertain expression. The man beside him did not look back.

'We think she may be able to help us find out if there are other doorways open,' Bishop Turnbull finally said.

Luca frowned in confusion. 'Excuse me?'

'We believe that her 'sensitivity' could help establish whether a suspected location is normal, haunted… or something worse.'

Luca sat forward. 'But she is more susceptible now to the influence of the other side. Yes, I do believe she might be able to sense if a certain location is actually an open gate, but she would also be extremely vulnerable to its power. She would be a double-edged sword.'

'One we would need to wield carefully,' the man with the Eastern European accent said.

'Luca,' Bishop Turnbull went on, 'the Church is worried about these gates. *Very* worried. The order has been given to try and find the existence of any more. If there *are* others, we must close them all. The thing is, we were lucky this time. If all the gates were open prior to closing Perron Manor, who knows how close we came to the end. And until you found that book, we had no idea such things really existed. The Church *will not* be in the dark anymore. We are going to be proactive and seek these things out.'

'I can understand that,' Luca said. 'But Miss Pearson is incarcerated. She—'

'We can see to that issue,' Bishop Turnbull said. 'In fact, we've already put things in motion to help her.'

Luca shook his head, incredulous. 'She's been through enough,' he said.

'She is a soldier,' the Eastern European man said, sternly. 'One now without a cause. Or a family. Make her see, Father Janosch. Show her she could once again have a purpose.'

'But isn't it dangerous putting her into these situations? We are taking the key right to a lock that should not be opened.'

'Well,' Bishop Turnbull went on, 'for now we know that Hell is at least one gate down. And we only need her help to find the gates. She will not be involved in closing them.'

'Sounds like you have it already planned out,' Luca said.

'To an extent. We need Sarah, David Ritter, and the others to remain silent. However, we understand what we are asking here, so we can offer something in return. They will be offered the chance to participate in our investigations, Church funded, and led by you.'

'Me?!' Luca asked, incredulous.

'Of course. You've already closed one gate; you have prior experience with a serious paranormal incident in Hungary; and you have studied *Ianua Diaboli* and the ledger already, if only briefly. You are perfectly placed.'

'If I refuse?'

Another man sat forward, the oldest looking of them all. His face was painfully thin, almost skeletal, save for his sagging jowls. 'I'm afraid it is an order,' he said. His accent was English, but with no regional dialect Luca could pick up on.

'From what we understand,' Bishop Turnbull said, 'David Ritter and his team are not coping well after the incident. And since we are going to need to insist on their silence, we can offer them a job in return. One that would be very well paid.'

'So in effect, you are buying their silence,' Luca said. 'Only, you don't have the dignity to just leave it at that. You're also going to insist they work for you and help you as well.'

'No, Luca. They would be helping *you*. Use them as you feel they are needed. If any of them aren't up to it, fine. We can let them go and come to another arrangement with them. But your role now, with Miss Pearson as a guide, will be to find out more about these gates and hunt down any that exist. When one is confirmed, Sarah and her friends will be immediately pulled out. They will be safe.'

'This is madness,' Luca said, feeling his chest tighten. He wanted to be done with the Perron Manors and Zsámbék Churches of this world. He didn't want to risk his soul any more... but now he was being ordered back into the mouth of Hell. 'You're putting their lives in danger. They're just ordinary people; they aren't trained for this.'

'*No one* is trained for this,' the Bishop said. 'That's the point.'

'So they're pawns?' Luca asked.

'Think of them more as willing volunteers.'

'What makes you think they'll volunteer?'

'Because you'll convince them, Father,' Bishop Turnbull said. 'Just like you'll convince Miss Pearson to give us the book. Make them see it as an opportunity. Tell them to do it in the name of their fallen friends. For Sarah, it can be in the name of her sister, or her lost sense of purpose. Whatever it takes.'

Luca slumped and looked down to the table. 'I'm not comfortable with this,' he said. 'Not at all. And I won't be strong-armed into tricking people. It isn't right.'

Bishop Turnbull looked to his right again. The large man nodded. 'I understand, Father. This is not easy to hear, I am sure. And it certainly isn't easy to ask. But think of what is at stake here. Is this calling really something you can turn your back on?'

Luca clenched his teeth together as he glared at the man opposite. Other than Bishop Turnbull, he had no idea who these people were. And yet they were asking him to go against his morals and better judgment.

But what choice did he have? Turning his back on the request—no, the *order*—would be turning his back on a world that needed his help, even if it didn't know it. How could he live with himself if he ran away?

Luca brought up a hand and ran it over his face. He let out a long, defeated sigh.

'Fine,' he eventually said. 'I'll do it.'

THE END

HAUNTED: POSSESSION

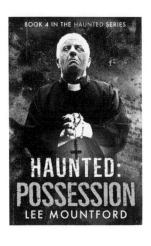

THE DEAD ARE SUFFERING...

Haunted: Possession

Book 4 in the Haunted Series.

A haunted cathedral. A possessed priest.

Sarah Pearson and her team are sent on their first assignment together—to investigate a case of possession in Kutná Hora, Czech Republic.

Father Hus, a respected priest, has reportedly succumbed to possession from a supernatural entity. On top of that, there are stories of a ghostly and bloody monk wandering the halls at night.

As the investigation gets underway, it becomes clear there is more going on at the cathedral than they first thought. The team realise they are in a fight for their lives against a terrifying enemy with a plan that dates back centuries.

Haunted: Possession is Book 4 in the Haunted series.
Buy Haunted: Possession now.

INSIDE: PERRON MANOR

Sign up to my mailing list to get the FREE prequel...

In 2014 a group of paranormal researchers conducted a weekend-long investigation at the notorious Perron Manor. The events that took place during that weekend were incredible and terrifying in equal measure. This is the full, documented story.

In addition, the author dives into the long and bloody history of the house, starting with its origins as a monastery back in the 1200s, covering its ownership under the Grey and Perron families, and even detailing the horrific events that took place on Halloween in 1982.

No stone is left unturned in what is now the definitive work regarding the most haunted house in Britain.

The novella, as mentioned in Haunted: Perron Manor, can be yours for FREE by joining my mailing list.

Sign up now.

www.leemountford.com

THE DEMONIC

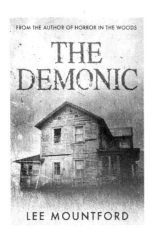

If you liked the Haunted series, you will love The Demonic.

Years ago Danni Morgan ran away from her childhood home and vowed never to go back. It was a place of fear, pain and misery at the hands of an abusive father.

But now Danni's father is dead and she is forced to break her vow and return home—to lay his body to rest and face up to the ghosts of her past.

But Danni is about to realise that some ghosts are more real than others. And something beyond her understanding is waiting for her there, lurking in the shadows. An evil that intends to kill her family and claim her very soul.

Experience supernatural horror in the vein of THE CONJURING, INSIDIOUS and the legendary GHOST-

WATCH. THE DEMONIC will get under your skin, send chills down your spine and have you sleeping with the lights on!

Buy The Demonic now...

OTHER BOOKS BY LEE MOUNTFORD

The Supernatural Horror Collection
> The Demonic
> The Mark
> Forest of the Damned

The Extreme Horror Collection
> Horror in the Woods
> Tormented
> The Netherwell Horror

Haunted Series
> Inside Perron Manor (Book 0)
> Haunted: Perron Manor (Book 1)
> Haunted: Devil's Door (Book 2)
> Haunted: Possession (Book 4)
> Haunted: Mother Death (Book 5)
> Haunted: Asylum (Book 6)

ABOUT THE AUTHOR

Lee Mountford is a horror author from the North-East of England. His first book, Horror in the Woods, was published in May 2017 to fantastic reviews, and his follow-up book, The Demonic, achieved Best Seller status in both Occult Horror and British Horror categories on Amazon.

He is a lifelong horror fan, much to the dismay of his amazing wife, Michelle, and his work is available in ebook, print and audiobook formats.

In August 2017 he and his wife welcomed their first daughter, Ella, into the world. In May 2019, their second daughter, Sophie, came along. Michelle is hoping the girls don't inherit their father's love of horror, but Lee has other ideas...

For more information
www.leemountford.com
leemountford01@googlemail.com

ACKNOWLEDGMENTS

Thanks first to my amazing Beta Reader Team, who have greatly helped me polish and hone this book:

James Bacon
Christine Brlevic
John Brooks
Carrie-Lynn Cantwell
Karen Day
Doreene Fernandes
Jenn Freitag
Ursula Gillam
Clayton Hall
Tammy Harris
Emily Haynes
Dorie Heriot
Lemmy Howells
Lucy Hughes
Marie K
Dawn Keate
Diane McCarty
Megan McCarty

Valerie Palmer
Leanne Pert
Carley Jessica Pyne
Justin Read
Nicola Jayne Smith
Sara Walker
Sharon Watret

Also, thanks to my editor, Josiah Davis (http://www.jdbookservices.com) for such an amazing job as always.

The cover was supplied by Debbie at The Cover Collection. (http://www.thecovercollection.com). I cannot recommend their work enough.

And the last thank you, as always, is the most important—to my amazing family. My wife, Michelle, and my daughters, Ella and Sophie: thank you for everything. You three are my world.

Made in the USA
Middletown, DE
21 August 2023